Jaret Bachmann travels with his family to his beloved grandfather's funeral with a heavy heart and, more troubling, premonitions of something evil lurking at the Bachmann ancestral home. But no one believes that he sees ghosts.

Grappling with his sexuality, a ghost that wants him out of the way, and the loss of his grandfather, Jaret must protect his family and come to terms with powers hidden deep within himself.

THE BACHMANN
FAMILY SECRET

A Companion Novel to the Realm of the
Vampire Council Series

Damian Serbu

A NineStar Press Publication

www.ninestarpress.com

The Bachmann Family Secret

Printed in the USA

Print ISBN: 978-1-64890-059-4

First Edition, July, 2020

Also available in eBook, ISBN: 978-1-64890-058-7

Warning: This book contains graphic violence, homophobic language, mentions of past murders.

To Becky—for being the sister most people only dream of having. With all my love.

Chapter One

Foreboding

I trembled at the thought of returning to Nebraska for my grandpa's funeral.

Even he told me not to return.

Of course, you can't explain the situation to your parents, or say your concerns out loud to anyone, without the world thinking you'd gone bonkers.

Still, after my uncle called Dad to tell us Grandpa died, Gramps tried for the past day to keep me at home.

Yeah, my dead grandpa warned me not to go to Fremont, which meant no way I wanted to go either. I trusted him dead as much as I trusted him with all my heart when he lived.

But what Gramps and I wanted did not matter. Because we all planned to get into Dad's Blazer and drive back to Fremont, to the big Victorian house that had comforted me so much my entire life as the embodiment of Gramps's love, to the small town we'd left behind years ago.

Unfortunately, none of these dreadful thoughts took me away from the reason I shut my eyes a moment ago and worked with all my power to keep them closed.

Sitting on my bed next to my suitcase and hugging my knees close to my body, I knew Gramps still stood in the corner with a frown. His ghost was upset, and his agitation had to do with my going to his funeral.

Keeping my eyes shut, I reached over next to me, at least comforted by the presence of my dog.

Then my mind played a fucked-up trick on me, as I giggled at my thoughts. I wished for a support group. *Hi, I'm Jaret, and I see dead people.* Like the frickin' movie, with what's-his-name acting in it. The *Die Hard* guy. Not that I ever wanted to see ghosts. Nope, never did. But ever since I was a kid, as early as I could remember, I saw them. And I learned pretty quickly to keep my mouth shut about my visions, no matter how many times I saw them. People would look at me like I went nutso if I told them such stuff. The other high school kids would freak. My own parents signed me up for the shrink farm when I was in third grade because I told them about the old man ghost in my classroom who made mean faces at me when I got an answer wrong. But could I blame them? My story sounded bonkers and scared the shit out of them. For all I know, the ghost sightings proved once and for all I am nuts.

Back to my senses, I took a deep breath and peeked over at the corner. Still there. Gramps shook his head, the way I remembered from when he wanted to teach me a lesson when I was little. The love had sparkled in his eyes even as he'd reprimanded me, and his ghost form adopted the same demeanor, despite his displeasure with my insistence on traveling to Nebraska.

I almost tricked myself into believing he still lived, except I had watched him materialize out of nowhere in my bedroom. One minute I stared at my hot picture of Captain America, the next Gramps blocked the poster from view as he appeared to me.

"Gramps," I whispered. "I don't know what you're trying to say." My head pounded with a headache, always a sign the dead had arrived for a visit. "Please help me. I don't know what you want. Or how *I'm* supposed to do it. I'm not in charge around here! You know I have no power."

He shook his head again, and the word "no" echoed through my skull.

"I got your message!" I yelled as a jolt of pain crashed through my brain. "You don't want me to go back to Fremont. But I can't not go. What would I tell my parents?" They'd scold me about making stuff up about ghosts again. Or could I even mention the episode to Jenn and Lincoln, my sister and brother? Too embarrassing. "Gramps, I'm sorry. I have to go. Please understand."

Again Gramps shook his head, but then began to fade away.

"No. Please. I miss you—"

He disappeared, and Darth whined next to me, her ears back, her big brown eyes worried. At least my head returned to normal, except my stomach turned over in knots. A very, very bad force lurked in Fremont, bad enough Gramps's spirit left his house to warn me.

I pulled Darth into a tight hug, so she pushed her snout into me. Even she tried to keep me from packing. She listened to Gramps's warning and took his plea to heart. *Yeah, I'm a strange case. I bond with dead people and dogs.* I petted her and she whined again. "Don't be sad. You get to go too." Of course, I figured my assurance might make the fear worse for her.

I sighed as I stood, Darth mimicking me, and then grabbed my suitcase and headed upstairs, Darth on my heels.

"Look at the bright side," I told her. "First we have a long car ride through Nebraska! And—Dad informed us no one can take a cell phone. How cool, right? No contact with the real world the whole time!" While Dad often flipped out about our being on our phones too much, he'd lost it with total abandon today. He forbade any phones on the trip, whatsoever. We all caved, though, because, well, first the order came from our dad. We never won those battles. And I think we all figured the phone rage related to his grief.

Darth tilted her head at me, trying hard to understand my words. "Plus, Gramps doesn't even have a computer!"

We always dealt with the old-world nature of visiting Gramps, but we needed to bury him, which made the whole thing feel like total bullshit. No phones. No computer. Like 1890 all over again. Not to mention the ghosts fucking with me more than usual.

All these dreadful thoughts continued to float through my head as one cornfield after another flew by on the trip to Fremont. I stared out the window the entire time. But my mind kept reminding me we hurried toward a black hole, with nothing good at the other end.

I stifled another inappropriate giggle. The latest horror movie, starring Jaret! The dark stairs seemed foreboding, so I headed right down them! The evil monster ran into the woods. I charged in there alone after the beast! Every movie watcher screamed to go the other way, but the idiot actor plodded right into the danger. Except I became the idiot. Fuck me.

Plus, my head hurt like I got it smashed between two elevator doors. No way to forget the bad premonitions when your head reminded you of them every second.

Thankfully, we all stayed pretty quiet for the entire trip, given the grief of the moment.

*

We arrived in Fremont the next afternoon, first driving by the cemetery to my left. Grandma was buried there. She died of cancer years before I was born. But Gramps missed her every day of his life. I sensed his sadness, even as a kid. Maybe he could go be with her. Or maybe not. There he was, again, standing in the cemetery, watching us pass.

My apprehensions almost exploded right out of my stomach, all over everyone in the Blazer. A sudden, debilitating headache paralyzed me and a white light blinded me. I turned my head toward the graveyard. In the middle of the bright light, Gramps glared at me through my pain, the one clear vision amid the piercing white light. His apparition hovered beside Grandma's tombstone, shaking its head back and forth with the same warning. "No. No." His stern face added a desperate plea to his words. "Go no farther. Turn around. Turn everyone around." His ghost appeared so real I thought I could reach out and touch it. No other ghosts from past visions had such tangible features or form. I saw right through them, but Gramps looked as if he still lived, in his actual body.

"Jaret? What's wrong?" my mom almost screamed but stifled the sound. I regained my sight and found my mother turned around in her seat studying me.

"What?" I asked with a lame tone of voice.

"You're pale. Are you sick?"

"No. Sorry. I was thinking about Gramps." My half-truth ended the conversation.

Mom reached back and placed her hand on my knee. Even my brother, who shunned physical contact, touched my shoulder, but their comfort hardly relieved my fears.

I almost blurted the truth out to all of them but bit my tongue. We drove through the rest of Fremont, with its small-town feel. I always loved coming here, with its throwback charm and Gramps's love all around, but the whole place creeped me out on this ride.

The sight of the gables on Gramps's old, white Victorian house almost made me blow chunks right there in the SUV. Gramps loved to tell me about its history, but like everything else, its presence felt off as we drove along. Built in the late 1800s and owned by subsequent Bachmann generations, Gramps said the first immigrants in our family came from Europe with a lot of money, part of which they used to erect the house. Rich. The uber wealth ended with them. But the house remained, with lots of charm, a huge porch, great stained-glass windows, all sorts of cool stuff. Except when it lurked over us as if alive, waiting to eat my entire family as we meandered toward the mansion.

Shit, I had to get a grip.

Upon rounding the corner, I spotted Aunt Alice standing on the porch and staring into the street as if lost. We'd pulled into the circular driveway and started getting out before she jolted out of her funk. What the hell? She'd never acted like a space cadet before.

"Well, goodness. I didn't even see you." She laughed and shook her head.

No shit.

She greeted all of us with a hug and ushered us inside. As I passed her, she almost grimaced but then returned to her welcoming smile, though her eyes maintained a hint of suspicion or fear. Great. Did she already sense my psycho-ward tendencies gripped me? Or did I give off an evil vibe? What the hell was going on?

I walked inside and started up the stairs, but made sure Darth followed me. No way I would go up these stairs alone, with all the shit happening with ghosts and feelings and death. I headed straight toward my usual room, ignoring the tingling in my head, the rumbling in my stomach, and all the bad thoughts racing through my mind.

On the second floor, I went by the hall down to Gramps's study, felt a nasty chill as I went by the door to the attic, and almost fell flat on my face. The hair on my arms stood straight up, and Darth growled a warning. After I regained my balance, I peered down the hall to see Gramps's apparition staring at me, as vivid as the one from the cemetery. He pointed to the attic door and shook his head. "No, no:" the same message as before but directed at a particular place. His stern expression reminded me of the times when he wanted to teach his grandkids an important lesson without seeming angry. Strangely, because of his demeanor, I no longer feared Gramps's ghost, though an unseen force terrified me to the core at the same time.

Dad's voice from below yanked me out of my funk and back to reality. "Hurry up. I'm hungry."

I sighed. More than ever, I struggled with carrying on with business as usual when freaky shit kept happening.

Also with Dad's shout, Gramps vanished. He'd seemed so alive, so real, I'd had the urge to race up to hug him. But what the hell did he want? For me not to go to the attic? All the effort, and that's all he communicated to me? Back home, he'd warned me against coming to

Fremont, but he now seemed to accept my presence, though he cautioned me against approaching a certain door without telling me what scared him. Was I too dense to figure his message out? Again my head spun in confusion.

Worried Dad would start yelling again, I patted Darth on the head to calm her and tossed my suitcase onto the floor in the bedroom. I returned downstairs to find everyone gathered at the front door, so we headed outside and into cars to meet the rest of the Bachmanns for lunch. I hated leaving Darth behind in the place with all the creepy sensations, but again I had no choice unless I revealed all the loony bin stuff occurring around me, or at least taking place in my head. I kissed her on the head and followed my family, refusing to look back at her because I knew she was staring at me like I betrayed her.

*

My uncle and cousins sat in a downtown café, eating and chatting with one another when we arrived. They all rose to greet us, sharing hugs and handshakes, the smiles and warm embraces dampened by the reason we came together. I fought against the tears welling in my eyes, especially when I noticed how Uncle Harold's lip trembled when he looked at Dad. Uncle Harold stiffened, stretched his back, and then parked himself back at the head of the table. "Sit, everyone." He motioned at the table for us to join him, so my cousins returned to their seats, Dad plopped down next to Uncle Harold, and Mom and Aunt Alice sat next to each other. Lincoln, Jenn, and I joined them at the other end.

Dad and Harold talked about work, while Mom and Alice quizzed the kids about everything: school, work, friends, hobbies. I answered with a short reply, not trusting my mind to manage the mundane without freaking out. Whew, Mom turned her attention to my cousin, Tony.

"So, how's the new medical practice?" she asked.

He grinned, an obvious pride at what he'd accomplished already in life written on his face. "Good. Real good. I'm excited they allowed me to join their practice already. I was tired of the ER, and the new hours are nice."

I giggled inside as the inquiries about his life continued. Though he was fifteen years older than me, Bachmann tradition locked a person into a certain generation and didn't let go until the older one died out. So, Lincoln, Jenn, and I felt like grade schoolers again, and even my cousins, grown with families of their own, answered Mom's questions like little kids.

After we all ate lunch and the chitchat of catching up died down, an uncomfortable silence fell across the table. Uncle Harold and Aunt Alice glanced at each other, a secret communication between the two, but awkward enough everyone else noticed and so waited for them to proceed.

"Well, I suppose we should tell them." Uncle Harold directed his remark to Aunt Alice, as if no one else could hear.

She nodded, stared hard at the table, and fidgeted with her napkin. "Go ahead."

Harold turned his attention to my dad. "I'm sorry I didn't tell you this before. I didn't know how to bring it up. My kids know though." He paused, an uncertain demeanor I seldom saw in the confident man. "We're selling Gramps's place so we can split the profits. I don't feel right about Alice and me moving into the house alone. If the kids still lived with us, maybe. But not just the two of us."

I was dumbfounded. I never planned to live in the house, but the thought of the mansion leaving the family—was so wrong. A betrayal of Gramps. Everyone avoided eye contact with one another, seeming to share my discomfort.

Dad pushed his chair back and cleared his throat. "If it's the money, forget about it. No one expects money out of the house. You and Alice deserve it. Hell, you've taken care of the place since Gramps got too old, anyway."

"That's not the problem." Uncle Harold waved his arm in the air for emphasis. "Money has nothing to do with our decision."

"Your health?" Dad scrunched his brow, his words reminding all of us of Harold's heart condition.

"No." Harold grimaced. "No. It isn't the money or my health. We're too old to take care of a big house."

Silence descended on the table again, with no one quite sure what to say. I, for one, thought Uncle Harold hid something. Too old never defined him or Alice, and the way they traveled, worked on projects, and enjoyed life never spoke of older people. Uncle Harold remained active his whole life, first by serving in the military, then working at a meat packing plant until retirement, and since then volunteering a lot for Habitat for Humanity.

"What's going on?" Dad asked.

Jenn and I stole a glance at one another when we recognized Dad's tone: he was calling Harold out on the lie. My sister and I communicated well with silent expressions or subtle motions, both of us straightening up in our chair as if waiting for a reprimand from our father.

Uncle Harold raised his voice, startling all of us. "You know damn well why we won't move into the death trap. Stop badgering us. Alice and I are scared. Do you feel better, now, making me say it? I think we should destroy the house, everything in it, and sell the property. No one should live there." Uncle Harold took a deep breath and stared back at Dad. "Mom was right. We've witnessed the truth now, Alice and me, and it's not good."

I stared at him. Harold never yelled. Not even in private. Never toward Dad. And glancing at the others, no one but Dad, Alice, and Harold knew what the hell they were talking about.

"Calm down." Dad scanned the restaurant, nervous. Only a few customers remained, but they all turned their attention to us. "Jesus Christ, I thought we'd forgotten about those stupid superstitions. Nothing haunts the house. And you've said so yourself a million times. You always agreed with Gramps."

Um, what were they talking about? I looked first at Harold and then at Dad. What haunting? I almost wondered if I invented the conversation because of the weird stuff happening to me. But unless I lost touch with reality, the Bachmanns sat in Fremont and popped the youngest generation over the head with a ghost story.

"Strange things happen there," Uncle Harold responded with a whisper. "I know different than to disbelieve. I saw what occurs with my own eyes."

"Dad, calm down." My cousin, Marie, put her hand on Harold's arm. "You can't get this upset. Just explain what you saw to everyone."

Uncle Harold took a deep breath and nodded.

"What are you two talking about?" Mom broke the silence when no one said anything.

Harold looked with disbelief at my father. "You never told her? Let's see what *she* thinks about the stories."

Dad spoke softly when he answered, running his finger around the rim of his glass as if speaking to the water instead of her or anyone in the family. "There's no proof about hauntings. And your Gramps and Grandma always disagreed about them. Grandma said things about ghosts but never explained her fears, and Gramps said the ghost stories were nonsense. He didn't want us telling the grandkids. I know other people claimed to see things or feel spirits, but there's no evidence. Just a bunch of damn superstitions and town rumors. You and I never experienced anything as kids. What changed your mind? You always agreed with Gramps about this."

"Alice and I can't find the jewels," Harold said in a low voice. "And when we looked for them, things happened. Stuff flew across the room at us. The spirit wants us dead."

Holy shit. I landed in a mystery movie set and outside my normal family. Jewels? What was he talking about? What wanted them dead?

"They're always under the stairway where Gramps hid them," my father said. He ignored the scary part— typical Dad.

"No. They've disappeared."

"Whoa," my mother interrupted again. "Back up. What are you two talking about? What hauntings? What jewels?" As much as the news surprised me to learn about those two tidbits, I was shocked even more to learn my mother knew as little as me.

Dad shook his head. Harold remained silent. No one else dared interject anything.

"If they want to sell the house, then sell it before this gets any crazier." Mom looked from Dad to my uncle to Alice. "No one wants the mansion, so get rid of it. Unless you want to explain all of this to everyone, I don't see much of a conversation going on. What's the problem?"

"We can't do anything until we find the jewels." Dad looked at her, worried.

"There you go again. Jewels?" Mom rolled her eyes. "What jewels? This sounds like we're after the Holy Grail."

"I told you about them." Dad looked at Mom. "My father owned valuable jewelry that came over with the first Bachmanns from Germany. The gems are worth a lot of money. Gramps never had them appraised, and he never wanted to sell them, so he kept them in a box under the stairs. He said he could never sell them because they reminded him of his brother, who treasured them and looked after them until he died, but Gramps said we could get rid of them after he passed away."

"Yep," Harold said, "and I checked for them first thing after Gramps passed. The spot where he kept the chest was empty, though the rest of the crap he stashed in there was still in the closet. I looked everywhere, but they're gone. And a couple times boxes fell on me, once a candlestick flew across the room as if someone threw it right at my head."

"Did Gramps get a safe deposit box?" Dad asked. Again, he ignored the most notable item to me out of Uncle Harold's mouth, about candlesticks flying across the room. What the fuck?

"I checked everything." Harold wiped his mouth clean and put his napkin on the table. "I thought maybe you'd know."

My head still whirled. I half expected Gramps's ghost to appear right here and add to my confusion. Instead, secretive adults and a bewildered younger generation sat around me.

"Tell them about the attic," Alice instructed Harold.

"What now?" Dad sounded impatient as he tapped his fingers on the table.

"I didn't check the attic for them." Harold took a deep breath before he continued. "Gramps never went up there. Even he hated the third floor. And the narrow steps scared him. He thought he'd fall. So they can't be up there." Harold paused and stared again at the floor. "I *tried* to check the attic. But the damn door wouldn't budge. It's jammed."

"You two, listen up," Alice raised her voice, speaking in a stern tone. "Some*thing* wants the attic locked. Some*thing* lives in the house. You can speculate for hours about mechanical problems or creaky doors, but I know the truth, and so did your mother." Alice stared hard at Dad, then back to Harold as her words sunk in. Her expression softened when she turned her attention to Mom. "Candlesticks don't fly on their own. Boxes don't materialize out of nowhere, to land on your head. Beth, there are ghosts in the house. Who knows where the jewels went? But if the ghosts put them in the attic, we'd best leave them there."

A tingling sensation ran down my spine. I felt a presence even in the restaurant and believed Aunt Alice because of the fear in her widened eyes.

"Calm down." Harold frowned at his wife. "Even if an entity haunts the damn house, it never hurt anyone. I think the ghost intentionally missed with those things, wanted to scare me is all. Maybe we need to try harder to get the attic door open."

"Let's get going." Dad got up and paid the bill, ending the conversation.

I shot out of my chair and hurried out the door because the whole scene freaked me out. The revelations yet continued unknown, the stares from other tables, and a lingering presence of evil, all caught up to me. Yeah, Gramps maintained his disbelief through all the episodes, but his ignorance bothered me all the more because Uncle Harold said a ghost haunted the place. Add the idea to my visions and, pardon my French, fuck me all to hell.

*

As we returned to Gramps's house after lunch, the revelations about Bachmann ghosts and history spun around in my mind when I tried to link them to my visions of Gramps's ghost from the last few days. Had he appeared to anyone else? Did anyone else feel his presence when they talked about these ghosts? If my grandmother knew about the haunting, as Dad and Harold mentioned in their conversation, then a ghost possessed the house before Gramps died, someone other than Gramps. Besides, the chill consuming me on the second floor felt malevolent, but in my heart I knew Gramps, even as a ghost, would never plague his family and drive them out of the house he loved.

No one talked during the ride, nor did anyone say anything when we pulled into the driveway. I jumped out of the Blazer and raced inside to find Darth, who stood wagging her tail and spinning in circles with apparent relief I returned home.

But as I pulled myself together, I ran up the stairs to my room and felt a chill when I walked by the attic. I hurried past, afraid to look, but then spun around when I reached my room door and saw Gramps again staring at me, standing in the middle of the hall. Accustomed to his visits, at first I almost failed to react and felt no fear. But I tensed today. His past manifestations always appeared so human, with a solid body I could almost touch. The apparition standing in front of me was transparent, the outline of a ghost but not the detailed human features from before. I shuddered and backed away.

Plus, he or it was pissed. Wicked angry. So I almost lost control of my bowels when he floated toward me and stopped a few inches from my face. My head flooded with a maniacal cackle as he stood in front of me, laughing harder and harder. Woozy and unsure of myself, I stumbled backward and then I saw Darth bound down the hall and snarl at the vision. To my relief, Gramps thrust himself toward the attic and retreated through the door, vanishing as quickly as he appeared.

I stood motionless while Darth barked and scratched with fury at the base of the door, angrier than I'd ever seen her. The hair on her back stood straight up and she snarled the entire time. I grabbed her by the collar and pulled her into my room, seeking safety and to calm her.

"It should be cool in here," I told Darth as I yanked her into my room. She grunted but otherwise relaxed.

I jumped and again almost pissed myself when a voice spoke behind me, "Don't start getting yourself worked up."

Mom stood at the door.

"Hey," I said, feeling lame she'd caught me talking to my dog.

"Did those stories from lunch get to you?" Her tone softened, and she looked concerned.

"A little. And Darth's been acting weird since we got

here." I stood in the center of the room wondering how much to tell her. She moved to the bed and sat down.

"Sit." She patted the bed next to her. "I know how these things get to you. But even though I don't understand everything going through your head, I love you. And you can't stop me from worrying. You act like a bundle of nerves."

I sat next to her and she grabbed my hand.

"I'm okay. Really. I just hate the ghost stories."

Mom brushed hair out of my eyes and smiled. "You always had an active imagination. Everything's fine."

I wanted to believe her. Every time we talked about my visions, I tried to convince myself to trust her, because she believed her words and she loved me. Except I also *really* saw the ghosts.

"Is anything else on your mind?"

"No." Well, a million things, of course, but nothing I wanted to divulge at the moment.

"I wanted to ask you another question. I think it may relate to your feelings about everything."

"What?" My voice rose an octave. Her comment did not sound good.

"Why didn't you ask anyone to the prom?"

Parents were so weird. What the fuck? Prom? Was she serious? I swallowed those thoughts before answering. "I told you already. I don't want to spend the money. I need cash for college next fall."

"Did you ever consider going for fun?"

"No. I never wanted to go. Dances don't seem fun."

"Oh. I'm sorry. No one's going to make you go."

Despite her words and fake smile, Mom's stiffened posture and tapping foot indicated she worried more than before we started the crazy conversation. And I felt more stressed about our talk than I did about the evil premonitions and nasty ass ghost of minutes ago.

"I'm going to help Alice in the kitchen. Maybe you and Darth could go for a walk?"

"Okay. See ya."

She walked out of the room, and I closed the door after her, my hands shaking, my heart pounding. Why did she ask those questions? "Prom?" I asked Darth, thinking the dog might clarify the situation.

I took a deep breath, afraid of my next thought. Did Mom know about my other secret? I never told anyone about it except Darth, but moms sensed shit with their kids. Maybe she suspected?

I collapsed onto the bed and put my arm around Darth, who cuddled next to me with her head on my leg. I rolled onto my back as the room spun around me and sweat dripped from my forehead. Then I moved Darth aside and sat up.

Fucking prom. Why did Mom care? I wanted to focus on Gramps's death and the funeral, but I also confronted ghost visits and weird stories about family hauntings and mysterious vanishing jewels. Mom added another layer, the very layer I buried deep and could not even admit to myself yet.

Deep inside, I wanted to tell her the truth when she asked me about the prom. I wanted to say, "I don't like girls that way. I never have. I don't want to date them. I think I'm gay."

The thought of saying those words sent tears down my cheeks. If only one person knew my secret, I'd feel like a huge weight was lifted off my back. But it was too risky. What if Mom and Dad kicked me out of the house? How would I pay for college? How could I leave my family forever? It was safer to bury the feelings and attempt to live a celibate life without stupid sexual feelings. I could adopt twenty dogs and live with them instead.

I rolled over, trying to stop the tears, trying to clamp down on the longings haunting me with even more force than any ghost. When I dreamed about the rest of my life, I always pictured another man by my side. When I fantasized about school dances or meeting the perfect person in college, it was always a boy, never a girl. And here I was, an eighteen-year-old virgin because to fulfill my dreams meant jeopardizing everything else important to me.

I knew there were rumors about me at school. So many girls tried to date me and even asked me out or offered to pay for the date, to the point I started inventing lame excuses to avoid going with them. But my dodging dates intensified my fear that it gave me away. So I went on a few dates to try to keep attention off me, but they always ended with a platonic goodbye, the girl never trying again. I bit my lip, fighting those tears.

Darth repositioned herself to snuggle closer to me, her typical response to my crying—she smothered me with attention. Kissing the top of her head and clutching her soothed my anxiety. I knew she would stand beside me, no matter what.

Finally, I jumped up and grabbed her leash and headed out the door. I had to get out of here, so I took Mom's advice and walked Darth around the block a couple times.

The house and yard covered one entire city block, so the house sort of hovered over me the whole time. Once again, I almost relaxed as I focused on how much Darth loved to sniff *everything*, when a vision in the attic window surprised me. I gulped in confusion. Two people looked down at me, too small from the distance to identify, but one looked like Gramps. His ghost again? But who was the second vision? Were they actual people? I hurried around the corner and up the porch steps, even though going toward the ghosts seemed crazy compared to running like hell to get out of Fremont.

I forgot, until I hit the second floor, that Uncle Harold said no one could get into the attic. I tried the door but found it locked. I breathed a sigh of relief, because despite my instinct to go up there, another part of me warned against the adventure. Instead, I returned to my room with Darth and enjoyed a little bit of peace and quiet while I worked on homework until Mom called me for dinner.

*

When Aunt Alice called all of us to the dining room, old habits and traditions continued to enforce family ritual. First, everyone complied at once, unlike at home when we often took turns wandering in late or forcing Mom to yell a second time to get to the table. Aunt Alice commanded compliance by force of will—an aura one never needed explaining but a power to fill us with a sense of dread at the consequences of disobeying—so forceful, to my knowledge, no one ever challenged her authority. Too, when Gramps lived, no one wanted to disappoint him by missing a family gathering or creating "unpleasantness," as he called it whenever we were scolded. Even in his absence, we filed into the ornate room, with its blue wallpaper printed with white roses, and sat in our usual spots around the table. No one took the head of the table, where Gramps always sat—a tribute to our fallen leader.

We settled into familiar chitchat again as we lost ourselves in the ritual of eating, another sign of both a family connected in deep love and, at the same time, one repressing the macabre reason for our gathering. The comfortable pattern allowed me to forget about the visions for a little while and, like my family around me, ignore the swirl of emotion inside. After we ate, we talked a little bit about Gramps, which made me feel better because the Bachmanns shared their feelings. Everyone took a turn telling a story, then laughing and crying, until Mom announced she was tired and headed off to sleep.

I followed Mom upstairs, exhausted from all my emotions, both expressed and hidden within me. But once in my room with Darth, a new energy took hold, and I felt ridiculous trying to sleep already. I opened a window to let in a cool breeze and air out the stuffy room, then sat on the bed next to Darth, who looked like she, at least, wanted to fall asleep.

The cool breeze felt good as it moved through the room, reminding me of the perfect time of year in Nebraska, once the winter cold blew away and the summer's heat and humidity were still a few weeks off. I liked the way the breeze blew my long hair around my face.

I patted Darth on the head and walked over to the window, peering into the darkened sky as I daydreamed. I imagined a boy my age standing next to me and wished I had a boyfriend who might run his fingers through my hair. I stared into the night for a minute, then turned off the overhead light to see better outside. My window overlooked the street. Gramps's neighbors used elaborate lamps and decorations to light up their houses, but Gramps still relied on one gas lamp in the front yard. A few streetlamps glowed but a lot of their light was blocked by the trees surrounding Gramps's property. And no one turned on the porch lights unless they were sitting outside. Too many bugs to attract otherwise.

As I watched out the window, I heard Mom and Dad moving around in their room next to mine, until I heard the click of their light switch. I knew Lincoln had gone to bed an hour earlier, and Jenn had decided to sleep in my parents' room because the stories from lunch weirded her out. If she knew what I saw half the time, she'd lose all her hair.

A loud noise next door startled me. "Dan!" I heard Mom call out. "Did you hear that?"

Jenn spoke next. "I didn't do anything! Did one of you?"

"Something slammed my suitcase shut," Mom answered. My father mumbled something in return, too quiet for me to hear, but they all fell silent.

My thoughts then turned to Gramps. Overlooking his yard reminded me of the fireflies Gramps and I had spent hours catching when I was a kid, before we moved to Colorado and afterward on our summer visits here. I remembered the special cages we'd bought at the drugstore for them, but they rarely lived past a couple of days. I didn't care. I'd go out and catch dozens more. And Gramps never complained, never let on he might have wanted to do something else.

The ghosts of their little lights blinked at me, as if calling from the past. I wondered why none appeared tonight, and then my grief overcame me, and I wished Gramps were still alive. I thought about his appearance earlier in the afternoon. Why was he so scary? And how come he didn't look as solid as he had earlier? He changed once I got to the house. What was going on? That wasn't the Gramps I knew. Maybe dying changed him. But I didn't want to believe anything bad about the man who loved us so much in life.

I also thought about the faces in the attic window I'd seen from my walk. I wanted to believe a family member got the door open and went up there, but I knew the attic door was still jammed. I didn't even have to try the knob to know. So who, then, was at the window?

Darth growled and I whipped my head toward the bed to see her staring toward the side of me. She snarled and rose to her feet, the hair on her back standing straight up. The hair on my arms rose, too, when I turned and saw Gramps sitting in the corner, rocking in a chair. I went over and turned on the lights to get a better look. He appeared solid again, human even, and his gentle face seemed loving and reassuring, not irate. Gramps smiled at Darth and made a peaceful gesture for her to sit down, which she obeyed. She stayed on guard, but stopped growling.

Then he looked at me and smiled. I smiled back. "I miss you," I said, and he nodded in a way he used to do, when he was sympathizing with me.

Again questions shot through my mind with no answers in sight. What did he want me to do? And how come I was the only one in the weird family he came to? His ghost stood and walked toward the door and looked back when he reached it. He motioned for me to follow, then waited.

Confused, I went with him, but made darn sure Darth came along. And even though he'd been so weird and pissed during the afternoon, I trusted him. *Lord*, I thought, *I'm talking about a man who's dead, but he's taking me on an evening stroll through his house.* I hoped my parents or someone in the family didn't decide to get up for a drink of water or anything.

Gramps took us to the attic door and, without making a sound or movement, opened it and pointed. Well, the door opened by itself. I stared at the opening, feeling a new sense of dread, and refused to move, refused to step inside the room with the horrible energy, with all the bad feelings in it. I had never gone up there while Gramps was alive, and I couldn't go now, even with Darth, even with Gramps's *nice* ghost encouraging me.

Gramps still smiled despite my resistance. He looked at me and signaled he loved me by placing his fist over his heart and then pointing at me. He next drew a necklace around his neck and pointed into the attic.

No way, I thought. Jewels? Is Gramps showing me the jewels? I watched and he lifted his fingers to his lips in the *shhh* gesture. He wanted me to keep the news a secret. But from whom? And how come I got to know? I started to ask him, but he disappeared and left Darth and me alone in the hall. The attic door closed and locked shut without a sound as Gramps's ghost vanished, leaving me more confused than before, if possible.

Okay, so Gramps shushed me. Did he disappear because I tried to speak? Was he mad again? A chill passed down my spine and the hallway became icy cold, as Darth resumed growling in the darkness. I strained to see what bothered her when I saw Gramps again coming down the hall, but he was frowning, angry, and back to the pissed-off version of a spirit. What was going on? He was no longer solid, either, as I stared right through his form. Plus, he appeared younger than he was when he brought me to the attic not five minutes ago. Had I disappointed him? Was he angry I started to talk?

He drifted up to me and opened his mouth, and like when his laughter filled my head, his voice flooded my brain. "*Where?*" he screamed as he circled Darth and me.

Scared shitless, I ran toward the stairs and dragged Darth behind me. The ghost—Gramps?—stayed in the hallway and moved in violent circles. I felt the air as it swirled around. Why was Gramps kind and gentle one minute and then attacking me the next? What was going on? And why did he tell me about the jewels and then get all pissed?

I sprinted across the first floor to the back door where Darth's leash hung, grabbing it as I opened the door and ran outside with her at my heels, not bothering to hook her to the leash until after we stood in the backyard well away from the house. My heart pounded, my entire body trembled, and I struggled not to slump over.

*

I glanced at the house to see if anyone followed me or turned on a light because of the commotion, but the scene appeared serene and quiet. Like no maniac irate ghost spun around like a madman in the upstairs hall. Good, because how was I going to explain what happened? *Oh, don't worry. Go back to bed, Mom. Just a pissed-off ghost in the hallway. No biggie. It's under control.* I needed to take another walk, get myself together. I started to turn away when Gramps looked out the landing window and glared down at me with glowing red eyes. Even angrier than a moment ago.

"What?" I whispered. "What did I do? Why are you so mad?"

I pulled Darth away and headed out the gate, down the street, with no idea where to go or what to do, except I needed to get away from the house and the furious ghost. I sprinted down the sidewalk, my entire body still shaking, paused after a few blocks, exhausted, and glanced back at

Gramps's house. Even from a distance, I made out its shape and saw the gables peeking out from behind the trees. Despite all the warm memories, the place felt like the devil's lair in the blackness of night.

Darth peered up at me as if I had gone insane, then strained at the leash to keep running. Half-obeying her, I caught my breath and headed downtown but at a walking pace. I liked the feel of downtown Fremont, which looked like time had frozen a part of Nebraska in the 1970s. I could wander past places from my childhood and daydream about times that seemed simpler because it was like Fremont never changed. The houses and storefronts stayed the same, even if they changed ownership or swapped out businesses, returning me to a carefree feeling of being little again.

I passed the old movie theater, the false front sticking out over the sidewalk with the old-school marquee with plastic letters to spell out the movie name. They'd turned the theater into a bookstore about thirteen years ago when even Fremont succumbed to the new megaplexes and stadium seating, making the traditional theater with one screen obsolete. Jenn, Lincoln, and I used to walk downtown during the summers to watch the kids' matinees for a dollar. Even then, I liked the pretend places films invented and always wanted to jump into those mysterious locations. I wished to jump into a fake location in the next two seconds. I sighed and Darth yanked on the leash again, because I had stopped without realizing it.

How did life manage to get so complicated since then?

Darth and I walked another block but slowed a couple of stores down, where people my age gathered, talking and laughing. I stopped, not wanting to get any closer to them.

Before I could get away, a person shouted at me, "Hey, you deaf?"

Startled, I turned to see who yelled, wondering if the person would be better or worse than the ghost at home. A guy about my age watched me, his hands in his jeans pockets, standing between myself and the other kids.

"Sorry. I guess I didn't hear you."

He stepped toward me. "It's okay. Who are you? I've never seen you around here."

My heart pounded when he spoke. Half from fear the stud would punch me in the mouth. And half from lust. His short brown hair, blue eyes, and nice, full lips, sent tingles down my spine, contradicting the simultaneous fear. Cute. Way cute.

He glanced around, taking a moment to observe the others behind him. I wondered why, since over here we were pretty much alone, or at least out of ear shot.

He grinned. "I assume you speak English? Or were those all your words?"

"Oh, yeah," I said. "Sorry." I pulled Darth closer, feeling nervous.

"Listen, if you come downtown, people are going to talk to you. It's what we do. Not much else to do in Fremont, and you're fresh meat. Anyway, I know who you are." When he pointed at me, I tried hard not to stare at the muscles of his arm. Super hunk. Maybe he played sports. Yep, a gold football pin right there on his letter jacket confirmed as much. "You're here for the Bachmann funeral, I'll bet. Are you staying in the haunted house?"

"Um— How did you know I came for the funeral?" I hated my soft voice and feared it sounded too effeminate. Did the tone give me away? Would he realize I'm gay? If he did, would he freak out? *God, he's so cute.* For the millionth time, I fought to get control of myself to no avail.

He shrugged. "Everyone around here watches the Bachmann house. Especially since the old man died." As he spoke, he kept looking over his shoulder toward the other people, still too far away to hear us. Was he nervous? Oh, God, maybe he figured me out and he was afraid a friend would see him talking to a gay guy. Or worse, maybe he plotted to play a prank on me or to punch me in the face, like so many lame jocks in the movies. I was glad for Darth. She'd bite him if he messed with me, even if I lost a tooth in the process.

"Um," I repeated the brilliant noise as I stared at him. Oh, wow. He looked into my eyes, which was so different than most guys my age, who avoided an intimate connection, all of us trying to figure ourselves out compared to expected masculine norms, or similar bullshit. And guys like him hated fags, remarking on their loathing often to remind everyone of their supreme heterosexuality. Had the guy figured out I'm gay? Why was he staring at me? Was he attracted to me? *Yeah, right. Like that would ever happen.* Then my head snapped back to needing to protect myself.

"I guess a lot of people think the house is haunted," I answered.

"Yeah, everyone but you crazy Bachmanns. Especially the old guy."

The jab came, a hostile move against me that always materialized when I was around boys my age, but at least it wasn't physical violence. But the mere mention of Gramps made my eyes tear, another embarrassing feminine trait for him to see. I wanted to disappear. Darth moved closer and bumped my leg with her head, at least continuing her canine sympathy and understanding.

To my surprise, he lowered his voice and in a gentle tone said, "Can I ask you more questions about the house? I'm sorry. I didn't mean to fuck with you. I sounded shitty." He sounded sincere even as he glanced around again.

"I don't know much about the house, though I think you mean the ghost," I snapped back, my sharp tone an attempt to defend myself. "The 'old guy' was my grandfather, and we were pretty close. As for whatever ghost stories you're talking about, I found out about them today. You know more than I do."

He stepped back, perhaps sensing my crazy vibe. "Hey, chill." He put up his hands in defense. "I didn't know. I'm sorry about your grandpa. Really." He paused. "So maybe you could take me on a tour of the house."

"Oh, yeah, sure. Maybe I could charge admission. Bring your peeps along."

"Relax. Why are you so angry?" He wrinkled his forehead. "Look, I could fill you in on what I know." Again, he sounded genuine and looked around to see if anyone saw us, which made me even more nervous, so I looked around too. What was he worried about?

"Listen," he said, "if anyone else sees us, it'll be worse. If you think I'm bad, wait till these bored Fremont losers see you. Do you want to go talk?"

I hesitated, still afraid. What did he want? I clutched Darth's leash to remind him she'd protect me, but he didn't seem to notice, and my crotch was giving me a different answer.

"Come on, I want to talk about the ghost. Please? Let's take a walk."

I reached down to pet Darth on the head, stalling for time. What if I went with him and he beat the crap out of me? He looked strong. Would Darth defend me? And if that happened, what would I tell my parents? A guy picked me up and then smacked me around because I'm gay?

But other thoughts continued to contradict the fear. His tone and body language never gave off a threat, and I already knew from experience Darth would launch at anything threatening me. Why not take a chance to have a few minutes with a hot guy, anyway. Tell him about the house and see where our chat goes. I could at least dream about him later.

"Um," I stammered out my answer. "Where do you want to go?" *Always brilliant with the dialogue*, I thought to myself. Idiot.

"My Jeep's around the corner. I know where we can go."

"I need to stay around here." A half-truth. I'd kind of snuck out of the house, so I already risked getting in trouble, regardless of where I went, but getting in a stranger's car was not a good idea, no matter how sexy.

"You got any other ideas?" he asked.

"Uh, we could walk. I didn't see anyone back toward Gramps's."

He smiled again. "Cool. Lead the way." He motioned forward with his hand.

Okay, so I still took a chance of going with a bulky stranger, but with Darth to protect me, I decided to head toward Gramps's house where I could also try to sprint home if the situation took a bad turn.

So I turned around and headed back down the street. We walked away from downtown in silence for a block as the lights illuminating Main Street like a football field dimmed to an occasional streetlight along our way.

Intimate. Kind of nice. Or stupid, because the surroundings were darker and could make pummeling a guy and leaving him lying there a lot easier.

When we got far enough away, he looked behind us, which made me nervous all over again. Every movie or book taught you NOT to listen to your penis when making decisions. Fuck. I clutched Darth's leash, afraid the guy would attack me, but the solitude of these quiet residential streets made me more comfortable, and I liked being alone with him without other teenagers lurking nearby.

"Yeah." He broke the silence. "I'd love to hear more about the house. Everyone talks about it, but no one knows the truth. The old man—uh, sorry. I mean your grandpa—laughed at people when they asked about a haunting. Truth is, everyone liked him, but those stories creeped us out. I guess he liked to keep people guessing."

My mind froze, unsure of how to respond, because all my first thoughts sounded stupid or, worse, insane. Being shy sucked. What could I talk about with a gorgeous guy? The longer we walked, the cuter I thought he was, which tied my tongue more and more. I worried he would leave or make fun of me for not saying anything but instead he kept talking.

"Hey, I didn't introduce myself. Sorry. Steve Williams." He held out his hand, and I shook it, intimidated all over again by his firm grasp compared to my grip and the tingling I felt at touching his skin. He released my hand. "Okay, so do you wanna know anything about me? I play football. Wide receiver. Do you like football?"

I stared at my feet, trying to figure out what to say to him, not even able to introduce myself in return.

"You okay? If you don't want to talk, it's cool, I can leave. At least give me your name."

I clenched my fists together for courage and forced myself to speak, though barely in a whisper. "I'm Jaret. And, uh, you already know my last name."

"No way. Did you ever live in Fremont?"

"Yeah." I studied Darth, who sauntered along wagging her tail.

"Did you go to kindergarten at Clarkson? With Ms. Guggenheim?"

I looked at him, surprised. "Yeah."

"We went to school together. I didn't recognize you. But I remember your name."

"Uh..." I didn't remember him.

"You sat in the back and you always knew the answers to everything. I'll bet you still know everything."

Just as I started to feel more comfortable, he turned back into a jock. What did that mean? Was his assertion about me good or bad? "I guess I study a lot."

"Do you remember me?"

"Uh, no."

He laughed. "We sat next to each other for the alphabet. When I got stuck, you gave me the answers."

A vague memory of working with a kid in class because our teacher encouraged cooperation came to me. Otherwise, I had no memory of playing together or even talking to the boy, who must have been Steve.

"I kind of remember." I nodded and glanced at him. "We worked together."

"Cool. But then you moved."

"Yeah, to Colorado."

"Good. I guess the formal introductions are done." Steve's earlier macho mood passed and he returned to a more casual tone. Though I found the whole jock thing kind of sexy, I also had no way of relating to his demeanor. "What's your dog's name?"

Darth trotted along, oblivious to Steve and me, her ears pinned back as she hustled along. She lurched forward when she heard a dog bark, so I pulled her back. I patted her on the head. "Darth."

"Awesome. As in Darth Vader?"

"Yeah, I'm a big *Star Wars* fan. Especially the old movies. I used to watch them with Dad." I smiled. "Kinda geeky, huh?"

"No. I liked *Star Wars* too. So how long have you owned Darth?"

"My parents got her for me when I was about seven. She's almost eleven now. But she doesn't act old."

"Wow. She's getting up there. But she looks good. Is she as mean as the real Darth Vader was?"

I hesitated to answer. I could explain her sweet nature, but then he might not think she would bite him if he attacked me. My instincts were relaxing, though, which dissipated a little of my fear.

"No, she's more like R2-D2."

Steve laughed and reached over to scratch Darth's back, to which she wagged her stub of a tail but otherwise continued plodding ahead. "What kind of dog is she?"

"Kind of a mutt. Australian cattle dog, but there's other stuff in there."

"She looks fast." Steve grinned at me, and my heart pounded again. With the introductions over, another awkward silence fell between us.

*

I wondered what Steve wanted? Sure, a haunted house was always interesting, but his interest felt like there was another element too. I tugged Darth's leash to get her away from a bush. Maybe I only wished for more. I almost wanted to throw up, I was so nervous.

We walked in silence past another large brick house, its lawn lined with enormous oak trees whose roots warped the sidewalk. Did ghosts haunt it too? Were they everywhere in Fremont, or just at Gramps's? I stepped over a big crack but Steve missed it and fell into me, and we both lurched away from the contact, though I enjoyed his touch. He smelled kind of like Axe body wash, a rich, clean smell. Yum.

"Sorry," he said.

I freaked a little on the inside. The little touch got me all excited. What if he noticed the bulge in my pants? Puberty messed up most teens, but hormones were super dangerous for a gay guy. I fought my feelings, but my effort wasn't working. Thank God it was dark. And thankfully, Steve spoke again.

"You said you didn't know about the rumors? About your Gramps's place?"

"No. I heard about the whole thing today. My family doesn't talk about the haunting, I guess. Protecting the kids, or they think so, anyway. Plus, my dad doesn't believe any of the rumors, though my uncle and aunt kind of got into an argument with him at lunch."

"That explains all the gossip about the hauntings. People love to talk about shit they don't know about. So if your family never says anything, the silence fuels the fire."

"What do people say?"

"It sounds more exciting than in reality. They say crap like 'A ghost haunts the Bachmann House! Beware!' No one knows when the rumors all started or what this ghost does. They pretend to talk about the spirit. Small-town crap.

"And your grandpa never mentioned the tales—which always pissed people off. If you didn't know, then seems like he didn't even tell his family about the ghost. He hated anyone in Fremont mentioning it. I don't think your aunt and uncle talk about the spirit either. Their kids graduated before I started high school, so I never met any Bachmann besides you. But everyone says they all refuse to talk about it. Is Jill your cousin?"

"Yeah."

"She's said family members think the house is haunted. My aunt went to school with her. But she never said more. Your grandma, though. She told a lot of stories about strange things happening in the house."

I looked over at his tight T-shirt under the unzipped coat and wanted to grab his chest to see if it was as solid as it looked, a fantasy doing nothing to quell the excitement in my pants.

Steve continued talking, however, without noticing anything going on with me. "She and my grandma played bridge together every week. I got most of my information from Granny."

"Your grandmother knew mine? My grandma died before I was born. I only know stuff my family told me about her. Everyone says she was nice and wonderful, but I don't know. Today Dad said she and Gramps argued about the ghost. Gramps told her the spirit didn't exist, but she said it did."

"Granny says the same thing. She and Mrs. Bachmann used to talk about the haunting because it scared your Grandma."

"What did my grandmother think?"

"Like I said, most of this is what Granny told me. I don't know if it's true. Your grandma told people a spirit lived in the house and protected a 'Bachmann heritage.' My Granny says the ghost even guarded the crib of Bachmann babies until they grew up. Otherwise the ghost watches over the house. Your grandma claimed she'd feel its presence around the children, and she said it moved things to protect them."

"Really? This sounds more like a bad movie. A ghost lords over Bachmann babies and moves shit around the house."

Steve laughed. "I suppose the story sounds crazy. Have you ever seen a ghost there?"

No way I was going to tell him about my crazy, freaky ability. Not yet. So I ignored the question. "Do you know anything else about the stories?" I asked.

"No. Granny spent a lot of time comforting your grandma and telling her not to worry. I never heard of the spirit hurting anybody." He shrugged.

"It's weird everyone kept the legend from me. Or at least Dad decided not to tell his kids, because I don't think my brother or sister knew either."

"Does seem weird." Steve turned around and walked backward a few steps to look at me, before turning around again.

"Even Mom found out today," I added. "So, what else have you heard?"

"Just rumors. I guess most of Fremont talks about the haunted house. I've heard people say an evil being is in the house, and I've heard other people say it's all made up. Of course, most of the talk comes from the high school. You know, kids love a good ghost story."

"Kids our age care about it? Why?" I asked.

"We spend time trying to see the ghost. People sneak into the yard to try to get a peek. No one I know ever saw anything." He looked at me, seeming to get how what he found humorous alarmed me. "I don't believe in the ghost. It's a rumor to ponder in a boring town. People hide like idiots in the bushes and try to look inside. Doesn't every town have a ghost house?"

"I guess so." I shrugged. "People in Estes think the Stanley Hotel is haunted. You know, where Stephen King got the idea for *The Shining*. But I think most people have better things to do than hang around a small downtown or sneak around looking for ghosts." I regretted my snootiness.

Steve laughed again. "Yeah, Fremont sucks. Still, people think they *did* see a ghost. Scared the shit out of them. Or maybe their stories fuel the fire and get more people to spy."

Shivers ran down my spine when I heard other people saw a ghost too. "What do they see?" I tried to keep my voice from quivering.

He leaned closer to me and whispered, I think for dramatic effect, and my nerves turned from fear of ghosts to fear he'd figure out how much his proximity turned me on. "They see a ghost who wanders through the halls with a sinister grin." Steve spoke with a mock threatening voice, like a B-movie horror villain, but it made me sort of dizzy, him being so close to me.

But the sexual energy fizzled as my brain comprehended his statement and as the hair on my arms stood straight up. The image sounded like the figure who laughed at me earlier, the angry Gramps chasing me out of the house.

"Do you believe what people say?" he asked. "You look scared."

Past experiences of being mocked for seeing ghosts reminded me not to say a thing to a guy I just met, no matter what my dick tried to tell me. No way I was going to say I saw a ghost, and it talked to me too. No way I would explain the spirit terrified the shit out of me.

"Um, I guess if somebody thinks they saw a ghost, it seems real." Lame. I wasn't even sure what I meant, but my comment bought me time.

To get a grip, I concentrated on the steady rhythm of Darth's tags clinking together as she trotted along, Steve's and my footsteps, and the sounds of crickets. Trees loomed above us, and I caught the twinkling of stars through the leaves. And then I realized Steve had stayed close to me, close enough to brush his arm against mine a little. Great, I thought. First I'm freaking out about ghosts and next I'm freaking out about hormones. Never thought fear and lust could mix together all at the same time.

He looked sideways at me again. "You okay?"

"Fine. I was thinking about what you said. I wonder if Gramps knew all of this."

"You called Mr. Bachmann Gramps?"

"Yeah. Why?"

"It's kind of like my grandma is Granny. What were you thinking?"

"I always felt safe in the house because of him. I remember good things, so it's strange to hear everyone in Fremont is so scared of my Gramps's." Except the mansion frightened me today too.

"Maybe because you're a Bachmann. Even your grandma, who hated the ghost, thought it protected the family."

"The ghost sure doesn't feel protective anymore."

"Do you believe there's a ghost?"

I hesitated. "Do you?"

"I don't know." He kicked a rock down the sidewalk. "It's exciting to think there's one. But I never saw anything." He turned a little red. "I even went ghost hunting a couple times. But we never saw anything."

Silence returned. His words and continued engagement made me want to tell him everything, but my revelation always went wrong so I stayed quiet.

Then his hand brushed against mine again. I leaned a little into him, brushing against him, but hoping my move seemed like an accident. I glanced down to watch our hands touch. I liked how his skin felt, but when Steve looked over, I stared forward and pulled my hand away, hoping he hadn't noticed anything.

Steve kept talking. "You never heard about any of this?"

"Nope."

"Did *you* ever see anything in the house?"

"Uh—" I stammered and pretended to cough.

"Does the rumor creep you out?"

"A little." I held up my hand and showed him an inch between my fingers for a visual explanation.

"Why?"

The hesitation crept upon me again, about how I had a hard time keeping friends after I told them, about my fear of rejection. Just the same, I wanted to blurt the truth out and maybe get the embarrassment over. Let him think I was nuts and be done with all the turmoil inside me. "You'll think I'm an out-of-town freak," I ventured with caution. He scrunched his brow at me but still smiled. "Okay, fine. Yes, I've seen a ghost there."

"The one everybody says is clear and laughs at them?"

"I suppose."

"You suppose?"

"I'm not sure. I've seen a lot of things there for the first time today. The ghost looks like Gramps a lot of the time, as if his ghost lives in the house. And the vision is so solid I want to hug him. But other times the ghost is angry and not solid at all. What you described matches the angry ghost I see, and I saw it again before I left the house tonight. It's not pleasant. The spirit scares the crap out of me." Once the dam burst, my words flowed out, and I failed to check them.

Steve played it cool though. "So, is your grandpa the ghost?"

"The ghost looks like him, except younger, maybe when he was thirty. But then again, the apparition can't be him because people have seen it for decades, including my grandma, while Gramps was still alive."

"Wow. Strange. But if it looks like your grandpa—"

"Gramps never scared the crap out of people for fun," I snapped. "And he wouldn't even after he died."

"Sorry. Relax." He reached over and patted my shoulder. More contact to thrill me. "I was thinking about what you said."

*

We walked without saying anything for a couple of blocks before he asked another question. "Do others in your family see a ghost?"

"Not in my immediate family. I can't tell for sure about my aunt and uncle."

"What do they think of your seeing the thing?"

I sighed. "A long time ago, I tried to tell my family when I saw things, but I stopped and would never tell them any of this." My openness surprised me, but Steve made me feel so comfortable and normal about the situation, I kept talking.

"Wait," he held up a hand to stop the conversation even as we kept moving forward. "You said you saw your gramps's ghost, or whatever haunts the house, for the first time. What do you mean a long time ago?"

I grinned in embarrassment. "Well, I see ghosts. My whole life. And my family freaked the first time I told them, which is why I won't tell them about this time."

Steve nodded his understanding. "What would they do?"

"They either don't believe me or think I've lost my mind and lecture me about my imagination. Please don't tell *anyone* what I told you."

Steve giggled a little, a surprisingly feminine sound coming from him. "How would I explain this to anyone? Or tell them how we met? I can imagine." Steve jogged a couple steps ahead, strutted like a jock, grabbed his crotch, and lowered his voice to a booming masculine tone. "Hey, guys, I went on a late-night walk with a Bachmann dude, and he told me about ghosts at the Bachmann house."

I laughed, wondering if he adopted his jock persona at other times or as a joke for me. "All right, I get the picture. You can stop. I'm sure it won't surprise you I don't hang out with a lot of jocks. I'm not into football." My confident words hid a sudden embarrassment about my skinny body. But Steve laughed. Then he put his arm around my shoulder and squeezed, like football players do after a great play.

"You're a funny guy." Then Steve slapped me on the back.

I liked Steve and got so comfortable I blurted out the entire story, of seeing Gramps's ghost in Colorado and everything that had happened to me since we got to Fremont, including the warnings for me not to come here.

"Oh," Steve skipped into the air, excited. He clapped his hands together. "I forgot this."

"What?"

"A pastor here thinks the Bachmann house is haunted. I can't believe I forgot. He's an old geezer who's been at the church forever."

"Which one?" I asked.

"Lutheran."

"You mean Pastor Schmidt?"

"Yeah. You know him?"

"He baptized me." I yanked Darth along when she stopped to sniff a mesmerizing bush.

"No way. Too weird. Anyway, my grandma told me about him too. She said he helped your grandmother, or at least tried. Granny told me he performed an exorcism on the house, but no one knows if the ritual worked."

"I hate to get all religious on you, but Lutherans don't believe in exorcism stuff. Sounds more Catholic." I remember asking my pastor in Colorado about exorcisms, and how he dismissed my question as nonsense.

"I know what Lutherans believe." Steve fidgeted with his hands. "Pastor Schmidt confirmed me." He grinned. "Yeah, he's Lutheran, but he believes a lot of the hocus-pocus stuff from a history of Christianity he studied. I never listened too much. I know he talked about magic and protective church rituals. We thought he was nuts. He made us promise not to tell people what he said because it wasn't in the catechism. But he wanted us to know the truth, he said. And Granny said he met with your grandmother and talked to her about exorcising the ghost. I guess his holy water and Bible didn't do the job."

It sounded like all of Fremont knew about the ghost, except my generation of Bachmanns, and my poor mother.

"Is that all you know about what he thinks?"

"Pretty much. He always hinted about strange things during confirmation. He told us about spirits haunting houses and warned us to follow the right path or they might come after us. Like I said, we thought he started to go senile. We tried hard not to laugh at him. But what you told me makes me think we ought to take him more seriously."

My feet ached a little from all the walking, but I worried stopping would prompt Steve to go home. I glanced at my watch, wondering about the time, more as a nervous twitch than because I cared at the moment. Two a.m.

"Do you need to go?" Steve asked.

"No." I jerked my head up to look at him. "I'm not ready to go back to the house yet."

"Cool. Follow me."

He turned and jogged half a block ahead. I walked behind, too sore to run, with Darth ahead of me and caught up with him at a huge park, set back from the street and dark because its one light had burned out. A sign warned the park closed at dusk and the police would fine and arrest violators.

"Ignore the sign." Steve pointed to it. "If we sit toward the back, the cops won't find us. The most they ever do is drive by and flash their spotlights, which means they can't see anyone through the trees. Except on the weekends. Then they check more often because this is a great make-out place."

An image of Steve kissing me bounced into my head, and my heart thundered at the thought.

*

Once at the rear of the park, I could see a lamp far down the street from our concealed position. In addition to the trees, playground equipment shielded us from the sidewalk and passing cars. Steve sat on a picnic bench and slapped it, a sign for me to sit next to him. Darth, also tired, curled up beneath my feet.

"I wish I had more to tell you about the ghost at your grandpa's," Steve continued our conversation. "I never believed till tonight. But I believe you. Especially since Granny also said the story was true."

"I'm glad I could talk without you thinking I'm nuts." I was a little surprised I revealed so much, so fast to a complete stranger after years of holding my secret inside, but the emotions of the past few days and the unique circumstances opened me to him. Steve's easygoing nature and nonjudgmental reaction helped too.

I was also amazed I talked to him at all, despite my total attraction. My hormones shut me right up most of the time. I worried he might figure out my secret and wanted him to like me at the same time, but I had no clue how those things combined. Was he a nice guy? What if my feelings repulsed him? Not that I intended to tell him. No way. Too risky. Just add him to the lengthy list of my secret crushes.

"You don't sound nuts. I believe you. It must be hard, losing your grandpa and now this ghost thing." He paused and looked at me. "Did seeing him bother you? I mean, he's dead, you came for his funeral, and now this ghost chases you around. That's gotta suck." He grinned at the complete oddity of the whole thing.

Which made me smile in response and shrug. Before I could answer, though, a lump caught in my throat. "It does suck." I choked back tears. "I loved him a lot. But this ghost thing, I don't know what to think. I think he wants to protect me. He feels so real and loving, like I remember. But then this transparent, angry vision comes and makes fun of me. I can't figure out what's going on."

Tears filled my eyes, mortifying me as one trickled down my face. I turned my head away and fought to regain control, then flinched when I felt a hand touch my back.

"It's cool," Steve said. "Let it out. I didn't mean to make you feel bad."

Steve rubbed my back and then wrapped his arm around my shoulder. He tugged at me, as if we knew each other well. His embrace felt wonderful.

Until I got all excited, about two seconds later, which sent my emotions spinning even more out of control. What if he noticed?

But he sat there like we were in the most natural position, not at all grossed out by the man-to-man contact. Even when we made eye contact, he stared straight back at me and then, without a word, Steve leaned forward and kissed me. He grabbed my face with both hands and pulled me toward him, then pushed his tongue into my mouth. Chills swept through my body as Steve ran his hand down my back and grabbed my ass and pulled me toward him as we kissed even harder. Oh, my God. His chest was rock hard, and it felt so good against mine. I ran my hands up his muscled arms, the thrill of touching and kissing almost making me pass out with excitement. I let go and wrapped my arms around his neck.

We kissed for a long time, making eye contact, his gorgeous face so close to mine as I explored every inch of his mouth. His eyes burned into me and his short brown hair glistened with sweat when we paused for a moment. "You're hot." He wiped the hair from my forehead and rested his hand on my cheek.

"I never did this before," I said, dropping my gaze to his chest, shy again.

"Me neither." Steve pulled me back and kissed me again.

We slid into the grass and lay next to each other, still kissing. The next several minutes shot by in a blur of excitement and energy, until we lay motionless, gazing up at the stars, my mind exhilarated and wondering what the fuck happened. I loved feeling his chest move up and down as he breathed, his arms holding me, until he propped himself up on his elbow and stared down at me. "I'm attracted to you. Like, a lot."

My stomach lurched with excitement. "This is your first time?"

"With another guy. I dated girls and shit. After tonight, I can't imagine being with a girl again."

"You kissed a girl?" I scrunched up my face, like I tasted a sour apple. "I never have."

Steve laughed. "Girls are okay!"

"Yeah," I agreed. "As friends and stuff. I have lots of them. But I never wanted to kiss one."

"Well, I felt obligated, because I'd much rather be kissing you." He followed through on his words by planting another one on my lips.

I laughed. "I plan to stay a girl virgin."

Steve jumped on top of me and pinned my shoulders to the ground. He tickled my stomach until I begged him to stop, but he continued to hold me there and then leaned over and kissed my cheek and licked along it to my lips. The sensation was heaven, and I hardly believed how much I already liked the guy, like we'd known each other for years.

"This is fucked up," Steve whispered. "I know I sound nuts. But I want to see you again. I *have* to see you again. No one can know about us, but we could still see each other before you leave."

I grinned. "Agreed."

"About what?"

"Everything." I twirled a strand of my hair on my finger. "We can't tell anyone. But I want to see you again too."

"I still have school. What works for you?"

"My family has dinner together, the whole extended group. Then they sit around and drink and talk. I can't leave until afterward. But I can sneak out again later."

"Cool." He flopped down onto the ground next to me. "My parents think I'm in bed. I climb out my bedroom window onto the garage roof and jump down all the time without them knowing. Where should we meet?"

"Beats me. You know Fremont better. You pick."

"Well, we gotta avoid downtown where everyone hangs and cruises around in cars because there's nothing to do. Most everything will be closed by then too. God, Fremont sucks. What if I come to the backyard? We can figure out where to go from there, and I'll think about it tomorrow. Listen, I'd text you, but my Dad is freaked about all the shit he hears on TV about what teens do. He thinks I'll shoot naked pictures of myself across the universe or text a dumbass comment. So he checks everything. I don't think I better call or text you. I'll come by."

He made me laugh because of my own dad's cell phone weirdness. "Sounds good. I don't have my cell, anyway, because of my father. It's a long story. Meet back in the bushes. It's quiet there and far enough away from the house no one will see. And I can even hide from the ghost there, if I need to." Okay, I sounded odd talking about the spirits during what should have been a typical conversation. Nervous, I giggled and wondered what he thought, but Steve smiled back.

"Makes sense. Be careful in the house. I don't want the ghost to take you away from me."

I blushed. His words and his ease with a new relationship melted me, even as we plotted to keep our relationship hidden. He was so easygoing, the exact opposite of me, which attracted me all the more.

Yet creeping doubt about myself and what he thought plagued me. It was insane to want anything from him after spending a couple hours together. "So did you talk to me downtown because of the ghost thing?"

He tilted his head in thought. "Maybe at first. Plus you were new. Fresh meat. But the entire time, I kept thinking you were hot. But I never thought I'd be telling you." He laughed. "I mean, I think guys are hot all the time without making out with them in the park. I have no idea what came over me tonight!"

"You're not afraid to say anything," I said. "I'd never have come up to you."

"Huh. It's what we do. Besides, I wanted to see your lips up close. And your ass."

My face burned with embarrassment, and I had no idea what to say.

"Plus, you're shy. That's hot." Steve tugged me toward him again and grabbed my ass. "Well, I'd better go."

Steve hopped up and reached down to pull me to my feet. As I launched into the air, he grabbed me around the waist and pulled me into himself. I hated when he let me go.

I looked at the ground, not wanting to leave him but knowing I had to. I patted Darth on the head to release my nervous energy.

"I'll be a zombie tomorrow at school." Steve grabbed my shoulders and pulled me into a kiss, then held me close. "Do you need an escort?"

The darkness did make me nervous, even with Darth, because I did not know what lurked in Fremont, be it human or ghost. But would my feeling appear wimpy or uncool to ask for him to tag along when he already expressed being tired and needing to get home? So, as usual, I stood frozen and silent.

"Come on." Steve grabbed my hand and pulled me along without an answer, as if reading my mind. Darth trotted beside us as we left the park and headed down the street until I bent over and grabbed her leash. Steve surprised me by holding my hand the whole way, which I gripped. Sure, at 4:00 in the morning the vacant streets did not threaten to expose us, but touching each other still made me nervous even as my heart tingled with excitement.

Outside the gate to Gramps's back yard, Steve pecked me on the cheek, like old time chivalry, and we said goodbye. I watched him start toward downtown, feeling giddy, like my friends at home who I made fun of when they started dating. I knew why they acted so crazy and why their hormones raged out of control. I was infatuated.

And Steve liked me too!

He spun around and waved, then blew me a kiss, before he turned the corner. I smiled a big sloppy grin and scratched Darth behind the ears before turning back to the house.

*

My euphoria evaporated when the house's shadow loomed over me. Dark and ominous, an awful presence lurked inside, waiting to consume me, a fear I felt deep inside my very soul. I moved through the yard and clutched Darth's leash when I reached the back steps. The second floor scared me because of the attic door. I thought about Gramps and the jewelry and wondered what was waiting inside as I opened the door, trying to be quiet.

The kitchen looked okay, nothing changed since I left. It even looked the same as when Gramps had eaten his morning Rice Krispies and chocolate donuts at the little table in the breakfast nook.

The hall to the front entry was normal, too, but the stairs came next. I couldn't go up them. I put one foot on the first step and froze, then felt the tension of Darth's leash as she pulled against going upstairs. Why was she still on her leash, I wondered, but then realized the combination of my fear and her resistance sent a clear message: stay the fuck downstairs.

So I went to the back porch and crawled into a hammock. Against her will, I lifted Darth into the hammock with me and cuddled next to her, watching her reactions for signs of the ghost. But she curled up at my side and put her head on my chest, so I closed my eyes and drifted to sleep with dreams of Steve holding and protecting me.

Just before sleep took over, my eyelids fluttered open for a second, and I thought I remembered Gramps sitting in the chair across from me, watching us lay there. But since Darth didn't move and I was exhausted, I went back to sleep, too tired to think about the vision.

Chapter Two

The Attic

The next morning, the smell of warm rolls baking in the kitchen floated through the screen door and onto the porch where I had slept without stirring despite the previous night's events. I clutched Darth to me, noticing she'd ended up on top of my stomach because the hammock smashed us together. She wagged her tail when I kissed her on the head, and then I helped her jump to the floor without jamming her paws into me. Grounded, she turned around to lick my face while I rubbed her back. Then she danced in circles to notify me we better get her outside soon.

I rolled out of the hammock and stumbled over to the side door that led into the fenced back yard. Before I even got the door open all the way, she darted outside and sprinted toward the grass, though she took time to run along the fence line before squatting to pee. Her simple happiness calmed my nerves a little, and Gramps's lilac bushes looked so fresh and welcoming they relaxed me even more. I reminded myself to act like a dog whenever possible and stay in the moment, instead of dreading what lurked around the next corner, even while stuck in a haunted house.

I stretched and, out the corner of my eye, spotted the chair where I thought Gramps had sat last night. Turning my attention to it, I saw the cushion still contained an indentation from a person sitting there. Could a ghost leave a mark? Or were my senses playing tricks on me? Because a human sat there at one point, too, before I even went to bed. One thing was certain. Daylight made things seem a lot less scary.

The sight of a pair of Gramps's reading glasses sitting on a small table brought my moment of peace to a crashing halt all too fast with the thought about how tomorrow the family would attend Gramps's funeral to say a final goodbye. A lump formed in my throat, and I tried not to cry.

A million emotions ran through my mind, racing around without a clear direction. Dealing with my entire family almost overwhelmed me, with their love for me countered by a sense of obligation to act a certain way. I was already stressed, still a little tired, and then add to those emotions the excitement of meeting Steve, of a total make-out session with him, but all the while fricking ghosts swirled around me. No one understood the stuff in my head, and everybody was going to be all Bachmann weird, depressed, and repressed because nobody would talk about their feelings, which made everything worse. Like a huge vise pressing into us, keeping feelings locked inside even as we could see in one another's faces a desperate longing to release them.

I smiled a little, though, when my thoughts returned to Steve. That must be what adults meant when they referred to teenagers and our fucked-up hormones. One minute, grief over Gramps and angst over my family almost overwhelmed me, and then I tingled with anticipation of jamming my face into Steve's again. Was I being shitty to Gramps because I kept thinking about Steve instead of focusing on the situation at hand? Shit.

*

The sound of the screen door into the main house opening behind me brought me back to reality. I looked over to see Mom.

"Good morning." She almost smiled, looking as tired as me.

Her hesitant manner as she stepped toward me sent alarm bells ringing. She wanted to talk and was nervous. Had she seen Steve and me come home together? Was she back to drill me more about prom?

"Morning." I stretched my arms above my head and pretended to look for Darth outside, thankful her presence was bringing my groin under control but still worried my excitement might show.

"You're tired." She patted me on the back and then sat in the chair where the ghost may or may not have watched over me.

"I just woke up."

Darth appeared at the door, so I let her back in and then plummeted to the floor in front of Mom.

"Do you have a minute?"

"Sure." I shifted around and grabbed Darth, to get her to sit beside me. Fuck.

"Are you okay?" she asked, her tone soft.

"Yeah." I nodded but avoided looking at her. "I miss Gramps. It's been pretty hard."

"We all do."

"Okay, well, it also bothers me no one talks about Gramps dying. Everyone acts like nothing happened. Like nothing's wrong. But something *is* wrong. Gramps is dead. He's gone. We should be talking about him. About our loss."

Mom reached down and grabbed my hand. "The Bachmanns don't deal with emotions very well. Maybe it's because they're German. And because that's how people live in the Midwest, but it's who they are. Your dad and I argued a lot about sharing feelings when we first got married. I needed him to share more with me. Expressing himself took him a long time, and it wasn't easy, but he came around. Or at least he got better. The rest of this family, though: they don't even know it's a problem. Your dad still has a hard time with emotion too."

I smiled. "Yeah, with his own kids."

"I know. Be patient with him. He loves all of you but doesn't know how to express his emotion. He shows he cares with what he does more than with words."

I loved my dad, even though he seldom showed emotion. I imagine I took my cue from him because I tried to hide mine all the time too. So at the same time, I had a hard time with Dad because I worried about disappointing him. Especially since I wasn't going to grow up, marry a nice woman, and have a bunch of kids. And how would we ever work through all of my issues if we never talked about our feelings for each other?

"You can always talk to me about Gramps," Mom said.

"I miss him. I don't know what else to say." I shrugged. "I feel him everywhere in this house. Everything I see reminds me of him. I can't accept he's gone." My eyes welled with tears.

"It takes time." She patted my knee. "There's no magic to make the feeling better or help you forget. Being sad is okay. You should be. I'd worry more if you didn't feel anything."

Part of me wanted to tell her more, but I was at a loss for words and afraid of what might come out, because no way I wanted to bring up ghosts. So instead I went simple, a repressed Bachmann response. "Thanks. I'll find you if I need to talk."

"And I'll do the same."

"What would you need to talk to me about?" I always forgot grown-ups dealt with shit too.

She shook her head. "You know how your imagination goes wild? You're not alone. Probably got the reaction from me. Because all night long I thought a ghost was nudging me and trying to get my attention. I hardly slept. The sensation was so real and frightening. It was all I could do not to get up and run out of the house."

Well, that bombshell forced me to pause. All the time she sent me to the funny farm for saying the same things, maybe this opened a door? No doubt her experience was with the same demon fucking with me. Except she dismissed the episode as imaginary, so I decided not to take the bait. Avoid, avoid, avoid. "That sucks." Brilliant teenage deductions always solved the problem.

She giggled. "Yes, it does. But I have one more thing."

My heart pounded in fear. Shit. Prom. "I was afraid of that." I grinned, trying for funny but sounding nervous with a quiver in my voice.

"You always could read me." She grinned, not all tense like me. "Why did you sleep on the porch?"

I shrugged again, not making eye contact as I searched for what to say without telling the truth, about how ghosts on the second floor kept me from going up the stairs. "No reason." Lame. Like she wouldn't see through my stupid excuse. "It was kinda hot upstairs." I think even Darth peered up at me in disbelief with my utter stupidity.

Mom nodded once but seemed unconvinced when I looked up at her. "I heard you leave last night. I thought maybe you slept our here so you wouldn't wake us up when you came home."

I stared back down at the floor. She cut to at least part of the truth, but her theory still kept the ghosts out of the conversation. "I went out with Darth for a walk to clear my mind."

"I'm not mad." She shook her head. "Be careful. Where did you go?"

"We wandered around Fremont."

"Okay. But don't let your father know. He has enough on his mind without thinking about you out at night after curfew. He'd worry."

"I won't tell him."

"Were you by yourself?" she pushed.

"I don't know anyone in Fremont," I hedged. "I could get in a lot more trouble back home if I wanted to." I wondered how long I could keep dodging the issue, when every thought of last night brought memories of kissing Steve.

Thankfully, she laughed.

"Remember, I went to college here. I know there's not much to do, outside of hanging out with people."

"And drinking." I smiled at her. "You talk about drinking a lot. Grasshoppers at the steak house?"

She laughed and shook her finger at me. "Don't think you need to do everything I did. Don't you ever forget anything we tell you?" She stood. "Why don't you come inside now? Your Dad's waiting."

"What for?"

"He and Harold recruited everyone to search the house for those jewels. Even your sister joined in. It's like a big Bachmann Easter egg hunt. After years of never mentioning these mysterious gems, they've become the most important thing in the world."

"Did you find out about the jewels yesterday?"

"Yes." A slight grin spread across her face.

"And they never mentioned the ghost thing before?" I probed a little for her reaction.

"You know too much." She smiled wider. "No one ever has talked about any of this. Not even your father when we were alone. I suppose he didn't know how to tell me. And I can see the next question in your eyes, so I'll tell you I was bothered they hid the story, but I'm not angry. I think your dad was embarrassed about the ghost more than anything, because he doesn't believe a spirit haunts the house. I'm sure that's what got me worked up last night."

As she guessed my next question before I answered it, I thought how well my mom and I knew each other. Which was why I suspected she already knew I'm gay but she didn't want to deal with my sexuality. "So you think Dad didn't know how to tell you?"

"In part." She nodded. "But he also never believed in the ghosts. He told me last night. I can't imagine anyone wanting to talk about a situation that might make their family look odd. And the jewels were Gramps's. I think everyone avoided them, because if they talked about what to do with them, they'd also have to talk about your grandfather's eventual death."

"Does it bother you, how Dad kept the family ghost a secret?"

"No. We talked about what happened yesterday. He apologized. I learned a long time ago to enjoy my time with the Bachmanns without worrying about the things unsaid or unknown. Like I said, they hid most of these stories because the rumors embarrassed them. If I took it personally every time this family kept a secret, I'd feel bad or be angry all the time. I take these things in stride, knowing they don't keep secrets to be malicious. Your father reverts to the behavior around the rest of the family."

"Plus Gramps hated any conflict." I remembered how hard Gramps would work to resolve any tension and scold any of us if we got mad at each other, even for a moment. "Since they disagreed about the whole haunted house thing, he wouldn't talk about the ghost to keep peace."

"How right you are." Mom sighed in agreement.

"So they want me to help look? Where else could the stuff be? We've already searched the whole house."

"I think they're in the attic. We went over every inch of this house except up there. And Uncle Harold went to the bank safe deposit box before we got to town, and they weren't there either. But they still can't get the attic door open." She moved toward the kitchen door. "Let's go. Aunt Alice has homemade cinnamon rolls."

Darth and I followed Mom into the kitchen. "Want a treat?" I asked Darth, who wagged her tail and sat in front of me. I reached on the counter for the bag of Snausages I brought from Colorado. "Gentle," I told her before letting her take one from my fingers.

As she gulped the treat down without so much as one bite, through the corner of my eye and down the hallway, I spotted the stairs. Not quite as scary in the daylight, but I still knew bad shit lurked up there.

And just what I always wanted. To scrounge around the house when evil didn't want us to. Thank God, Darth was with me. Sounds stupid, but she could read my mind, had a ghost radar to warn me when they approached, and so far, always agreed with me on when to get the hell out. I picked up one of Alice's cinnamon rolls, still warm, and ate it. Delicious.

*

When I finished eating, Darth and I went into the living room and plopped into a chair together to wait for everyone else. Anything to avoid going upstairs.

Lincoln meandered in first. "Avoiding work again?"

"I didn't feel like going on a lost treasure hunt."

Lincoln flopped himself onto the couch. "Such sarcasm."

"Bite me."

"Where did you learn to talk like that, young man?"

"Whatever. What do you want?"

"To annoy you. And it's working. Are you going to help us today?"

I shrugged. "Do I have any other options?" Darth jumped to the floor and lay in front of me, so I lifted my leg over the arm of the chair and sat back. "It's not like there's a lot to do in Fremont. But I might go on a walk with Darth. They won't look all day for the jewels, you know how Dad and Uncle Harold like their breaks. They'll get hungry, and they never miss a feeding time. Besides, everyone knows the jewels are in the attic."

"You're right, smart guy." Lincoln tossed a throw pillow into the air. "But we can't get the attic door open. The situation feels like Gramps nailed the door shut from the other side."

"We could use dynamite."

"Oh, yeah. Great idea. Let's tell Dad." Lincoln laughed as he got up and pulled me out of the chair, making me laugh, too, more at him than anything else. Darth led the way. She followed the smell of food to Dad, who was eating in the dining room with everyone else.

"Hey girl," Dad said and threw a piece of his roll to her. She caught the morsel midair and gulped it down.

"Don't give her people food," I scolded.

"It's just a little bit."

I rolled my eyes but knew he would never listen to me. He mumbled and took another bite.

"Jaret thinks we should blow the door up to get in the attic," Lincoln announced as he came in behind me.

Everyone laughed.

"Is that the best plan you turkeys can come up with?" Uncle Harold asked.

"Yeah, aren't you two helpful." Dad ate another bite of his roll. "We can blow the door up like you used to blow up your army figures with firecrackers. It's amazing you both have all of your fingers."

"Well, who bought us the firecrackers?" Lincoln asked.

"Harold and I gave up on the door for a while." Dad scraped his plate clean with his fork. "We need to think about what to do. Maybe a box fell down the stairs and blocked the door."

"Or maybe a *thing* doesn't want us up there." Aunt Alice dropped her fork onto the table with a clang.

"Ah, Alice, don't start again." Harold frowned but avoided eye contact with his wife. "We'll get the damn door open. We have to find those jewels."

She scowled at him. "You and Dan need to think a little more before you go and try to force the door." She held up her hands in surrender. "Your mother never took the strange things happening in this house for granted."

"Damn it, Alice." My uncle's face went bright red. "Enough. I don't want to live in this house any more than you do, ghost or not. But we need to find where Gramps put everything, and the less you nag about the situation the better."

The room fell silent. I had never heard Uncle Harold talk that way to anyone, let alone my aunt.

She glared at him for a long moment, then stood and walked out of the room with her plate.

Dad broke the awkward silence. "Hey, honey. Bring those rolls and coffee while Harold and I try to figure this out."

I cringed. Could my dad be ruder?

"Please?" Mom asked.

"Yeah, okay."

My mom rolled her eyes but she got up. I wondered if all hetero couples acted the same way? Or was their behavior generational? With the men growling orders and the women telling them to shut up but obeying the order anyway? Maybe being gay wasn't so bad. I sure hoped Jenn would never even date a guy who treated her that way, even though I knew how much Dad loved Mom.

Besides, all the talk of attic doors, family tension, and ghosts was stressing me out. "I think I'll go take a shower."

"Thank God," Lincoln said and threw a piece of roll at me. I ducked and the food fell on the floor, where Darth cleaned it right up.

"Quit feeding the fucking dog," I said more with more force to Lincoln than Dad.

"Are you going to help when you're done?" Dad asked.

I gave him a thumbs-up and bounded toward the stairs, Darth chasing me. Before climbing, I paused, took a deep breath, and then sprinted up, down the hall to the guest bedroom, and slammed the door behind me. In the morning light, the room was a typical guest bedroom, with my suitcase lying open on the floor and an unslept-in bed. Darth sniffed around the perimeter, doing her doggie security sweep, but nothing required her immediate attention, so she lay down on the floor next to my suitcase.

Okay, so nothing scary here. I hoped the same applied to the shower too. I grabbed my toiletries and towel, called Darth to follow me toward the bathroom, hoping a shower would calm me, and then hurried out the room and to the safety of the locked bathroom.

Being alone made me think about Steve. Yeah, I needed a shower because he got me all sweaty and bothered.

I washed and rinsed superfast, because I didn't want to give any ghost an opportunity to catch me naked in the shower. Maybe that was stupid, but enough weird stuff had already happened, so I wasn't taking any chances. Another crazy trait. Nutty people laughed at thoughts running through their own mind. I finished up and dressed in a hurry, then checked myself in the mirror. I liked the way my shirt hung on my chest, and hoped I looked nice for Steve later. I had enough muscle to give the outline definition, even if I didn't have a football player's build. For the first time ever, I felt like a giddy kid preparing for a date. Ghosts or no ghosts, I was so into him.

*

But the crazed up and down of emotions continued when I got into the hall to find Dad and Harold playing with the attic door, still with no success. Their tools and new attempts failed again.

I continued toward my bedroom but stopped to watch them from the doorway, trying to ignore the negative energy floating through the air, from their annoyance at the project, from my fear of what haunted the place, and maybe from an evil presence?

"Hand me the hammer." Dad's face was bright red as he strained against the door.

"Maybe we should leave this alone," Harold said. "I know you and Gramps agreed about the house and ghosts. I did, too, for a long time. But Alice and I are worried. Do we need the jewelry? Is finding the gems worth the trouble? I mean, I've experienced stuff, like Grandma. Maybe she was right, not Gramps."

His tune had changed from the one he sang at breakfast. My ears perked up with interest.

Dad paused. He put the hammer down and placed his hand on Harold's shoulder. "I understand what you're saying. I know Mom said the same thing. She and Dad went round and round about the ghost. I don't blame you for wanting to sell this place. But I want to find those jewels. You and I have everything we could ever want. I don't want the money for myself. But I worry about the kids. Selling these jewels would help them. College. A house. Getting started."

Harold nodded. "Do you think I've gone nuts? I never thought this shit would get to me."

"Don't worry about it." Dad looked straight ahead and concentrated on the door. "Maybe it's the stress. I never doubted Mom's sanity when she talked about spirits, even though I didn't agree with her. The same's true for you."

"Do you mind if I tell Alice what you said? She's more worried about what's going on than me."

"Tell her whatever you think she needs to hear."

Dad and Harold paused and stared at the door in an uncomfortable silence.

"Then let's get the damn door open." Uncle Harold's gruff determination returned and helped the two men get beyond their awkward emotional exchange. "Here, rip off the doorknob."

They picked up tools and went at the brass handle with gusto. But all of their prying, banging, and cussing failed to do anything but scratch the door until, after another curse at the handle, Harold bent over and fell to his knees.

"Harold?" Dad looked at him, worried.

My uncle gasped for breath. "I—I—need my pills."

"Where are they?"

"Help me...up. Just help me." Harold lifted himself off the ground, still struggling for air, and slid over to lean against the stairway banister as color returned to his face.

Dad yelled for Mom and Alice, who ran up the stairs.

"Sit down," Aunt Alice commanded. "I'll get your pills."

I was paralyzed with fear. Emergencies always freaked me out, and knowing my uncle's heart problems made it even worse. I did not want to lose my uncle on the same trip when I buried my grandfather.

Harold ignored Alice's advice, shrugged off Dad's attempt to stop him, and fumbled down the stairs. Dad and I followed. He staggered into the living room and eased into a chair. Alice raced into the room and put a pill into his mouth as all of us gathered to watch and hope.

The medicine made a difference at once. He took deep breaths and his face went from crimson to peach again. Still, no one said anything, until we heard a car in the driveway.

"Who?" Alice asked.

"Jill and Tony," Mom answered.

A minute later, my cousins walked into the house. They looked around, seeing something wasn't quite right. Tony figured the problem out first.

"What are you doing?" Tony hurried over to Harold. "What's wrong?" The doctor in Tony took control, making me feel a little more at ease with his expertise.

"He had another attack," Alice said.

"I'm okay," Uncle Harold growled. "That's why they gave me the medicine. Let me rest. Getting away from the door ended the episode. He won't keep coming for me unless I go back."

Dad and Tony exchanged worried looks, but I knew what my uncle meant. The ghost attacked him, it wasn't some random physical event.

"I need to check you out, Dad. Sit up."

Harold obeyed without a word but scowled the entire time Tony examined him. "You may have had another mild attack, but I think it was a warning. You need to relax and stop trying to do so much. You can't keep ignoring the stress you put yourself under. I think we should go to the hospital."

"No." Harold frowned. "We don't have time. I can't sit on my ass all day. We have a lot to do. I'm fine as long as I stay away from the door."

"Dad," Jill intervened. "Tony's a doctor, remember? You should listen to him."

"He's not my doctor."

Jill huffed out her exasperation in a huge breath. "Then rest, Dad. We'll help out with the jewels or whatever. What do you want us to do?"

"Like you said, we're looking for the jewels." Harold pointed toward the stairs.

"If you've got any ideas, let us know," Dad added again to the conversation by deflecting from the argument. I realized Gramps wasn't the only one to avoid and hate family tension.

"I don't have any idea." Jill shrugged, her expression reflecting her wonder of why on earth they focused on that problem. She grinned at me. "But let's have lunch before we look again. Can Dad have food?" Jill asked Tony.

"I can have anything I want."

Tony and Jill smiled at each other and then headed toward the kitchen with Mom and Alice in tow.

Dad, Lincoln, Jenn, and I sat in the living room with Uncle Harold, waiting for lunch and not knowing what else to do. Very Bachmann-like. A bunch of small talk about the weather and sports took over the conversation as if nothing major had occurred. I almost fell out of my chair when Dad and Harold started talking about the Huskers defense and worried about the starting quarterback. Crazy. I decided to go feed Darth and get away from the insanity.

*

I started toward the stairs when a chill passed through my body and the hair on my arms stood straight up. Darth looked up toward the second floor with a snarl. I paused at the base of the stairs, afraid to continue, but I did, anyway. At the same time my fear told me to stay downstairs, another notion compelled me forward, until I halted on the landing. The second floor felt even more ominous than the night before, and even the daylight stopped brightening its atmosphere.

"You'd better hurry, lunch'll be ready soon," Dad called after me from the living room.

I headed up the remaining stairs to shut him up, dreading every step, yet curious, driven to continue despite the circumstances. Darth, with her hair standing straight up on her back and growling, stayed close to my side, perhaps forging ahead because she refused to abandon her stupid master. Nothingness surrounded us, but I still feared what lay ahead when we reached the top of the steps.

Horror. Nothing else describes how I felt but horror when I stared down the hallway. The sun shone through the opened doorways in to various rooms and everything looked in order. But one door in particular stood open, with a ray of dust-packed light shining in from the stairway's confines. The eerie scene, despite its warmth, paralyzed me. Darth kept growling. No visions of Gramps confronted me, but there the attic door stood, wide open, like a kind of horrible beacon. The door neither my dad nor uncle—two big, strong men with a lot of tools and determination—had been able to budge.

Darth growled again, a low, guttural rumble and glared at the sunlit doorway. I reached down to pat her on the head, more to reassure myself, but she lunged forward and raced toward the door in attack mode.

"Darth!" I grabbed for her collar too late and tumbled to the floor as she sprinted up the attic stairs, barking. I leaped to my feet and ran after her. But I halted on the landing halfway up to the attic, stunned to find myself inside the place. A musty odor filled the air and filth blew everywhere. I saw Darth's paw prints in the dust on the stairs but didn't hear her. Oh, no. Not Darth. Please, no. Slowly, needing to check on her but still afraid, I kept going, up into the room where evil swirled in little dust bunnies and patches of light.

I concentrated on seeing the wooden stairs and walls with the gray flaking wallpaper as I climbed upward. A bit of the wallpaper littered the steps while other parts of it clung to the wall by a thread. My weight on the stairs made creaking noises, which meant I could not continue without making noise, so I kept on, jumping a couple of steps at a time, otherwise my fear would have had me running back downstairs because I expected to see ghosts staring at me when I got to the top, or worse—my dog dead from a paranormal attack. "Darth?" I said in a stage whisper, like ghosts couldn't hear.

I entered the room, looking for her, looking for ghosts, and instead saw a typical attic full of a family's treasures, discarded junk, and boxes. A layer of grime covered everything, but Gramps had organized the room well. Trunks lined one side of the attic, while rows of boxes filled the other, everything labeled with care. I didn't turn a light on, so the windows on either end of the attic illuminated the room. The one above the stairway, behind me, shed the ray of sun falling into the hallway downstairs. The walls up here matched those in the stairway, with a fading wallpaper, crumbling off at various places, its faint floral print visible. The slanted plaster ceiling remained intact but dirty.

"Darth?" I called again. "Come here, girl."

I jumped when something in front of me moved, then saw Darth's familiar face peer from behind a box. She relaxed enough to sniff around a bit before joining me. I crouched and hugged her. "Don't fuck with me." She licked my face, and I wondered why she had charged up the stairs like a bat out of hell in the first place. I wanted to believe a dog thing drew her attention, like the scent of a rodent, but I knew better than to dismiss anything happening in the house.

I gave Darth another squeeze before I stood up. One thing in particular caught my eye right away: a phonograph, out of place because the old machine was the one unpacked item in the room. The phonograph sat on an antique table underneath the opposite window. It was old, like right out of the twenties. And no dust covered the surface, though everything else was dirty.

I surveyed the room again but only the phonograph seemed unusual. Then I felt the same tranquility that seemed to have calmed Darth. I didn't even freak out when the turntable started to rotate and the sounds of a band filled the dank air. I recognized Glenn Miller because Gramps had played his music all the time.

Mesmerized, I didn't move. I stared at the phonograph when Gramps materialized out of nowhere and started dancing with a woman. Seemed like the most normal thing in the world. See? Fucking crazy. Scared shitless one minute, then hanging with ghosts the next like I spent time with spirits all the time.

Gramps smiled as he twirled the happy lady on his finger. They moved in perfect rhythm with the music. The woman had to be my grandmother, at least according to the pictures I recalled seeing of her. You could tell from their smiles they adored each other.

Gramps swung around and dipped my grandmother. As he did, he glanced up and winked at me. I cocked my head, wondering if he meant to acknowledge me or if he even knew I was in the room.

Darth sat down beside me, panting and watching the show too. The fear and turmoil from earlier disappeared with the scene. Unlike most people who wonder where their loved ones go when they die, I, at least, knew a partial answer. They remained as spirits, whether angels from heaven or souls floating remained unknown, but Gramps and Grandma were peaceful, happy even, which made me feel better about losing him.

They wore the same clothes as in their wedding picture hanging in our home in Colorado, as if they stepped out of the photograph and came to life. Gramps was again the loving man who watched me sleep the night before and cautioned against coming to his own funeral, in contrast to the angry Gramps, so mad his rage seemed to make him transparent, like he couldn't hold himself together. I felt as if I could step forward and fall into a group hug with them, tangible beings dancing in front of me.

The big band sounds of Glenn Miller turned into the rhythmic beat of Count Basie, but no one changed the record. Gramps and Grandma picked up the pace and laughed. I loved seeing him so happy.

Yet underneath my pleasure a tingle of alarm shot through me.

Gramps stopped dancing and turned toward me, as if in response to my concern. The music faded, as did the phonograph and its table. Grandma blew me a kiss and touched Grandpa on the arm before she disappeared with the furniture. Gramps's spirit walked toward Darth and me. He stopped a few feet away, placed his hand over his heart, and pounded his chest a couple of times before pointing his finger at me. For whatever reason, Gramps communicated through motions, gestures, and acting— only when he was angry last night had he screamed words into my head. I touched my heart and returned the gesture to him with tears in my eyes. Here was the love I remembered and would always miss. What was going on, and why was I up here?

Gramps seemed to have read my mind, and his eyes widened. He scanned the attic, watching, as he shook his head at me.

"No? No what?" I spoke aloud, and then caught myself. Gramps glared hard at me and put his finger to his mouth to silence me.

But Darth stood up, lowered her head, and growled. Gramps drifted back toward the other window, looking all around, terror in his eyes. He stood against the wall as if stopped by its solid structure and stared into my eyes. And then I heard him. I heard his voice in my head. "I will never, never hurt you. But there is danger. Everywhere."

What danger? I tried to think my answer back at him, but nothing seemed to register. *Explain what is going on!* I screamed in my mind, but still nothing from him came back to me.

The attic's aura felt wrong all of a sudden. Darth ran in circles around the walls' edges, sniffing and growling. The hair on her back stood up and she snarled at an enemy I couldn't see.

Gramps faded away with a furrowed brow, either unwilling or afraid to help me. My heart thumped in my chest. I whipped around in circles to see what was here as a chill swept through the air and dust whirled around Darth and me.

Darth lunged again at her hidden enemy before us, but I grabbed her collar to keep her close and to try to get out of here together. She strained against me but I pulled her toward the stairs, her claws scratching at the wooden floor. Pulling her along, I started down and almost fell off the first step, when cold air swept up the stairwell and took my breath away.

I released Darth as I gasped for air. Barking like a maniac, she spun around in one leap and placed herself on the second and third step, between me and the advancing frozen air. A low, guttural laugh filled the room. The noise wasn't in my head—the cackle was real. And whatever produced the sound was fucking pissed.

I yanked Darth back into the attic, where we could both stand on more solid footing without almost crashing down the stairs.

Then, talk about scaring me shitless, the frigid air transformed itself into a ghost, the same one who had chased me out of the house the night before. Evil Gramps. I could see through the ghost's form, unlike the solid one dancing with my grandmother moments ago. The figure's outline faded in and out but was an image of a younger man. The angry apparition of Gramps reversed the aging process.

It—he?—glared at Darth and me with a fierce rage, lowered its chin, then glowered, its eyes glowing red. The laughter stopped but the stare pierced into my soul.

"You cause trouble," the spirit said in a determined but calm voice.

Darth stood her ground and barked with more urgency, though I could hear the ghost through her tantrum.

"Gramps?" I sputtered out the words, bewildered.

"Silence." The thing held up its hand in front of me. "You know too much, because you see the other ghosts in this house. They see me, and therefore fear me. You will too." The figure spun around and circled me three times while bellowing out his awful laugh again to send shivers down my spine.

Weird. Fucking weird. The image looked so much like Gramps's pictures when he was younger, but the voice included a slight accent I couldn't place. And who and what was it talking about? Who saw him? What other ghosts? Grandma?

Darth kept barking and tried to bite the apparition, which knocked a stack of boxes over onto my head. I pushed Darth out of the way and put my arms up to protect myself as I fell on the floor. The spirit shot down the stairs, still cackling away, while I scrambled to free myself.

I heard the attic door slam shut, and I knew before I tested the knob I was locked in.

*

Scared, but relieved evil Gramps was gone, I stopped struggling with the boxes and lay still. After I regained my breath and could move without shaking, I pushed the last of the boxes off and went down the creaky stairs. Sure enough, the door once again was shut tight.

Panicked again, I rattled the doorknob, hoping I could get out. No deal. Locked, with me on the other side. But I could unlock the door from here, right? I tried, but no. The turnkey was broken inside the keyhole. So how was the door locked? What the fuck was I going to do?

I clenched my teeth to keep from screaming, and despite my predicament, afraid of how to explain my appearance on the other side of the door to my family. What if they still couldn't open the door? Everybody would think I went insane and locked myself in the attic, and then they'd accuse me of keeping them out.

I sat on the stairs, defeated, and Darth plopped next to me, exhausted from her guard dog duties. I wish I had her ability to focus on the moment, when she reacted to immediate threats by barking and attacking but, once the risk evaporated, returning to a calm.

I put my arm around her as tears welled in my eyes. I had always told people when things got bad I wanted to stop the world so I could get off. Locked in the attic, captive to an angry spirit, my world stopped spinning.

Ghosts, funerals, and fags swam in my mind. I sang a little song to Darth about the situation, trying to make myself feel better, even laughing at the lyrics I made up. See, I was cracking.

As further proof of my increasing insanity, my next thought was to worry about my plans to meet Steve. What would he do if I didn't show up? What if I was trapped up here for hours? I got mad at Dad, wishing for my cell phone, but no! We had to go old school. Fuck. I switched between despondence, terror, and resignation a million times before I heard a person walking down the hall on the other side of the door.

"Hello?" I called out, pressing my head to the door. "Hello?"

"Jaret?" Jenn sounded uncertain as she talked.

"It's me!" I exclaimed.

"Where are you? We started lunch without you."

"I'm stuck in the attic. Try to open the door." Sweat dripped down my forehead.

"How'd you get up there?"

"It's a long story, and the door locked again. I can't get out of here."

Jenn rattled the doorknob, but nothing happened.

"I can't open the door. Should I get Dad?"

"No!" I yelled, not wanting to deal with him.

"Chill. I guess you'd rather stay in there."

"Sorry. I want to try to figure this out without them. They'll get mad."

"Then what do you want me to do?"

"Good question." I had no answer. "Try the handle again."

I heard her jiggling the knob around on the other side, but the door remained shut. Feeling desperate but also wanting to keep adults out of the problem, I decided to try one more thing.

"Twist the handle and pull hard, and I'll shove the door from my side at the same time."

Jenn laughed, amused by the whole thing. "Ready?" she asked through giggles.

"I'm glad you find this hilarious. Yes. Now!"

At the sound of Jenn grabbing and twisting the knob, I stepped back and then rammed into the door full force. I expected to meet resistance in the form of a hard wooden door, but instead the door flung open. Jenn fell backward into the wall and onto the floor, and I came lurching out of the stairway on top of her. Darth scampered down after me and stood panting above Jenn's face, then gave her a big kiss.

"Gross," Jenn said, but still laughed, before she turned her attention to me. "You don't look so good. How did you get up there?"

Sweat poured down my face as I caught my breath. I always told Jenn everything but hesitated today, worried about involving her in the sordid affair and endangering her in the process. What if angry Gramps flipped out on her next? "Thanks for saving me," I stated to avoid the question.

"What's going on?" Jenn was having none of my avoidance.

I got to my feet, then pulled Jenn to hers. "I wish I knew."

Before I could further delay the conversation, we both jumped when the attic door slammed shut of its own accord. No one touched the door, and no wind blew through the room.

"Did you close the door?" Jenn asked.

"Of course not!" I half yelled. "Freaky shit."

"So what's going on?" she asked again, with more force.

"Listen," I sighed. "I'll explain all this later. I promise. Just try to help me right now." I reached for the door, assuming it would open and close, yet the handle was locked as before, as if I never went through the doorway and up those stairs. A shiver went down my back when I realized nothing changed. "It's locked again."

"You sure we shouldn't tell Mom and Dad?" Jenn's voice quivered.

Fuck. I hated dragging her into the mess. "Give me another day, okay? It's on me if we get in trouble, and I'll tell them."

She nodded but frowned at me. "If you tell me what's going on. You're keeping secrets, ever since we got to Fremont."

I looked at the floor. I wanted to share everything, and I always trusted Jenn, more than anyone else in the world. But how could I keep her safe at the same time? One glance in her eyes told me I was too late, she knew more than she admitted already. Too wise for her age, as my dad often said. She forced me to come clean.

"Come on," I said. "Darth needs a walk."

Jenn, Darth, and I headed down the stairs to the kitchen, where I grabbed a couple sandwiches for lunch and a bag of chips. Mom tried to make us stay, but we insisted we had to get to the park and have a picnic for old times' sake, so Jenn snatched up a couple pops and out the door we went.

I loved her too much to keep the secrets bottled inside me that I knew she would understand. Still, my stomach twisted in knots as we walked down the sidewalk.

Chapter Three

Jenn

Jenn and I turned toward the park, thoughts of which turned my face bright red, with Darth pulling ahead at a brisk pace. We walked in silence for a couple blocks, waiting to get farther away from the house before talking and opening the chips to munch on as we went. Moments ago, I sat trapped in the attic, but again I fled from the house like the night before. However, I left because I promised to explain everything to Jenn. *Everything*. Shit.

My head spun with wanting to forget about telling her anything, to avoid reality for as long as possible, then whipped to wanting to launch into the entire story, from ghosts to being gay to Steve. Typical of her, Jenn waited and walked by my side.

"You know these crazy ghost stories we learned about?" I asked.

"Yeah." Jenn glanced at me.

"What do you think about them?"

"Dad said it's made up. But I'm not sure. I don't know what to think. Kinda scary."

"Do you think I'm crazy to think ghosts exist?"

She shrugged. "A lot of people believe in them. How could they all be nuts? I never thought about your sanity much."

My mind froze again, but I forced myself to continue. "Okay, here goes." I took a deep breath. "I see ghosts all the time. I don't think I'm insane, but I know I see them."

I waited for Jenn to speak but she walked along without a word.

"Please don't tell Mom and Dad." Panic set in. "I tried to tell them once, and that's why I had to go to a counselor. I don't know why ghosts come to me, but I see them, and I wanted to tell you. I'm so sorry. Please don't tell them."

Jenn reached over and touched my arm. "Stop. I won't tell anyone. And I believe you."

"Thanks." I sighed with relief, then bit into a chip to stall for a moment. "So, it's intense this time. More than ever before, and the premonitions started before we even left Colorado. I saw Gramps, or at least his ghost, at home and then again here. It's like he wants to tell me a secret but can't. I think he wanted us to stay in Colorado. Before I got trapped in the attic, I was up there and I saw him and Grandma." Jenn shot me a surprised look. "I'm serious. And before, when I was going to my room, Darth and I saw the attic door open. She went nuts and ran up there. I was so creeped out. I shouldn't have gone up there, but I had to get Darth. Next, I saw Gramps and Grandma. Or at least ghosts like them."

Relieved at sharing my secret, the story and all the gory details flooded out.

"Oh, and get this! When Gramps appears in the transparent form, he's always mean and young, like we've seen him in pictures. He circles me and laughs. Not like anything's funny, but like a villain in a movie. I can't even describe how pissed off he is." I paused. "So, do you want to admit me to a mental hospital?"

Jenn laughed. "No. I believe you. Can I tell you a secret?"

"Of course."

Jenn looked to the ground. Then she took a strand of her long, brown hair from over her shoulder and twirled the hair in her fingers. "I've seen stuff on TV to make me believe you and other people do see things like ghosts. Whatever you call the ability, I know you see things we can't. Mom and Dad don't like what you see, by the way. But you knew. They're afraid other people will find out and think you're strange. I never asked you about the ghosts because I didn't want to embarrass you. But I believe you. I love you. I don't think you're nuts. Or at least not completely." Jenn smiled.

I laughed at her teasing. "Thanks. I hide my sightings from everyone because they freak out if I say too much, not just Mom and Dad. I even wonder if what I see is all a make-believe land I created in my head. I was even scared to tell you."

"Well, I like how you shared the truth with me."

As we neared the park, enjoying the peace of being together, away from the others, Jenn glanced over, her brown eyes burning.

"What?" I asked.

"I think I've seen things at Gramps's house too. I can't tell if what I see is a ghost or my imagination, so I never thought about my visions too much. They look so real I thought for a long time the ghost was a person. It looks like one. But then I noticed it's kind of clear, like you can see through the apparition. But I don't know anything else about the spirit. I never see it for long—real quick here and there. A man walks down the hall, or by a door, and then disappears."

"Why didn't you tell me?"

She looked at me like I was an idiot. "Same reason you didn't. I convinced myself the ghost wasn't real, thinking my vision was me being all upset about Gramps." Jenn shuddered so I put my arm around her and pulled her close.

"It's okay. That's what I see. We can deal with the situation together."

"I can't tell if the ghost knows I watch or see it. It never looks at me or says anything. Or is it a *he* instead of an *it*? I don't know. But the spirit feels like he knows I'm there. He scares me."

Her story alarmed me more than any vision I experienced, because I would be more distraught than ever if something happened to Jenn. The thing she described sounded an awful lot like the angry Gramps who yelled at me, even if he meandered around for her. Fuck. How was I going to protect her? We fell into silence again.

*

At the park, I crumpled up the empty chips bag and threw it into the garbage. "We ate half our lunch before we got here."

Jenn and I laughed, then settled down at a picnic table to eat our sandwiches and drink our pop.

"I'm afraid," Jenn said. "What if the ghost attacks me? What does he want?"

"Listen to me." I swallowed a bite before talking. "I don't think he wants to hurt you. Even the laughing ghost who seems so angry has never tried to hurt me. He dumped a bunch of boxes on me in the attic to scare me. But if the spirit had wanted to, he could have hurt me bad. I don't know what's going on or why, but right now I think we're safe. I'm not lying to make you feel better, I believe what I said. Okay?"

Jenn nodded as she ate. "Okay. At least we can talk about what we see." Her brow was still creased in confusion.

"Maybe we should make a plan." I drank the last of my pop and crushed the can. "Or at least have a way to tell each other."

Jenn giggled. "Too bad Ghostbusters don't exist for real."

"Very funny. Hilarious. So we can't trap the ghost in a vacuum cleaner." When we stopped laughing I continued with my idea. "If you see a spirit, even if you think a ghost might be there, find me, and I'll help. I know I sound lame, but being there for each other is at least a promise. Then we can try to figure what to do out together."

Jenn finished the last of her sandwich, so I collected our garbage and took it to a nearby trash can before we continued talking.

"Do you think other kids deal with this?" Jenn asked me. "Or are we weird?"

"We're weird." I grinned and shrugged. "But who knows? It'd be even crazier to think no one else ever dealt with crazy shit like this."

We sat for a minute, both thinking about our conversation. I loved my sister so much. Unlike all the stories of sibling rivalry and constant arguments, we almost always got along. Our relationship meant the world to me.

"Oh!" I thought of another idea. "Darth can help too. She watches for the ghosts and hates them even more than we do."

Jenn squinted at me in disbelief. "Are you serious?"

"Yeah. Watch her when we go back to the house. She doesn't act like herself. She looks through doorways and stuff. Like she's always on guard. Whenever one of the ghosts comes, she knows even before me when it's on the way. Goes apeshit when the angry one appears."

Jenn leaned over and scratched behind Darth's ears. "Good girl. A dog Ghostbuster."

Darth ignored both of us, having laid down to take a little nap.

"So we won't tell Mom and Dad, right?" Jenn confirmed.

"Not right now. Other people, Mom and Dad in particular, look at me funny when the ghosts come up. So unless we need to, let's keep things to ourselves. Can you imagine how much Lincoln would make fun of us if he found out?"

"He already thinks we're nuts."

The discussion about ghosts wound down. We talked about Fremont, Darth, and reminisced about the park and the times we came with Gramps.

*

When my stomach started turning over again, I remembered one other thing I needed to tell Jenn. My heart raced at the thought of revealing my secret.

Before anything escaped my mouth, however, Jenn moved us in a different direction. "Fremont never changes. It's so weird. I remember all this from when we lived here. And we moved when I was in first grade."

"Yeah, like the ice cream place we walked to from home. Remember it? I saw the building last night. Still looks the same." My mind recalled the picture of the aluminum siding, no more or less faded than ten years ago, a pale deep blue with light blue splotches.

"I do! We should get everyone to go again. But Fremont is almost scary. I can't imagine being trapped in this place. Thank god Mom and Dad moved us to Colorado."

"But Fremont was a good place to raise us," I pointed out. "The town was safe. I mean, they let us run all over without watching us the whole time. I never want to live here again though. Just visit."

"None of the buildings change." Jenn swept her arm through the air, pointing toward the rest of Fremont beyond the park. "The stores are still the same. I'll bet they held a parade when the Starbucks opened. What a radical change! A new thing in Fremont."

We both laughed.

*

"There's not much exciting to do." My voice quivered as nerves took hold because I decided to transition to my next announcement. "I couldn't fall asleep last night so I walked downtown with Darth. All of the high school kids cruise on Main Street. I think they gather every night."

"Boring. Did you stay long?"

My heart skipped a beat. "No, Darth and I checked things out and left."

"Did you talk to anyone? Did they even notice you? I figured an outsider would excite them. Oh, I forgot. You're shy." She poked me in the side and giggled. "You'd run away if a stranger talked to you."

"Shut up." She knew me too well, but I knew how to shock her too. "Actually, I *did* talk to a guy."

"You talked to a stranger?" She stared at me in disbelief.

"Yep, without anybody's help."

"I bet they approached you first."

I laughed at the truth. "Well, yeah. But at least I talked. It was like you said, he wanted to figure out who this new person was. Everyone wondered, but he talked to me."

"They're so weird here. Did he just come over and ask why you came to Fremont?"

"Sort of. He already knew. Speaking of ghosts and stuff, he asked me if I thought ghosts haunted Gramps's house. Everyone knows Gramps died, and he guessed I came for the funeral. They talk about all sorts of rumors about the house, ghosts, and stuff. He even told me they sneak over and hunt for ghosts."

"See, what he said is proof. They have no life in Fremont."

"Except the house is haunted for real! Yeah, they want a haunted house to keep them busy. But the story is true. Even Steve said most people here are too sheltered."

"His name's Steve? You must have talked to him for quite a while."

"Yeah." I fidgeted around. "We talked for a long time. Our conversation kept my mind off Gramps and ghosts. Anyway, pretty good for a shy guy, huh?" I sat up with pride, making Jenn laugh again.

"Not bad. Who would've guessed you'd make a friend in Fremont before me? I'm jealous." Jenn was a social butterfly. "Take me with you tonight. I need to get away from everyone. The house is too stuffy."

I hesitated, unsure how to respond. I always took her along back home when she asked, and I understood her wanting to get out of the house. But how could I explain Steve? And what if we wanted alone time? I did *not* need to get into that conversation with her.

"What is wrong?" Jenn put her hand on my shoulder. "You okay?"

"What? Yeah. Why?"

"You look scared. Did you tell me everything about the ghosts?"

"Of course. Why wouldn't I?"

"Then what's bothering you?"

The moment had arrived. Time to tell her. I glanced at her again to reassure myself. She tilted her head and smiled.

"You promise you love me? You won't go nuts on me?"

"What are you talking about? I love you. Nothing can change how I feel. Sit down. I didn't freak about the ghosts, did I?" When I saw her look at me, I got nervous all over again.

I surveyed the park, which always felt vast and open, with playground equipment dotting the landscape and huge expanses of grass between each exciting ride. I remembered growing up nearby and running from the swings to the merry-go-round to the iron rocket and thinking they were so far apart. But today everything felt smaller. The trees loomed over us, the bushes hid dark unknowns, and the sidewalk seemed too close. I don't know if the ghosts, Gramps's death, or what I intended to tell Jenn caused the anxiety, but I was nervous as hell.

To stall for more time, I grabbed a tennis ball we brought along for Darth, unleashed her, and threw it to the other side of the park. As always, she dashed away, scrambled to snatch up the ball, then bounded back to us with her prize. Playing with her kept my mind from exploding, and we laughed when Darth over ran the ball the second time, turned too fast and slipped, then growled at the ball when she got it and tossed it in the air to herself.

"So, you going to tell me or avoid the subject all day? This isn't about the ghosts, is it?" Jenn asked.

"I'm trying." I stared at Darth running again for her ball, afraid to look at my sister. "Do you ever feel different from everybody else? Like no one in the world will understand? Part of me wants to run away and hide, and the other part wants to let everyone know."

"You sound like aliens abducted you."

"So you see little green men too?"

"They make me have alien babies. Fifty in one night. Then they bring me home in time for school."

"Aren't you too young to be a mom?"

"Enough. This is getting gross." Jenn took the ball from me as Darth lay back down to rest. "You're avoiding me. What is it? You look like you're going to have a stroke."

"Dad could save money and put me in the same casket with Gramps."

"Stop!" But again I had her laughing. "Talk."

I got nervous again, and my heart convulsed. Even my knees shook and I stuck my hands in my pockets to keep them still. "So, did you understand what I meant with the whole thing about no one understanding?"

"I guess. But I don't believe you're alone. We talked about ghosts. If I understand you see ghosts, what could leave you alone?"

"I'm not sure how to say it."

The words "I'm gay" stuck in my throat. They sounded too threatening, too exposing. I liked other guys but did not want Jenn to associate me with being gay. Sure, I knew enough to see the thought as my own homophobia, but learning about stuff–like big word psychology ideas such as homophobia–on Twitter and the internet, or accepting other people being gay, felt so different from applying the label to myself. "You know Steve?" I danced around saying *gay* out loud and applying the idea to myself.

"The guy you told me about?"

"Yeah, the Fremont dude."

"Not personally." She smiled at my delay tactics.

"He and I kinda clicked yesterday. We spent almost the entire night together, talking and stuff. We have a lot in common. You see, well, I guess I want him for a different reason."

My entire body shook. Jenn grabbed my arm and looked at me.

"What do you want from him?" Her voice softened, her body language opened, all as if calling for me to share with her.

"I want him to be my boyfriend." My voice quivered. I shook even more, and waiting for Jenn to talk seemed like an eternity. At least I avoided the word "gay." I could not get the word out.

"Are you gay?"

My ears burned but the tension flooded out of my body. Jenn knew, and nothing could take back my revelation.

"Yeah," I whispered. "That's what I needed to tell you."

"I'm glad. Thank you."

*

I never expected anyone to thank me for telling them. My heart told me all along Jenn would understand, but the fear still overwhelmed me, to the point the shaking continued even after her positive reaction.

"I'm kinda relieved." Jenn sounded chipper, her usual content self. "You made this seem so serious. I thought you had drastic news, like you wanted to run away or were a serial killer. Why would this change my opinion of you?" She scrunched her forehead up in total confusion. "I love you. If being gay makes you happy, then it makes me happy."

"A lot of people freak out when this comes up. At school, guys are too macho and make fun of gays all the time. I know the topic upsets people. I tried to fight the feelings, but they kept coming back."

"I think being gay is normal." She shrugged. "People are just gay. Ignore the idiots who have a problem with it."

"I wish I was like you. You do your thing and don't worry about how people view you like I do."

"You could too. Not everyone freaks out. If your sexuality is part of you, let yourself be." Jenn often sounded wise for her age when it came to understanding people and emotions. Her acceptance of others felt to me like her love went on forever.

"I always had these feelings." I pulled my hands out of my pocket as my body settled down. "I didn't know what to call them. And I don't feel bad about being gay, personally. I worry about what other people will think. I hope I still have friends."

"Give me a break." Jenn smirked. "You'll always have friends. You may lose assholes, but do you like them anyway? And wait until you start meeting other gay people."

"Yeah, I guess. It's scary, you know? Do you think Mom and Dad will hate me? Will they kick me out of the house?"

She stared at me in disbelief. "Now you do sound nuts. They'd never hate you, or any one of us. I'm sure they'd worry. That's what they always do. And they might get upset, because that's what they always do too." We both laughed. "Remember the time they found Lincoln's *Playboy*?" The memory sent us into hysterics. Jenn continued after we calmed down a little. "So I'm not sure what they'll do at first. But they'll always love you. When do you think you'll tell them?"

"I don't know." I picked at a splinter on the table. "I'm not ready. You know, no one else."

"What about Steve?"

I grinned. "Yeah, he knows too. But no one else."

"There's no rush. One of my friends thinks she's a lesbian. But I think she says she's one for attention. Everyone figures their own story out on their own time."

"I feel weird talking about being gay. After all these years of keeping the secret inside, I'm not sure what to share with other people. Thanks for listening, it means so much to tell you about myself first. Are you angry I waited until now to tell you?"

Jenn thought for a minute. "No. No, I'm not angry."

"But?" I asked.

"Did I hurt you? Why did you wait so long to tell me? Did I make you uncomfortable, or tell a stupid joke?"

"Now it's your turn to chill. I wasn't ready to tell anyone. I mean, if I hadn't met Steve last night, I don't know if I would've been ready today. Steve came to me first, and he made me ready to tell you."

"How long have you known?" Jenn asked.

I wrinkled my nose. "I'm not sure."

Jenn looked at me funny and we laughed.

"I'm not lying. I mean, I always knew I was different from everyone else, even before any sexual feelings. I remember in about fifth grade I started to feel an attraction to other boys. I already knew, too, not to act on the urges or tell anyone. I didn't know what the feelings meant or anything. I liked boys but knew to keep the sensation a secret."

"So you always knew you were gay?"

"Kind of, but not really. I never used the word *gay*, even in my mind. Figuring out to apply it to myself shocked me. I was stunned to learn my feelings toward other guys meant I was gay. Hard to deal with the word."

"What word?"

"Gay."

"Makes sense." Jenn nodded. "Do you care if I ask questions?"

"No, I feel good talking about myself."

"Are you okay with the gay thing? I mean okay, not appease Jenn okay?"

"I'm okay with my feelings. I guess, though, using the word scares me. I can handle my attraction to guys but not saying I'm gay."

"I know. You didn't say *gay* until I said the word first."

"Saying the words makes them more real. I want people to like me. After I decided I was gay, I felt like people watched my every move. Straight guys glare at me, as if they already know and hate me for my sexuality. Mom and Dad look suspicious."

"Yeah, you naturally think all that, but I think the problem is all in your head. Most straight guys don't have a clue about who's gay. Think about Lincoln. He would never guess."

"We need to make a new brother-sister pact," I said. "Since you know, you have to protect me from straight guys. Neither of us could stand up in a fight, but you can use your charm to ward them off. They won't hit girls. Besides, you're cute, and you could distract them."

"Okay," Jenn said and then laughed. "I'll protect you from the straight guys. We wouldn't want them to scar your pretty little face."

I punched her arm. "Stop it. I already think I act too much like a girl."

"So? There's nothing wrong with acting like a girl. Do what feels comfortable. Don't act a certain way because people think you should."

"I know. And I'm cool with who I am most of the time. But if I get stuck in a room full of guys I get nervous. I need more sissy friends." I thought again about all the gay people out there and how I never met any of them. In a more open day and age, how on earth had I avoided every gay person in Colorado?

"Are you sure no one else knows?"

"Just you, Darth, and Steve." Adding Darth made the list feel longer, and she learned before anyone else, before me, I bet. She continued to fetch the ball, sprinting to catch it, and then running back to return the slimy thing to me. "Why is that hard to believe?"

"Liking guys is such a big part of who you are. I can't imagine keeping your story inside for this long."

"Can I ask *you* a question?"

"Sure."

"Do you think other people can tell when they see me? Do I act gay?"

Jenn grinned. "You asked a trick question."

"Be honest."

"I think most people don't have a clue. They walk around and never see into a person's soul. Like I said, straight guys miss a lot of stuff. Most stuff, except what they want to see. But gay people, and a lot of straight women, have gaydar. And you set it off."

"What?"

"*Gaydar*. You know, like radar but to spot gay people."

I marveled again at how much Jenn knew despite being younger than me. "I heard the term on a TV show once, but I thought they made it up. The idea is too much. I've never heard of that before. Do *I* have gaydar?"

"You'd better or your life will be deficient."

"Can you teach me?"

Jenn shrugged and tilted her head. "You watch for things most gay guys do."

"Like what? Girl stuff?"

Jenn punched my arm. "I swear, you sound more like a straight guy than a gay one. Girl stuff isn't even a thing."

I laughed. "You know what I mean."

She pressed her lips together. "How am I going to explain this to you? I thought gay guys were hardwired to find one other. I know! We can go to the mall and practice. Practicing will be easier for you there, because all you need to watch is how guys look at you. If they give you more than a glance or stare back at your eyes, they're gay most likely. The eye stare doesn't mean they're out, but it means they're interested. This strategy works, trust me."

"Because of all your experience as a gay guy?"

She slapped me again. "I know things. You need to get out more anyway. You're too sheltered."

"So besides the eye contact thing, you watch for guys to act gay or feminine?"

"There you go again." Jenn sighed. "How they act can be a clue, but some hide their sexuality better, so you have to watch. And some straight guys are effeminate. You said Steve's a football player. I bet he doesn't give off any of those vibes. So eye contact is critical."

I pictured Steve in his letter jacket and jock demeanor, acting straight at first glance, like a typical guy. But I sensed a vibe in him last night. Maybe "gaydar" told me to follow him. I was safe and he was interested.

"So back to my question. Do I set your radar off?"

"*Gay*dar." Jenn tried to speak but laughed too hard. "It's *gay*dar. Don't worry so much about yourself. Who cares? Be yourself, and you'll find a whole lot of people will respect you. True friends and people without hang-ups hate fake behavior."

"You're avoiding the fact I look gay."

I guessed a long time ago I was more effeminate than most guys. Today, the idea fascinated me more than anything, though inside I knew in the past the idea bothered me because I felt vulnerable. I sucked at sports and liked hanging out with girls more than boys, but starting to deal with being gay made it easier to accept myself. I almost missed Jenn's snicker as I thought about myself.

"What?" I asked.

"You want me to be honest?"

"Tell me."

"You act pretty gay." But her smile became sympathetic, no longer mocking me. "Does that bother you?"

"No." I shook my head. "I kinda figured out what I'm like on my own. I wondered if everyone else saw how I act."

"Your behavior isn't a bad thing. It's who you are. You don't like all those boy things, like sports and chasing girls and farting. And you're so pretty and soft-spoken. I like how you are. But I think a lot of people miss the signals because they don't look for signs of being gay."

"If you thought all this, why didn't you ever ask me?"

"I didn't want to offend you. Or scare you farther into the closet. Don't you think it's best to let people decide for themselves when to come out? Plus, just because a guy fits the stereotypes doesn't guarantee they're gay, or they'll ever come out."

I had never felt so comfortable or free talking about myself. Yeah, anxiety about telling other people lurked in the background, but to have at least one other person, a person important to me, affirm what I felt and still love me meant the world right then.

I started laughing. Memories of growing up with Jenn reminded me of all the gay things we played as children.

Jenn laughed without knowing the joke. "What's so funny?"

"Thinking I could hide this from anyone who knew me growing up. No wonder you already knew."

"Remember playing Barbies?" Jenn snorted.

"I *loved* Barbies."

"We took them everywhere and set up houses and things to do with them. Did we even have boy Barbies?"

"No, we didn't want boys." I shook my head. "We owned Ken because a friend gave him to me, but we didn't use him as much. We always sent him on business trips.

We also used the G.I. Joe I got as a birthday present for a Barbie husband, but we always sent him with Ken."

Jenn and I laughed so much we stopped talking.

"We also pretended to be teachers." Jenn laughed so hard she bent over. "You always wanted to be the teacher, even though most of yours were women."

"I never remember wanting to be a woman. I wanted to act like one and do the same things, like teach. We even pretended I had husbands when we played, remember?"

"Oh my gosh, too funny. And you used Darth as your child." Hearing her name, Darth picked up and took her ball to Jenn, which prompted Jenn to pat her on the head and throw it. "She hated staying with us, but we trapped her in the room as the baby."

"I think you made me play these girl games to make me gay. I'm sure this gay thing is on you."

"Uh, you came up with most of what we did, and I followed along."

We laughed until another memory dawned on me. "You know, if you think about it, Mom and Dad were pretty cool not to freak out. They let us play and never said anything about my playing Barbies or school."

"Well, Lincoln is macho enough for both of us."

"True. But he didn't tease me about who I am either." Talking about the rest of the family tweaked the butterflies in my stomach. "Telling Lincoln scares me more than telling Mom and Dad."

"He might not struggle as much as you think. He cares a lot about us."

"But he's so conservative. Like those televangelists."

"Stop your nonsense. You're out of control. Maybe we can tell him together, so you don't feel alone."

"I'll think about when to tell him. I want to tell Mom and Dad first, but not yet. I'm not ready."

*

We stopped talking for a few minutes and watched Darth chase her ball. The park, with its solitude and distance from the problems lurking a few blocks away felt so peaceful I hated thinking about returning to the house.

"How did you meet this Steve guy anyway? What's the story?"

"We hooked up and talked."

"Bullshit."

"I don't know what to tell you." And besides, I was embarrassed to talk about Steve, but I would never let Jenn know. She smiled as she waited. "We met downtown and took a walk. I suppose his 'gaydar' went off when he saw me. He introduced himself."

"He walked up to you out of the blue?"

"Yeah. Darth and I were standing there watching the people when he came over and said 'Hi.' He scared me at first. I didn't know what he wanted. But he convinced me he was okay, so we went on a walk."

Butterflies returned at the thought of Steve, but in a fluttering, positive way. I swooned at seeing his face in my mind as he hovered over me before we kissed.

"Do you know anything about him?"

"Not much. He plays on the football team and doesn't like living in Fremont. He's not out or anything. I'm not sure why he came over to me. We talked about stupid stuff all night and wandered around the park. Darth likes him too."

"The park? Late at night in a park means more happened than just chatting." She arched an eyebrow at me.

A big, stupid grin spread across my face. "Well, we made out for a while. Isn't this getting a little personal?"

"That's all I need to know." She waved her hands in front of me as a sign of surrender. "Are you going to see him again?"

"We're getting together this evening."

"I get to go along. Steve has to show me Fremont too." Jenn patted me on the arm. "Stop with the worried face. I'll give you plenty of time alone. But I need to get away from the house and family as much as you do. Deal?"

I laughed. "You can join us for a while. Then you have to leave us alone."

"Trust me, watching my brother make out with a football stud won't do a thing for me. I'll leave long before. How do you think he guessed you're a Bachmann?"

"Because there was no other explanation for a stray kid in downtown Fremont."

"Did you tell him why you came here? Or about the ghosts?"

"He already guessed why we came to Fremont. I told him the whole thing, which surprised me how I shared so much, and even weirder I think he believed me. At least he didn't run away. He told me a lot of people believe a ghost haunts the house."

"How do so many people in Fremont know about what goes on in Gramps's house? They're so nosy."

"Is Fremont any worse than Estes? I think it's what people in small towns do because they're so bored. Besides, we know Grandma always told people she thought the house was haunted. Steve heard about the ghost from his grandmother, who knew Grandma Bachmann."

"But how do *all* the kids know? We never hear about strange spirits in Estes Park."

"You must have never listened when people talk about the Stanley Hotel. Who knows? We do other dumb things, like gossip about the people who take drugs."

"Because drugs are a problem at home. A serious one."

"And the ghosts at Gramps's aren't a problem?"

"Still, what do they do when they talk about the ghost?"

"Steve said they sneak around outside the house trying to see a ghost. Since we've seen stuff, maybe they do too. That would explain the rumors."

Jenn fell quiet. I let her think for a moment before saying anything, reaching down to scratch behind Darth's ears after she got tired and lay down to rest.

"What is it?" I asked when her expression grew troubled.

"I wonder what Gramps thought about all this stuff. He denied the rumors about a ghost, but since so many people thought they were true, and with Grandma telling people about the haunting, he must have at least wondered."

"Whatever Gramps believed died with him." I patted Jenn on the back to try to comfort her as I reminded myself I dealt with ghosts for as long as I could remember, but real ghosts who haunted us were new to Jenn. "But when I see the vision of his ghost, Gramps knows about the truth now. If only everyone else believed us."

Not able to avoid the inevitable any longer, I stood up, grabbed Darth's leash, and hooked it to her collar. "We better get back." Darth wagged her tail, excited to get to walk again and then lunged at a squirrel, who scampered up a nearby tree and chattered away at Darth in defiance from a high limb. Jenn and I giggled at the moment of comic relief as Darth barked and spun in circles, agitated by her furry antagonist.

After a pause, Jenn got off the bench, and we proceeded out of the park and plodded along, going much slower than our journey here.

"Do you think we should tell anyone else?"

"No." I pulled Darth away from a piece of candy melting on the sidewalk.

"I want to tell Lincoln. If we can convince him, maybe he'll help us."

She voiced a common difference of opinion between us. Jenn trusted people, while I thought the worst of them.

"You can tell anyone you need to. It's up to you. But please don't tell him what I think. He'll make fun of me, which always pisses me off."

"You don't think he'll understand?"

"No." My fear of telling Lincoln was about his personality, not his love for us, because he took after Dad. I was afraid he would think we had gone nuts if he knew what Jenn and I thought about ghosts.

Gramps's house appeared, the attic gables first popping above the trees. The windows were dark and dusty. I used to love the bright white home, which symbolized all the love Gramps gave me as a child. My vision of happiness turned to a dull dread festering like a nasty sore in my mind. The house was no longer inviting—it mocked me instead.

"Hello?" Jenn knocked on my head.

"What?"

"You zoned out to Mars."

"Thinking about everything. And isn't Mars where they keep your alien babies? What'd you say?"

"I asked if you'd mind going with me to talk to Lincoln."

"I'll go." The words came out despite dreading the very idea. I couldn't leave her alone when she needed me.

We got to the house and she charged inside on a mission. I sighed and followed.

"Lincoln!" Jenn stepped inside the front door and screamed. "Lincoln!"

"What?" he yelled back and walked into the room. "Don't you have any manners? Proper little ladies don't scream in the house."

"Shut up. I need to talk to you."

Lincoln looked to me for a clue, but I shrugged and concentrated on maintaining a blank face. Darth trotted toward the kitchen for water, while the three of us headed for the living room. Thankfully, the room was empty—of both the living and the dead.

Lincoln jumped on the couch and stretched out while Jenn sat across from him. I plopped down on the floor, waiting for Darth to return. She'd be my support system again.

"You promise you'll be serious the whole time and not make fun of me?"

Lincoln answered Jenn with a nod, though he looked puzzled.

Jenn stared hard at Lincoln. "Ghosts haunt this house. I see them. Can you help me tell Mom and Dad, or figure out what to do?"

Lincoln kept his composure, not even his usual smirk in evidence. "I think you're tired. With Gramps dying and everything, you're under a lot of stress. We all are."

"I'm not nuts."

"I didn't say you were. I think this has you stressed out."

"So you won't help me?"

"What do you want me to do?" Lincoln asked.

"Forget it." Jenn's temper flared.

"How did you get away without saying anything?" Lincoln looked at me and threw his hands up in the air.

"Leave me out of this. Jenn and I already talked about the issue."

"So you believe the ghost stories?"

"Let it go. You're right. We all feel a lot of stress."

Jenn sat despondent as I tried to calm us down.

"All right, all right." Lincoln put his hands up in submission. "I'm going upstairs. Listen, guys, find me if you need me." He stood up and put his hand on Jenn's head then walked away.

The minute he rounded the corner, she erupted again. "He pisses me off. If we don't think like him, then we're wrong."

"Forget about him." I resisted the urge to tell her I predicted his reaction. "That's why I don't tell anyone. They don't understand. They never experienced a ghost, so the idea doesn't make sense to them. You can't get mad or they'll think you're psychotic."

"I wanted him to believe me."

"It's all right," I said. "Maybe he'll come around. I think he did believe you think you see things. I'm going to my room for a while before dinner."

"Yeah, hours of fun. I think they are weird when they make the whole family gather for dinner and then never talk about anything important. Like no one will say anything about Gramps."

"Our family operates that way. We'll get through this problem. We can laugh at them later."

"And I can still go with you to meet Steve?"

"It's a deal." I gave Jenn a thumbs-up.

*

Darth and I trudged up to my room because I needed time alone to think about everything. But a few minutes of being alone in my head got old fast, so I turned my attention to staring at myself in the mirror and trying to look as good as possible for Steve. I combed my hair, changed my shirt, brushed my teeth, and waited for dinner. As I sat down to read for a little bit, without any ghosts popping in for a visit, a knock on my door interrupted me.

"Jaret?" Mom called out.

"Yeah. Come in."

She opened the door, looking confused. "You have a phone call. I don't know who it is."

I didn't either. Again I got pissed about Dad's stupid rule about cell phones because the lack of one invited everyone into my business. And the call seemed to upset my mother for an unknown reason. "Huh, wonder who it is?"

"Did you give your friends this number before we left?"

"No."

I followed her down the hall to Gramps's upstairs lounge and the nearest phone but paused before going in. I'd avoided the room since we arrived because his study reminded me so much of him. He used to sit and read in his favorite chair for hours by the fire, even in the middle of the summer.

"I'll be downstairs if you need me." Mom touched me on the back before turning to leave.

I stepped into the room, overwhelmed by the memories and afraid a ghost would interrupt the whole thing. After taking a deep breath, I walked over and picked up the receiver, laughing a little. Gramps still owned an old rotary phone, and I bet most of my friends never even saw one, let alone used one.

"Hello?" I asked the mystery caller.

"Hey babe. What's up? I hope it's okay I called."

My heart jumped at hearing Steve's voice. "Hi. I had no idea who was calling me in Fremont. I'm glad you did."

"So my calling won't cause problems, will it?"

"No, it's cool. You're not canceling on me?" I hated to sound like a desperate schoolgirl, but the shoe fit.

"No way. Not for a million bucks. I wanted to make sure nothing changed."

"Yeah, same plans. But can you meet earlier? We're eating in a few minutes, so I could be ready in an hour."

"Cool, the more time the better. What do you want to do?" he asked.

"Nothing in particular. But, and I know this sounds weird, can my sister come along for a while? She's bored and wants to look around Fremont."

"Does she know?"

My heart beat fast, afraid he'd be mad at me for telling her. "Yeah, I mean, about me. I'm sorry I got you into this."

"You worry a lot. I trust you. It's cool. Relax. As long as you don't broadcast our relationship to everyone in Fremont. I'm not ready to come out."

"Okay. Anyway, she promised not to stay with us the whole night."

"Listen, I gotta go. I'll be there in about an hour."

"See you then. Bye."

"Later, hot stuff."

I hung up, feeling wired and exhilarated by the send-off. He called me by nicknames already, and though our getting together seemed pretty fast, I wanted to go with the feeling for as long as possible. In fact, I melted every time he used one. Why not have a little infatuation for once in my life, after seeing all of my friends going gaga over the opposite sex? For the first time, I understood why they got so giddy weird at the start of a relationship.

Seeing Jenn walk by down the hall, I shouted at her. "Jenn!"

She jumped a foot in the air. "Shit!" She laughed and came into the room. "You scared me."

"Did you pee your pants?"

"Sneaking up on me is mean right now." But she grinned as she spoke.

"Sorry. We're meeting Steve in an hour, right after dinner."

"Good. I need to get out of here. And speaking of dinner, Mom sent me to find you to come down to eat."

*

Jenn and I headed downstairs to the enormous cherrywood table. The room, more than any other, reminded me of the family's original wealth. I had never been in any other house except museums that included a formal dining room and table capable of hosting over twenty people. The opulence embarrassed me a little, a room running so contrary to how anyone of us lived. Mom, Dad, Lincoln, my aunt and uncle, and my cousins were sitting around the table already, chatting about the day. Without a word, Jenn and I joined them and started eating.

Dinner went as expected. The family sat and talked without acknowledging anything weird, no mention of Gramps, the ghosts, or my uncle's health. We acted as if we drove down the block to dinner, not across the entire state of Nebraska to bury a loved one. As dinner wrapped up, my heart raced and I twitched my leg, wanting to get out of there to meet Steve as soon as possible.

"I need to take Darth out," I announced as an excuse. Before I left, I jerked my head toward the door and stared at Jenn to signal her. She nodded with a slight motion as I left the room.

When I opened the back door, Darth shot outside and did one of her rituals, which involved circling the entire yard and sniffing the edges, in what I called her perimeter patrol. When she got to the far end of the yard, however, she reared up, growled, and the hair on her back stood straight up. And then she barked.

I sprinted across the yard to stop her. "Darth!" I yelled. "Shut up!" I grabbed her collar and held her snout to stop her, but she wiggled around and persisted with her rage at the bushes.

"Steve?" I whispered. "Get out of there. No one can see you from the house."

Steve stepped out of the bushes, straightening his back and stretching. He smiled and glanced around. "Hey, babe." He pecked me on the lips and patted Darth on the head. She went from attack dog to wanting attention in seconds after she recognized Steve. "Where's your sis?"

"On the way. We left separately so no one asked questions. How are you?"

"A lot better now."

He grabbed me around the waist and pulled me into an embrace and deep kiss, and crazy hot passion swelled inside me. I struggled a little with how fast we got involved—we met one night ago—but I loved the sensation and did not want to slow down, nor did my hormones.

"I'm getting too excited," I explained as I tried to pull away, but he held tight.

"Isn't that the point?" He blew into my ear.

"Yeah, sure, I mean, we can't right now."

Steve laughed and let go. "Do you guys want to cruise around? I'm not sure what else to do, although we could catch a movie."

"I'd rather hang out."

"What does your sister want to do?"

"She'll go with whatever we decide."

As I finished, Jenn bounded toward us. "You must be Steve. I'm Jenn. Jaret's shy so I won't make him introduce us."

"Nice to meet you," Steve said. They sounded and looked all grown up as they shook hands.

"We thought we'd go look around Fremont and not do anything specific," I told Jenn.

"Good. I had to get out of the house. They're talking about Fremont politics now. Boring."

"Come on." Steve motioned for us to follow him.

Once outside the back gate, we walked a block away to Steve's Jeep—bright red with a black cloth top. The perfect car for a football player. I guessed Steve's family did all right, since their son was driving a new car, a powerful and sexy one. The whole scene turned me on. We got in and Steve drove us through Fremont, honking and waving at a few people but also pointing out things of interest and chatting about what changed since Jenn and I moved, which wasn't much. A lot of times he mentioned a business changed owners, even though the building looked the same.

Steve, like Jenn, seemed to have no problem talking to strangers, so I spent a lot of time listening to them. In addition to Fremont, we chatted about normal stuff like teachers, movies, and music, then compared the assholes he knew in Fremont to those we knew in Estes, finding mutual comfort in the fact people did stupid things no matter where you lived. Thankfully, no one brought up the Bachmann ghosts or even Gramps.

We drove around Fremont for an hour, stopped and got ice cream, and then Jenn said she needed to get back to the house, I think more to give Steve and me time alone than from really wanting to go home.

But as Steve pulled into the front driveway, my anxiety about what to tell my family came back. I worried someone would see his Jeep and interrogate me later about who he was, where we met, and blah, blah, blah. I knew I was irrational to think seeing a car would lead them to think about two guys having sex, but logic came hard after so many years of hiding being gay.

"Nice to meet you," Steve said to Jenn, again with the fancy adult talk. "I'm sure we'll see each other around."

"I know you'll be around if Jaret has anything to say about it."

"All right." I poked her in the side. "You're done. Get inside."

"I'll leave you two lovebirds alone." She slammed the door and ran away. Steve and I laughed as he drove away.

*

"I like your sister, but you're so different from her. You were shy last night. I kind of expected the same from her, but she's pretty outgoing. I love how you get along so well. My brother and I fight all the time."

"What about?"

"Everything. Unless we're talking about football."

"Does your relationship with him bother you?"

He shrugged. "I suppose a little. But what can you do about it?"

Two streets later, Steve hit the brakes at a stop sign, looked in the rearview mirror, then jerked the Jeep into park. With no one around, he grabbed my hand and squeezed it, then leaned over and kissed me, his tongue running along my teeth.

"I'm glad we're alone," he whispered.

"I thought about you a lot today."

"Can I take you away?"

"Sure. I'm all yours. Where?"

"Home," he said.

I didn't respond, not sure I wanted to meet his family.

Reading my mind, he laughed. "Don't worry. My parents left for a business trip and my bro's at college. I have the house to myself. How else do you think I wandered around so late last night? They would've killed me if they were home."

We rode the rest of the way in comfortable silence, still holding hands, my mind fluctuating between absolute thrill and apprehension. Thrilled at the hot guy wanting to be with me. But apprehensive because, how well did I know him? Was he safe? Instinct told me not to worry and for once in my life go with the moment, even though I also thought about a movie I saw about Jeffrey Dahmer in his high school years, already getting ready to kill gay boys.

We arrived at a large, colonial brick house with enormous pillars in front and white trim around the windows. Twice as big as our home in Colorado, this was even bigger than Gramps's house a few blocks away.

"Nice house."

"Thanks." His tone suggested he did not understand why I complimented his home as he grinned and jumped out of the Jeep, so I followed behind, still nervous and giddy at the same time.

We walked into a huge entryway, like on TV. The living and dining rooms to the right and left were immaculate and unused, right out of a magazine, and a crystal chandelier glowed as it hovered above us. Steve took my hand and pulled me toward the huge staircase that wound in a circle around the walls of the house's middle. We turned to the right at the top and into a bedroom.

"This is my room."

I looked around at a very tidy space, everything in place and dusted, even though he hardly seemed the type. I wondered if they hired a maid. His double bed sat against one wall, opposite a bookcase full of sports trophies. As I took in the scenery, he hugged me from behind and kissed my ear.

"Welcome to my lair," he said in a sinister voice. "You're now captive to my every whim." He licked my ear, whoa—total excitement, paralyzing me as he took charge of my weakness. He spun me around to look into his steel-blue eyes. "I missed you today. Are you comfortable?"

"I don't think I've ever been this chilled out." My heart raced with excitement. He ran his hands down my back, grabbed my ass, and pulled me toward him. Kissing him again sent thrills through my body.

Steve moved us toward the bed and pushed me onto the mattress, then took his shirt off, so I ripped mine off too.

I was making out with another man! I'd always thought people were kind of corny when I read stories about their first times, how they saw fireworks or felt so enraptured they almost fainted, but I learned you had to experience the moment to understand. As we finally lay on his bed and relaxed, I felt amazed and lost myself in the sensation of him combing my long hair out of my eyes.

"You okay, babe?"

"A lot more than okay." I stared into his eyes, feeling like a hopeless romantic.

"I know you avoided this all night, but I want to say something."

My heart raced. *Oh, no. Maybe he doesn't like me that way.*

"Relax." He read my mind and petted my head to soothe me. "I want to make sure you're handling the ghost thing okay. Do you need to talk?"

"I like ignoring the topic." I hated the thought of the ghosts, but the tension spilled out of me because the topic beat him dumping me already.

"I can imagine. But don't be afraid to talk to me. I mean, experiencing ghosts has to be lonely, and strange. I thought about this a lot today. I want you to know I believe you and everything you say about the haunting, and I want to help."

I wrapped my arms around him and squeezed. "Just hold me."

He returned the hug, and we stayed in the embrace for a long time.

Chapter Four

The Hospital

"So, what's your favorite food?" Steve asked after we snuggled together for quite a while in contented silence. Then he licked my ear.

I giggled, then turned and bit his ear in return. "You."

He laughed, then bit my ear. "You taste good too. But if you could eat anything, what would it be?"

"Pizza. You?"

"Still just you." He licked my cheek and kissed my eye.

I grinned and grabbed his head in both my hands. "Be serious."

"Okay, steak maybe. I have a hard time picking."

"What's your favorite hobby?" I asked.

"Watching football on Sunday."

"Even after you practice all week and play on Friday?" *What a jock!*

"You can never get too much football."

I groaned. "I guess I'll have to watch sports with you." I ran my fingers along his bicep.

"Well, we'll be together for a long time, right? Fuck living in separate states. We'll go to college together, have a ceremony, and watch football every Sunday together."

A clock chimed in the hallway, so I avoided my initial response to the thought of a lifetime of watching football on Sunday by counting them aloud. "Shit," I yelled when I finished. "It's midnight." I jumped up and scrambled for my shirt, while Steve propped himself up on one elbow and tilted his head at me.

"Do you turn into a pumpkin at midnight, Cinderella?"

"My parents will kill me if I'm late."

"You stayed out later than this last night."

"They didn't even know I was gone. I have a curfew. They'll freak if I'm late."

Steve got out of bed, but wouldn't move until I kissed him again. We headed toward the front door, but when we got to the entryway Steve grabbed my arm and pulled me back to him.

"Give me one second," he said. "I like you. Call me if you need anything. I'll be here alone tonight." He wrote his cell number down for me, reminding me again of my irritating father because I could not click my phone to his to exchange numbers. At least Gramps used a phone, even if he owned a rotary one.

He leaned over and kissed me again before we went out to the Jeep.

I was relieved at first as we headed toward Gramps's, sure no one would notice I was a few minutes late. As I relaxed a little, my head started to pound. My brain hurt as if a demon slammed a hammer inside my skull. I closed my eyes and held my head.

"Babe, you okay?"

"Yeah," I lied. "I got a headache. Stressed with the ghosts and shit."

Steve reached for my hand as we turned onto Gramps's street. I fought the panic and against the pain as I focused on Steve.

"When can I see you again?" Steve glanced my way, concern in his expression even though he attempted casual conversation.

I rubbed the side of my head. "I don't know. Gramps's funeral is in the morning. I'm not sure how long I'll need to stay with my family."

"Okay. Well, let me know. I'll be thinking about you." He squeezed my hand.

I nodded and shook my head to clear my mind. But when the house came into view, looming above like a monster, the hair on my arms stood straight up and the pain in my head increased to the point I was blinded. My vision returned to the scene of the white gables glowing in the night, daring me to enter, and the whole place gave off an evil aura, like the house itself hated me.

"I'll call you later." I gripped his hand before letting it go. "Maybe we could at least talk a little and see when we can hook up again." I wanted to say a lot more, to tell him how much the house scared me, and to beg him to keep driving and maybe we could go be out and not deal with hateful people, or ghosts and spirits, or even family.

"Sounds good. I'll wait up." He slowed the Jeep to a crawl and kissed me on the cheek one more time. "Are you sure you're okay?"

"I can handle the problem. I'll explain more later."

The driveway appeared too soon as Steve pulled into it. "This place *is* way creepy at night." He stuck his head out the window to get a better view. "Maybe I feel weird because of what you've told me."

"Or maybe you feel odd because the house has got a lot of fucked-up things going on inside those walls. For real."

"You still going to give me a tour?"

I laughed. "After you said the haunted house creeped you out? Maybe, though I have no clue why you want one. I go in because I have to."

He smiled. "I'll protect you."

I returned the grin. "I'd better go. I'll call."

"Good. Be careful."

"I will." I jumped out and ran toward the house, fighting against my desire to stand and watch him go out of fear someone might see me and ask questions.

*

As my foot stepped onto the porch step, I forgot about Steve when my headache blinded me again, and dizziness swirled around. I grabbed onto the banister to steady myself.

I paused and then managed to stumble up the remaining steps, across the porch, and through the front door, where Darth greeted me with a wagging tail. She nudged my hand with her nose, seeming anxious and almost afraid. My headache subsided a bit, my vision cleared, and I looked up to see the entire first floor glowing an ominous color. Like candlelight flickered, but with no candles in sight. Nothing moved and the air was still. Why were all the lights off? Only a sliver of light from the streetlamp outside offered actual light beyond the eerie candlelight.

Echoing my fear, Darth whined and pushed into my leg. I stood, unsure, and listened to the silence before I patted her on the head to ease my own nervousness as I walked toward the staircase. But I heard nothing upstairs. The house was dead.

That did not stop my head from throbbing again, my vision from blurring, and my stomach from turning in knots. I fell to my knees and reached for the banister but missed and slammed onto the hardwood floor on my stomach. Darth licked my face, trying to revive me and urgent to get my attention.

As I fought to regain control of myself, the air got colder and colder and no matter how hard I tried, I could not get myself together to stand up. I was paralyzed. All I could see was Darth dancing around, the hair on her back up, and then she growled. *Oh, fuck.* I could see my breath.

A horrid creaking broke the silence, like every joint in the house screeched at me, and then the windows rattled and another blast of frigid cold swept down the stairs. I knew what was coming before I saw him, because his laughter filled the house. Evil Gramps's ghost.

He descended the stairs, laughing and staring into my eyes.

Why was he so angry?

"You know why." He came toward me, frowning. "Who else sees me? Who else understands me?" He stopped laughing and smirked instead.

He read my mind, which might have freaked me out, except a pissed-off angry ghost materialized and sauntered down the steps, chatting me up like a bad horror movie. So reading my mind felt right on target, predictable, not worthy of mention as my head ached from the continued pounding inside my noggin. "Kind of creeps me out, how you look into my noggin."

"Correct, young man. I see your soul."

"What do you want?" My body shook, my cocky words not covering the terror consuming me.

"Very well, then. You must guard this house, protect this symbol of the Bachmann legacy. I tried to tell you about this mission from the beginning, but you disregarded me. Now I must make my point with more clarity." He smiled, an awful, conspiratorial grin. "Do you know what I did?"

I shook so hard I thought my bones might rattle apart. "I don't know. A hateful shitty act, I'd guess?"

"Alas, a car approaches." His smile disappeared and he leaned over to hover a foot above my head. "Be warned. Others will suffer similar fates unless you obey me."

"Obey you? And do what? And why do you sound like a dude out of the nineteenth century?"

*

But he disappeared in a splint second, neither answering my serious questions or reacting to my snotty one. My headache disappeared, the house warmed again, and lights flickered to life. The creepy candlelight gave way to electricity. I sat up to comfort Darth, who was shaking and pacing around me, when I heard a car pull into the driveway. I sat there until a few seconds later, when the front door flew open like a hurricane shot through the yard.

Mom charged inside, frazzled, angry, and a little unhinged. "Where have you been? Come on, we need to go."

"What's wrong?"

"Come on."

She grabbed my arm, yanked me to my feet and out the door, then raced around the Blazer as I climbed into the back seat. Dad was driving, and he put the SUV into reverse the minute the doors closed. I sat in silence, unsure why I was in trouble, but more than anything terrified the ghost hurt my family.

"You can't wander around Fremont without telling us where you go," Mom spat. "This isn't the time to goof off." I stifled an inappropriate laugh about her old school language, my near smile disappearing as she continued. "We were worried to death, and when something happens, we need to contact you. And you never answered my question. Where have you been?"

"I hung out with a friend I met the other night. We drove around Fremont so I could see how it's changed. If I had my cell phone, I could've called you." Oops, did that fly out of my mouth? Mom shot me a look, but lucky for me Dad stared forward.

Mom took a deep breath and sighed. "Honey, you can't be disappearing. You need to stay with us."

I gulped back the fear of not seeing Steve, knowing it was not the time to challenge her.

"These late-night wanderings need to stop," she continued. "If you want to talk about your grandfather then come to us; don't spread things around Fremont."

I muttered an affirmative.

"Listen, I'm sorry I sound so harsh. I was worried. *We* were worried. And I need to know how to get hold of you in an emergency." I almost bit my tongue off, having to stop another cell phone comment from flying out. "I'm sorry I yelled at you."

We turned onto Main Street and then I saw the hospital. *Oh, no.* What happened?

"Uncle Harold had a setback," Dad said. Maybe he could read my mind too.

"What? Tell me." As we barreled toward the hospital, I wanted to shout "What the fuck does setback mean?" I already knew that ghost had something to do with whatever happened.

"We don't know for sure. Everyone else went to the hospital. It happened after dinner." He gripped the steering wheel with two fists as he drove ahead. "We were all sitting in the living room and talking for a while and the next thing we know, he's almost falling out of his chair. Tony stabilized him; then we all helped get him into the car to go to the hospital. Everybody else went along, and your mom and I looked for you. Jaret, you've got to make it easier for us to reach you. We've had a bad time since Gramps died, and we need to all stick together." Seriously, they begged for another smart-ass comment about my phone, but I did feel bad and kind of guilty because my uncle's sickness happened while I was having fun with Steve. We pulled into the parking lot and hurried into the ER, where the entire family sat waiting in silence.

"Any word?" Dad asked Aunt Alice as he strode toward her.

"Tony's with him." She was pale and sat in her chair like she had a rod down her back. "He's stabilized. Tony told us to wait."

I went over to Jenn and sat next to her. After making sure no one was watching, she smirked and squinted her eyes at me. Despite my worry about Uncle Harold, I fought to stifle a grin, instead patting her knee to acknowledge her and communicate I was still alive and survived our parents' wrath.

Nobody said anything else, just noise from a TV tuned to the news and soft beeps and whirs from medical machinery filled the air.

After what felt like a century, Tony walked into the waiting area and blew out a breath of relief. I had never seen him in an official capacity, with a doctor's coat and respect from those who looked his way. "Everything's fine." He reached over and rubbed his mom's shoulder. "Nothing shows up with his heart. It was stress. He needs to rest, but he'll be okay."

Alice bowed her head and exhaled like she'd come up from being underwater. A few feet away, my mom wiped away tears.

"I want you all to go home," Tony instructed. "You can visit in the morning." Then he looked at me. "But he wants to see you. I okayed going to see him, if you make the chat brief."

I cleared my throat and my hands trembled. "Me? Okay." A million questions raced through my head about his request, but I sat there without saying a word.

Tony turned to my dad. "I'll bring Jaret to Gramps's when we finish." Tony motioned for the others to leave after hugging Aunt Alice and his sister. He placed a comforting hand on my mom's back too. "It's okay. He's fine. Worn out."

The Bachmanns filed out like ducks in a row while I stayed in my chair. Jenn again gave me a weird look before she went outside, but Mom and Dad ignored Harold's desire to see me and went their merry way. Typical. No one said anything else.

When they all departed, Tony turned to me with a gentle smile. "Thanks, Jaret. I know the request must seem weird. Not sure what Dad wants, and he's a little confused right now because of the medication we gave him. If he says anything strange or that doesn't make sense, it's best to agree with him."

"Okay." I stood up and followed him down the hall, trying not to look into any of the open rooms, noticing we went through doors marked staff only. I hated hospitals. They always smelled like medicine and sick people, and all the patients looked like they'd given up or wanted to get the hell out.

We entered one of the rooms, and Tony pulled open a curtain, where Uncle Harold sat in a hospital bed, looking super pale and weak, maybe a little bewildered. They'd covered him in blankets up to his chest, and he wore one of the flimsy hospital gowns around his shoulders. He looked like he'd lost fifty pounds since morning.

"Hi," I said, trying not to freak out and wanting to explain how glad I was he was alive. But what words could explain my emotion without sounding morbid, or like I wrote him off for dead? Instead, I stood in front of him, shuffling my feet back and forth.

"I'll wait outside." Tony nodded to me before he left.

Uncle Harold smiled and motioned for me to sit next to him on the bed with a finger attached to a device with a wire that went under the covers. The oxygen tubes in his nose made him look worse than Tony had made his illness sound.

I sat next to him, careful not to slam against him or sit on a cable or anything as a million thoughts raced through my head again. But I knew one thing for sure. The evil ghost caused his illness. He was responsible. And I was involved too.

Uncle Harold's smile faded and a half-serious, half-scared expression spread across his face. He spoke in a whisper. "I know you see things." I stopped my instinct to protest and conceal my visions, knowing the moment called for a different reaction. "Mom, your grandma, had the same gift." He put his hand on my arm. "I never believed. I didn't *want* to believe." He paused, taking a moment to breathe. "Your grandma knew a bad entity was in the house. So listen, because only you can protect this family. Whatever's in there—it's evil. Pure evil." His hand fell limp beside me from the effort of talking.

I wondered if I should get Tony, or if Uncle Harold fell asleep but sat paralyzed, bewildered by yet another turn in the saga. When I leaned forward to leave, Uncle Harold placed his hand on top of mine to stop me. "Let me get this out." He regained his breath while I sat frozen next to him. "You alone can understand. The demon did this to me, but you can help protect others. Trust your instincts, like your grandmother did."

My stomach hurt, flipping over and tightening up. What was *I* supposed to do about a badass angry ghost?

"Whatever's in the house," he said with a gasp, "takes the spirits of our departed loved ones and turns them against us. I think Gramps is haunting us now."

One of the machines attached to Uncle Harold beeped, and seconds later, Tony raced into the room.

"I didn't do anything," I told him when he looked at me. "He was talking and got tired." I got up and moved toward the door as Tony monitored Harold and fidgeted with the machine, but Harold said one more thing.

"Be careful. Don't trust the house." He fell onto his pillows, out of breath and distraught.

*

"Okay, enough." Tony motioned for me to leave, so I did, more afraid than ever, and walked to the empty waiting room where I plopped into a chair. Tears streamed down my face. I felt alone, with even more responsibility on me, despite being a kid. A kid with the misfortune of seeing shit no one else could. I sat, miserable, and after twenty minutes of staring at the clock on the wall near the TV, Tony came down the hall.

"Ready?"

No, let's stick around here for another hour, I thought. Instead, I nodded and followed him to the parking lot. We drove to Gramps's without a word, good Bachmann men repressing whatever thoughts swam through our minds.

When Tony pulled into the driveway, I said good night and got out, but I waited until he drove away before I walked toward the house, which was more dark and frightening than ever. Darth was waiting for me, her tail wagging, her little face an expression of relief and joy. Finally, a friendly face. I leaned over and kissed her on the head.

We went upstairs, walking as fast as possible past the attic door, and into my room where I closed the door behind me. I thought maybe I would see Mom and Dad, since they were so concerned with my whereabouts. But no one cared since Tony watched over me, so I was relieved not to deal with them. I cried myself into exhaustion until I couldn't cry anymore and then I stared at the ceiling until I remembered Steve. Shit. I'd promised to call him. I jumped out of bed and told Darth to follow as I hurried down the hall toward Gramps's study and the phone, which was around a corner and down a short hallway.

I rounded the corner and then jumped because a light glowed from underneath the study door. Gramps always kept the door closed, as did we, with the light off. I knocked on the door to see if anyone else was inside, but no one answered, so I pushed it open, pausing after each inch to see if a beast attacked me or if I heard anything from the room, but instead of seeing or hearing anything, a supernatural sensation swept over me.

On instinct, I grabbed the doorknob and pulled the door back, not closing it but blocking off any view of the room. No way I wanted to confront a nasty ghost, no way I would ignore the ghost alert going off in my head.

Yet I stood there without retreating, also observing how my inner senses remained calm. Glancing down at Darth, who freaked when nasty shit visited us, I noticed she was chilled, too, leaning toward the door and attempting to push the bottom open with her snout.

Though a little apprehensive I might misread the situation or get tricked, I grabbed Darth's collar to keep her by me and shoved the door all the way open. The wood hit the doorstop with a gentle thud.

But I was too afraid to examine the room, instead focusing my attention on Darth. Her tail wagged and she strained against my hold to go inside, so I released her to charge around. Her head stayed close to the ground as she sniffed along, bouncing into the room like she did when she was excited or a family member arrived home.

I was struck by how the room continued to glow, a soft welcoming light, so I lifted my head to see what was going on. The light came from the fireplace, where gentle flames created an inviting scene, though the warmth felt more appropriate for December instead of spring. I followed Darth inside, no alarms going off in my head, the calm soothing me, but still much more cautious than my dog. After all, a ghost, or other entity built the fire but stayed quiet when I knocked.

I closed the door behind me, again the instinct to obey Gramps's behavior taking over, as Darth returned to my side, calm and happy. No evil ghost vibe so far.

I jumped a little when I looked toward the fire again but chilled right after. Gramps sat in his leather lounge chair, watching the fire, his legs crossed, not making a sound. He glanced at me as I inched toward him and smiled. Yep, he looked like my grandpa, loving, caring, and nurturing. Nothing scary about him, and no bad feelings welled up within me.

Gramps motioned toward his desk and pointed at the phone. Had he read my mind? Did he know why I came in here in the first place?

He nodded agreement to my unspoken questions, so I walked to his desk and sat.

Gramps turned back to the fire and stared into the flames.

As I dialed Steve's number, I marveled at going about my business as if I came to an empty room, without the spirit of a loved one or a magical fire blazing away. Weird. But then, weird shit got weirder and weirder since arriving in Fremont, so I went with the weirdness of the moment. I almost never disobeyed Gramps while he lived, so why start?

"Hello?" a groggy voice answered.

"Steve?"

"Yeah. Jaret?"

"Sorry I called so late. I tried to get away sooner, but there was a problem."

"What? Are you okay?"

"I'm fine." Then I fell quiet. I wanted to tell him everything, but at the same time I didn't want to unload a bunch of problems on him, and I wondered how much to say with Gramps in the room.

"Okay, I'm awake now. Something's wrong. Talk to me."

"I'm sorry for calling this late. I hope you're not mad."

"Relax. I fell asleep waiting. I would've felt worse if you hadn't called. Tell me what's wrong."

"My uncle was taken to the hospital. When I got home, Mom and Dad took me there. Uncle Harold asked to see me, so I talked to him alone. Visiting him weirded me out. He's going to be fine, at least."

"What are you talking about? Are you okay?"

"I'm okay, but—"

Steve interrupted me. "Can you get out of the house? Can we meet? I'm worried about you."

"We can figure a meeting out." The crack in my voice at his concern surprised me.

"Okay, babe. Take a breath. Let me think for a minute. How about if I come over there? My parents won't be back until tomorrow."

"Okay. But I should stay close to Gramps's. The funeral's tomorrow. Plus, with my uncle in the hospital I need to be here, or my parents will freak." Then the perfect place came to me. "The guest house!" I almost shouted. "We could meet in the guest house. It's above the garage."

"Cool. Hang tight. I'll be there in a few. I'll park around the corner so no one sees the Jeep. Do you want to meet in the bushes again?"

"I'll be there."

"Bye, babe."

I forgot Gramps amid my infatuation with Steve but remembered him right after I hung up his ancient phone. I glanced over to see if he had left, but he sat there, waiting by the fire, his hands folded in his lap, his face a mask of quiet contemplation.

Then a jolt of anxiety put my stomach in knots, not because of a bad omen, but because I wondered what Gramps learned from my conversation.

Gramps patted his knees and rose out of his chair, the speed and mannerism like the last time I visited him. He stood there, looking at me and smiling. My eyes teared and a loneliness swept over me, and I was missing him, afraid about coming out, and wondering about all the ghost stuff. I was overwhelmed as I thought about the unquestioned love the man always provided me. Gramps leaned toward me and started to speak, but no words came out. I cried even more. Then he walked toward the fire, glanced into the flames, and thought for a moment before he returned his attention to me. He closed his eyes and took a deep breath. As he did, a couple of the flames in the fire jumped out of the fireplace and into the room. Nothing burned, but the flames danced on the floor at Gramps's feet.

That got my attention and yanked me out of my pity party. The display of magic was amazing.

Sitting at my feet, Darth watched the display, as mesmerized as me. I started to grab her collar when she stood, thinking she might attack the dancing flames, but she sat back down and leaned into my leg. After a moment of pyro-magic, the blaze shaped itself into two people dancing with each other. They took the form of two men, not a man and a woman, and twirled in each other's arms. One of the male flames clutched the other tightly to him and dipped him, like men did to women on TV, or as Gramps had done with Grandma when I found them in the attic. As the fire continued its waltz below us, Gramps looked at me. Then I figured out the meaning of the fire dancing, again not because of any magic or supernatural hocus pocus, but from watching the scene and looking at Gramps. Though caution kept him from verbalizing anything, he created the scene of two men together to tell me he was okay with my being gay. He still loved me. And here came the tears again.

Gramps pretended to clap his hands together but made no noise. He grinned, then ushered me to the door and laughed silently, shooing me out. I think he must have known Steve waited outside. Before I left, I blew a kiss to Gramps, which he grabbed as he waved goodbye. I left with Darth, grabbing her by the collar to keep her with me. I felt the most secure since Gramps died. Here was the grandfather I remembered in life, and here was the safe house where I'd spent my most happy time as a kid.

With soft steps into the hallway, I inched toward the stairway, afraid to alert anyone to my presence and ruin the rendezvous. Nothing in the dark hallway, though I heard chatting down in the living room. I hurried down the stairs, still bent over to clutch Darth by the collar, and turned a sharp corner toward the kitchen before anyone in the living room could see me when I hit the first floor. My heart pounded when I got to the back door and stopped to listen to figure out if anyone heard me or came to check on any noise. There was still the faint sound of people talking.

I hooked Darth's leash to her collar and took my time opening and closing the back door, making sure not to make a sound.

*

On the porch, I took a deep breath of the cool night air. I pulled Darth close to me, afraid she'd bark when she heard or saw Steve, but noticed she was pretty calm. I was too. More chilled than in quite a while, though excitement welled inside me at the thought of seeing Steve. Down the few steps and into the yard, I spotted Steve lurking again under the bushes like a burglar. Darth, too, spotted him and tugged hard on her leash to charge ahead. I slowed her from a full sprint but allowed her momentum to hurry us forward, sending me into a slow jog.

As we rushed across the yard, a big, dopey grin spread across my face.

Steve smiled, too, as he whispered hello and reached over to touch my arm. "Follow me," I whispered.

I led him to a side gate and out onto the sidewalk, where we walked fast around the corner to the side of the garage. Neither of us spoke, but he grabbed my hand as we went along, causing my heart to flutter like a stupid princess in a Disney movie. A minute later, we climbed the stairs to the guest quarters above the garage, where I took out my key and opened the door.

I anticipated cobwebs, dust, and general neglect because no one ever used the room, but instead found the place was pretty clean. Gramps must've kept the cleaning up, even after Grandma died, even though no one ever used the guest house. We always stayed in the main house with him, and it's not like he hired any house staff who needed a room here. Or rented the room out or anything.

I closed the one window shade and switched on a bedside lamp. A tiny bathroom was located to one side, and there were two twin beds with a nightstand between them. Nothing else fit in the room that I bet looked the same at least since the 1970s, based on the decor. The lamp didn't give off much light, but I was afraid to turn on the overhead because someone might notice the glow from the house, shining from the cracks between the shade and window. I hurried to the bathroom and checked for mold or dirt, but the bathroom was like the bedroom—tidy and clean. I turned around to go back toward the beds, but Steve blocked my way.

"Hey." He grabbed me by the arms. "Slow down." He pulled me into him and squeezed me against his so hot and so hard chest. "You gotta relax. Are you always this jittery?"

I lay my head against his shoulder, feeling safe in his arms. When he let go, we walked to the bed, where he sat and pulled me onto his lap.

"Is there a way I can help you? What happened tonight?"

"Uncle Harold had another heart attack. He has health problems, and they think the stress of Gramps's death got to him. But I think the ghost got to him."

"But he's okay now?"

"Yeah. My cousin Tony—he's a doctor—checked him out at the hospital and said he'd be fine. But I'm still worried. I'd feel better if I believed my uncle had a health problem. I know I sound weird, but this scary ghost can do anything. Anything."

Steve nodded, seeming to accept the ghost story without question. "And the funeral doesn't help either. What else?"

I paused, running my finger along his muscular arm. "I'm kinda afraid to tell you. I'm surprised you don't already think I'm nuts. I mean, I told you I think a ghost went after my uncle. The story gets even stranger."

"Stop." Steve took my head in his hands and forced me to look into his eyes. Despite my anxiety, I melted at the feeling of his strong fingers clutching me and his chest against mine. I stared into his beautiful blue eyes against my instinct to look away. Teenager all over the place again! Fear and nervous embarrassment mixed with affection and a huge dose of lust.

"It must be hard to trust me," Steve said. "We just met. You're scared. But try to believe me, because I believe you. Maybe I'm nuts too." He made his eyes go big and stuck out his tongue like a crazy person before continuing while I laughed. "Maybe I'm blind because you're so hot. But I believe you. I wish you didn't feel so alone, you know? People who haven't helped you piss me off."

My face must have turned bright red. "Thanks. I'll try. When I got to the hospital, Uncle Harold asked to talk to me, which was pretty strange. He didn't ask for my aunt, my dad, or his own kids. He wanted me. The experience was awful. He could barely breathe. My uncle's a strong guy. He fought in Vietnam, so I was scared to see him so weak and vulnerable. He told me to fight the ghosts for the family and said the house was evil. He's the first adult who's understood what I see, like he knew about the ghost. But he can't do anything because he's in the hospital. I think Tony thought he was looped up on meds."

"At least he's on your side. Did he tell you what to do?"

I rolled my eyes. "No. Not helpful. I can see the threat. I sense the spirit wherever I go in the house. But I don't know how to fight him." I shrugged. "I almost can't cope with knowing the thing is there." Thinking about the ghost or demon or whatever I should call it, caused me to shake. I burst into tears, hugging Steve.

Steve squeezed me harder. "What else? Sweetie, you gotta tell me."

"What happened was fucking awful. The evil ghost showed up and confronted me. After you dropped me off, the spirit yelled at me. Told me to leave his plans alone and forget anything I'd seen. That's when Mom and Dad came back and took me to the hospital. So I've got a psychotic ghost after me, I have to protect the whole family, and I have to fight him by myself. I don't know how much more I can take."

Steve petted my hair as we sat in silence for a few minutes. "Yeah," he sighed. "That's a lot. But here's the deal. First of all, I won't leave you alone." He grabbed the back of my head for emphasis. "We might not be able to kiss in front of everyone, but I won't let you face this alone. You have to let me help." As he talked, Steve ran his fingers through my hair again. "Besides, I know you want to help your family and do what your uncle asked, but you can only do what you can handle, right? You can't let anybody pressure you into anything. Do what you can handle. Unless you find a manual on how to handle ghosts or an expert gives you better instructions, take it one step at a time."

"But I need to protect the family." My eyes welled with more tears. "No one else even knows this thing is after us."

"I know, babe. But you can't do everything by yourself. Not this second." Steve held me tighter with each word.

"You'll help?" I felt small and scared, but if Steve was going to stick around, at least I wasn't alone.

"However I can."

"But you'll need to be around more. How will we explain?"

He gave a dismissive shrug. "We'll figure out what to say. Our friendship doesn't have to be a secret from your family. Besides, they're old. If we stay out of their hair, they won't worry about the details. Guys hanging out don't freak them out, unless we make out in front of them."

He made me laugh. It almost sounded easier to plant a huge kiss on Steve's lips in front of everyone and be done with the coming-out shit.

"Besides"—Steve grew serious—"I want to protect you."

Steve lay back on the bed, and I rolled on top of him, grabbing his bicep with my hand. I put my head on his chest and let him rub my back.

"Your turn. Promise not to think I'm nuts?" Steve's voice dropped to a whisper.

I looked up into his eyes while he played with my hair.

"I won't think you're crazy."

"I like you." His voice quivered a little. "And I want to stay in touch. Not as friends, but maybe something else. I've thought a lot about us. I mean, since the night at the park, you're all I think about. And I sound crazy and impossibly stupid, but I wanna try to stay in contact and be, well, your boyfriend. Maybe we could at least try."

I hadn't expected *that*. I'd hoped for a boyfriend, but didn't think I'd ever get so lucky.

Steve waited for me to respond, his leg twitching. I wanted to blurt out everything I thought but couldn't find the words. Instead, I cried. "I want to try too."

"That's it?"

"Well, no." I giggled. "I mean, I agree with everything. I don't know what else to say. I'm afraid you think this now but will get tired of me and move on."

"Didn't you hear me?" Steve hugged me. "I've been honest with you all along. I'm not going to leave you all of a sudden with the ghosts and all this other shit. Babe, I don't know what else to say, but I like you and want to explore this. Like I said, I know being together will be hard. Hard enough you live in Colorado, but worse, we can't tell anyone. But I want to be with you."

"What about the ghosts? Are you telling me the truth that my visions don't freak you out? I've never told anyone this stuff. Or at least the few I ever told thought I was nuts and wanted me to get help. Nut farm city."

He laughed, despite his next comment. "I told you: ghosts freak me out. Not how you see them, but how they're after you. Nothing makes me think you're a loony bird. I told you already." He pulled my head to his chest and held me. Then he laughed again.

"What's funny?" I grinned despite not knowing what made the situation humorous.

"When I met you downtown, remember how I wanted you to give me a tour of your grandpa's house? I wanted to tell everyone I'd gone inside the haunted mansion? I thought the rumor was a big joke. Now I'm lying in the guest house, afraid of what's next door. Mom always tells me to be careful what I ask for, because I might get my wish."

"You won't be as amused if you ever see the shit going on in there."

"Are we safe out here?"

"I have no idea."

"Comforting." He smiled. "Okay, what else?"

"I don't know. I feel like we should plan, but I don't know how." I took a turn to laugh. I couldn't believe I thought we could attack a spirit. The mere thought *was* crazy.

"Now what's funny?" I felt him laughing underneath me.

"I sound like a ghostbuster. Have you seen the movie? It's kinda old, but pretty funny. I asked you how to fight a spirit running around my family's house scaring the crap out of me. Hello, most people don't believe in ghosts.

Sure, Uncle Harold does, but he's laid up in the hospital and thinks Gramps haunts the place. I think Aunt Alice knows, too, but won't say anything. Jenn, you, and me, we know. Oh, and Darth. How are three kids and a dog going to fight a ghost? We *do* need ghostbusters."

We both laughed, but then Steve got serious. "We'll figure out what to do. This is kinda nuts, too, but I always wanted to protect a hot guy. All the guys on the football team have girlfriends. I get jealous when they give their girl a coat, or open the door for her. Or when they exchange class rings. I want the same thing, but with a man. I know I can't do those things in public for you. But I'll do whatever I can. Right now, protecting you means helping you with this ghost. And, I like to call you nicknames. Do my names bother you?"

"No. I love them."

"Cool. So, back to the subject at hand. I think we'll have to trust our guts. But I think you need to focus on the funeral tomorrow. That's gotta be hard. I mean, your grandpa died."

I nodded, unable to say anything because of the lump in my throat. "Can we meet tomorrow?" I whispered and managed not to cry.

"Of course. Let me know when and where."

"Okay."

*

We lay for a while as I thought about Gramps, the funeral, the spirits, and how good I felt to have Steve with me. The swirl of emotion punched me in the gut, but I kept reminding myself at least I met Steve. At least I started another journey, one to help me deal with a whole other kind of secret.

"Does this mean you're my boyfriend?" I asked him.

Steve rolled me over and pinned me to the bed, which turned me on a little. A lot. "I'm your boyfriend, and you're *mine*."

"Are you going to college or are you going to stay in Fremont?"

"C'mon, give me credit. I want to get the hell out of here. I'm going to find out where you apply and go there."

"Are you serious?" My eyes lit with excitement.

"Totally." He locked his lips to mine and kept my arms pinned. When he stopped, he kept our noses touching each other. "So, where am I going?"

"Not sure." I shrugged from beneath him. "I still need to decide. We could choose a place together."

"Cool. Let's go where we can tell people." Steve licked my ear. "Like New York or LA."

"My family went to Chicago once, and I saw two guys holding hands. We were visiting a friend of my mom's, and I still remember Dad asking her why she lived in the *gay area*. Like living there was weird."

Steve settled next to me. "Okay. Go on."

"We drove down this street and I saw gay flags flying from half the buildings. My dad talked about how bold 'the gays' were in Chicago with all of their flags and crap. I don't think my mom's friend was too happy about what he said. She defended her neighborhood and said Halsted Street was the friendliest place she'd ever lived." I paused. "Why did I tell you this story?"

"We're picking a college where we can be openly and safely gay."

"Oh, yeah, so we can add Chicago to the list. Denver has potential, too, though I'd rather get away from home."

"Then Denver's out. We'll pick a few places before you leave."

"We'd better hurry. Deadlines have already passed. At least, we both like to procrastinate."

Steve leaned down and kissed my forehead. Then the eyelid. Then on the lips. I closed my eyes and lost myself in the physical sensation, in the pure instinct to smash our bodies together, in the absolute teenage lust.

Which came crashing to a halt when Darth, laying on the floor next to the bed, let out a persistent and guttural growl. Steve ignored her at first, tracing his tongue across my neck toward my ear, but a second later, a hammer started slamming against the inside of my head, and I opened my eyes to see the Evil Gramps hovering above us, squinting in anger.

My heart almost pounded through my chest as I pushed Steve aside and gasped for air. The ghost grinned, an evil clown kind of grin, then winked and floated through the air and out the window. Steve lay next to me with his arm around my chest.

"What the fuck?" he asked.

"I saw—"

And then the door flew open, and Mom marched into the room.

"Oh, God," she exclaimed. "What is this? Is this what you've been hiding? What were you two thinking? How could you do this?" She stared at us, and I wanted to jump out the window and run away.

Steve had shifted a couple feet away from me; my mom stood there frowning, and we were all speechless. Darth freaked out, too, scampering over to the corner and panting.

"You should leave," Mom instructed Steve.

Steve got up, straightened his shirt, and walked to the door. Mom ignored him, instead glaring at me the whole time. My stomach rumbled as I watched him walk away. At least he turned before he walked out the door and looked back at me. From behind my mom, he mimed holding a phone to the side of his head and mouthed call me before he left.

*

The second the door closed, Mom fired more questions. "Jaret, what—I don't even know where to begin. What will your father think? What will other people say?" Her tone softened, at least, losing the sharp edge.

Darth crossed the floor and scurried the last couple of feet onto the bed, where she lay next to me with her ears back. She understood, and I started crying for the hundredth time in one day, holding onto Darth as if she were a life preserver.

Mom sat on the edge of the bed next to me. "Shh. Calm down. I saw the light on in here. That's the reason I came up, because I thought somebody left the light on by accident. I wasn't spying on you, but honey, I didn't see this coming. Not tonight, and I can't deal with it right now. We'll talk, but not now. Not here. Please, stay away from the boy. Think about what this would do to your father, if he found out tonight." She patted my leg, but the touch didn't help. *Stay away from Steve?* I couldn't believe what I was hearing.

After another silence, Mom walked toward the door. Too emotional, my warning to her caught in my throat after I saw the ghost hovering above her again. The ghost flicked her hard on the ear, which caused her to look all around as her eyes grew wide with fright. "Get out of here." I didn't know if she meant that for me or the ghost, but she grabbed the door handle and walked out without acknowledging anything else.

And she ripped my heart out on the way. I so wanted to at least hear she still loved me. But she departed without saying a word and sobs made my chest heave as I rolled over and buried my head in the pillow, still holding Darth with one arm. I didn't care about the spirit in there, almost hoping he would come over and crash the whole roof right on top of my head.

I cried until I was exhausted; then I got up and straightened the room a little before I turned off the lights and left, relocking the door. I descended the stairs in the darkness with Darth in tow, at least grateful I didn't see anybody else around, living or dead.

I let Darth roam the backyard for a while to do her business. She brought me a huge stick she found under one of the trees and I threw it for her, fighting another round of tears. If only I could lose myself in chasing after a stupid branch for a little while. I set the stick aside and we went into the kitchen when she half ran, half walked to retrieve it. Darth headed for her water bowl, and I stood watching her, listening for any sounds or seeing if anything alerted my senses. From the silence, I assumed everybody had either gone to bed or left. My senses indicated the ghosts did too.

Good. I didn't feel like dealing with anything else. So when Darth finished drinking, we went upstairs. On impulse, I turned toward Gramps's study instead of going to my room. I sat in one of the leather chairs, grabbed the old school phone, and dialed.

"Hello?"

"Steve?"

"You okay?"

"Yeah. You?"

"I guess. I'm so sorry. Did she tell everybody?"

"No. She doesn't want anyone to know."

"Good. I mean, you know, it's hard."

"Sorry to call. I wanted to apologize."

"I'm glad you called. I couldn't sleep anyway. When can I see you?" he asked.

"She wants me to stay away from you. But I won't. I can't. She'll keep our secret, because she can't deal with my being gay."

"You sure you're okay?"

"I'm pretty freaked out and tired. But I'll survive. Promise you won't forget about me."

"Babe, you can't get rid of me so easy. Listen, we'd better get to sleep. Call me tomorrow?"

"I will, as soon as I can after the funeral."

"Sounds good." He paused. "You still there?"

"Yeah."

"Listen, just so you know, I thought about you all day. And, since I left you tonight, my stomach is in knots. I know I sound kind of cheesy, but I'll be thinking about you tomorrow too."

"I'll think about you too."

The minute we hung up, the isolation of the mansion hit me full force. I listened for anything, friend or foe, but heard nothing. Even the attic door hinted at nothing more than a silent house at night as I crept toward my bed. In my room, I went to bed with Darth curled between my legs. As tired as I was, thoughts whirled through my head. What was I going to do? Mom knew I was gay; I was banned from Steve; my uncle thought I had a kind of super power to beat an angry spirit; and Gramps's funeral was tomorrow. What a mess. No answers popped into my head, but at least I fell asleep. Or passed out.

Chapter Five

A Funeral Haunting

The 7:00 a.m. alarm surprised the crap out of me, so much so, I almost fell out of bed reaching over to slam the clock off. Getting to my room the night before, I figured no sleep would come to me with everything racing through my head. Instead, I must have passed out, and by the looks of the dog, Darth did, too, because she picked her head up to look at me and then lay back on the bed. I groaned and stared at the ceiling. Gramps's funeral was today. I stumbled out of bed to find my clothes that were both organized in piles on the floor and inside my suitcase.

My head hurt, but just a little, maybe from the ghosts, maybe from the lack of sleep, or maybe from all the shit piled together. Despite wanting to crawl back into bed, I grabbed a T-shirt and my jogging stuff, thinking a run would make me feel better. I leaned over to tie my shoes and got a big kiss from Darth, who had figured out my plans and leapt out of bed the second I touched my shoes. Then she spun around, her tail stub wagging, unable to hold still. When I took too long to tie the second lace, she nudged me with her nose, ran to the door, and yelped at me to hurry.

I tightened the last lace, picked up Darth's leash, and opened the bedroom door to a quiet house. Which was good, because I didn't want to talk to anyone—ghost, human, or otherwise. Darth and I went down the stairs, out the front door, and into the cool morning air. After hooking her onto the leash, I trudged along, setting a moderate pace as Darth tried to tug us faster. She finally gave up and settled into running beside me, taking the slower speed to mean she should attempt to sniff various things we passed.

Fremont was dead at the early hour, with empty streets and no sign of life. I stayed on the side streets and back roads, running along with Darth, and trying to prepare for the rest of what was sure to be a crappy day.

Darth jerked me out of my thoughts when she lunged for a squirrel. I pulled her leash to slow her down and told her to chill out, but she of course ignored me. I turned down another street, which forced her to follow, though she looked back for another minute at the squirrel and then darted ahead to attack a blowing leaf.

Without intending to, without knowing how to get there, I ended up jogging past Steve's house, which gave me little thrill. He'd already left for school because the football team lifted weights together before class, but I enjoyed thinking about him. After running awhile more, Darth and I crossed the street onto Gramps's sidewalk, where his property pretty much took up the entire block.

Just as a bounce returned to my step from the exercise high, however, the headache that always preceded ghosts slammed into my forehead. Bam! Needless to say, I dreaded what might come next. The third floor came into view as I passed a row of shorter bushes, and eyes stared at me from the attic window. The face looked like Gramps, maybe, but I wasn't sure. Was Grandma next to him? I was still a bit too far away to see them, but a sense of sadness filled my chest when I remembered today's event. My head hurt more, and I turned away, trying to keep my focus and make the image disappear.

But I glanced back to see they still peered down at me. I sped up and turned onto the walk to the front door and, against my better judgment, peeked up at the attic. Through a small, round window, I saw a glowing, bloodred shape floating in front of the glass, like a haze of crimson smoke floated there. I stopped dead in my tracks and yanked Darth toward me when a face appeared through the haze, a scarlet and transparent image with white eyes and bright teeth glowing when the image smiled, like a predator about to kill its prey, like an evil villain caricature come to life.

The face came into focus enough I recognized the evil ghost who had warned me last night. Was this ghost Gramps too? A second ago, I swore I saw Gramps in the other window with Grandma, and next, his exact likeness, though younger, glared down at me. And then the spirit was gone, and I stood staring up at clear glass.

"Are you going inside?" I jumped at the sound of my mom's voice coming from the porch where she stood wrapped in a blanket.

I walked toward the house, like a man toward his death sentence, and up the steps without answering. I didn't feel like talking to her. Not after last night.

"We're eating breakfast in a bit and then going to the funeral."

I remained silent and instead unclipped Darth's leash from her collar.

"Hello?" She tilted her head sideways at me. "Are you there?"

"Yeah. Okay. I'll go shower."

I tried to pass her, but she reached out and held my arm. "Come here for a minute."

Oh, shit. Here we go.

I sighed and followed her inside, to a small parlor off the main living room, where Grandma and Grandpa used to read together. There were a couple of chairs in here, and I took one while Mom sat in the other. I waited, wishing I could be anywhere but here, maybe even in the attic with the creepy red ghost.

Mom took in a deep breath. "Please don't disappear again today. I need you with the family. Your father will need all of us."

I rolled my eyes, no longer able to contain the emotion. "It's Gramps's funeral today. Why would I not be around?"

"Okay, fine. But could you be a little more attentive and engaged? And don't pout or get cranky?"

"Sure. Whatever. I've got a lot going on, as you know." I winced because my headache was getting worse, but from stress. And then I got pissed. "Look, I've tried to deal with this crap since I was a kid, and I'm tired. I don't care what you think, and I don't even care if you call another shrink, because nothing will change anything. There are ghosts in this house. I can see them, and they communicate with me. I didn't ask for this, and I can't explain what I see. Yes, I know how you and Dad feel about my visions. But I'm telling the truth. And what I see has nothing to do with my being insane." Even I was surprised by my statement.

Mom looked like I spit in her face. "What are you talking about? Are you upset right now, and needing sympathy? Is this how you're grieving?"

"Sympathy for what?" My words sounded tense. "Grieving?"

"You know what I mean."

"You think I like this whole ghost thing? You think I want sympathy?"

"No. You brought up the ghosts, not me. I don't want to find you with a boy again."

Tears filled my eyes, and I stared hard at the ground without speaking for a long while. "If I could go back and do it over again, I would in a second," I whispered.

"Your actions affect more than you. You got me so worked up, I thought a ghost was after me up there. Maybe you should have thought about things before you snuck into your grandfather's guest room."

I stared up at her like she tried to stab me with a knife.

She took her turn to look at the floor. "I'm sorry. I didn't mean to sound crass."

"Yes, you did." I felt like the most insignificant person on the planet.

"Jaret—"

"I *hate* what goes on inside my head. I see ghosts. I know they exist. That's bad enough." I threw my hands up in the air. "But my feelings about guys haunt me every single day too. If I could erase myself from this family, I would. Because you have no idea what it's like to know you're not normal; to behave and not create problems means I can't be who I am. I wish I could leave to spare all of you from my pain and the embarrassment of having an abnormal son." I'd cried a river by the end of my speech, and Darth bumped her head against my knee and pushed into me with concern. I petted her, trying to comfort her, and wiped my face with the bottom of my shirt. When I looked up at Mom, she was crying too.

"What have I done?" she said in a soft voice. "I ignored this for too long. Oh, Jaret, I don't know where to begin."

My tears continued and Darth pushed her snout into my lap.

"No one wants you to disappear," Mom said. "I love you. I never stopped loving you. I'm sorry I've hurt you. I'm trying to figure all this out. I am having a difficult time. Please let me take this one thing at a time. Let's get through the funeral first, okay? But never think anyone wants you gone or we don't love you. Give me time. But please don't hate yourself. Whatever haunts you, we'll work on making you better."

"Okay," I whispered, though I still felt worthless, like I'd let her down.

"Can we agree to focus on the funeral?" Mom slumped, and she looked tired.

"Yeah, fine." At least for today. I needed a break, and the truce seemed to relieve some pressure. "It'll be hard enough to say goodbye to Gramps."

"Let's get ready." She stood and put her hand on my shoulder. When I got out of my chair, she surprised me with a tight hug. "I love you," she whispered.

"I love you too." More tears. I could get through the day, at least, having heard those words from her.

I hurried to the bathroom, took a quick shower, and got my suit out. My suit and the dark tie made Gramps's death real, unlike before, on an even deeper emotional level. The same sense hit me in the hallway when I saw Jenn, wearing a black dress and a pair of earrings from Gramps last Christmas.

"Hey, you," I said.

"You look nice." She pulled at my suit jacket. "Sounds weird to say nice things on our way to a funeral."

"Yeah. But you look very nice yourself. Come here." I motioned her into her room. "Mom found out about me."

She stared at me with confusion until recognition lit in her eyes. "Wow. What happened?"

"She caught me with Steve."

"She found you with Steve? What were you doing?"

"Kissing," I hedged. "I didn't mean for her to see us. It was a shitty way for her to find out."

Jenn giggled. "Not one of the top ten recommended ways to come out to your mom. Did she freak?"

"Pretty much. She got pissed and made Steve leave and then told me not to see him again."

"She told you not to see him?" Jenn almost shouted her response.

I nodded. "Things this morning went a little better. She gave me a hug. She doesn't want me to tell Dad yet. We agreed to get through today before dealing with anything else."

"Okay. I suppose you can't ask for much more. I mean, that's a harsh way to find out. She'll get over her issue." Jenn hugged me in sympathy.

"We'll see." Jenn's support felt good, but I wished I had her same confidence about Mom. "Then I was stupid. I brought up the ghosts, which she didn't like any better. I was upset though."

"What did you expect? They always freak about you and the ghosts. Did she act like Lincoln did when we told him?"

"No. More of a scolding, and she didn't run off like him."

She studied me. "You worry too much about what they think. Your constant concern isn't good for you."

"I'm hurt. I hate how they treat me like a mental patient. I know I must sound insane when I talk about seeing things, but why can't they even try to understand? Why do they tune me out and patronize me? Instead of shrinks, maybe look for someone else who can help me with this shit. It's not like I wanted to be able to do this."

"Being you is tough. When you first told me, I thought the ghosts sounded kinda crazy too. I took a while to understand. And you gotta remember Mom and Dad are harder to convince about things. They never believe us. I think they freak when you talk about the visions because they worry you're not okay. It doesn't have anything to do with the ghosts. They don't even hear the ghost story."

I pointed at Jenn to stop her. "Except they're experiencing the spirit too! Mom admitted she had. The ghost went after her, a few times, but she decided the experiences aren't real and my getting worked up about a spirit got her thinking about ghosts. Their reaction will drive me crazy, not the ghosts."

"They want you to be okay, and you're not, so they freak. I guess the same idea explains how Lincoln reacted too."

"He thought he was helping." I contemplated for a second. "I suppose Mom and Dad think the same thing."

"Give Mom time."

"I promised her I would. I'm just hurt. It even surprised me how much I needed a hug when she gave me one."

"You can always talk to me."

"I know. Thanks. That's why I pulled you in here. We'd better get down there before breakfast is over." I sighed. "Today is going to suck big balls."

Jenn started laughing.

"Well, the day *will* suck."

"I know." She giggled again. "But saying it so simple makes me laugh." Then she grew more serious. "I miss Gramps. I keep thinking I'll see him, alive and well in the house when I walk around."

"Be careful what you wish for." I led us down the hall, with Darth right behind.

"Don't even joke about ghosts." She frowned at me. "So not funny." When we got to the top of the stairs, Jenn paused. "Do you see Gramps a lot?"

"Quite a bit. Especially since we got here. I've seen him, Grandma, and maybe others." I thought about stopping there, but since Jenn had seen things, too, I decided she should know everything. "Listen, this may be nothing, so don't panic. But I feel things going on in this house today. I mean, more than usual. I even saw weird stuff. I get headaches—premonitions, I guess—of things, and there might be trouble with supernatural shit today. Be careful. And let me know if anything happens. I almost didn't tell you, because I don't want you to worry. But I thought you should know."

"I'll be careful." I hated how concerned she looked.

"Good. Keep an eye out, okay?" I patted her on the shoulder, and we had started downstairs when I stopped in my tracks. "Wait. I forgot Gramps's crest." Darth froze in confusion but decided to follow Jenn down to breakfast. I hurried back to my room, where I unzipped the pouch where I placed the lapel pin Gramps gave me when I turned ten. The design wasn't anything special, a gold emblem with a lion, stars, and a cross. The signet indicated the Bachmanns' status in Germany. Gramps loved the crest and wore a lapel pin with it all the time. Remembering what the symbol meant to Gramps brought a tear to my eye. I stuck the crest on my lapel and hurried to compose myself before going to breakfast.

*

But when I turned to leave, the evil spirit blocked the doorway, mocking me with his creepy smile. I'd been too busy with the pin and thinking about Gramps. Only with him in front of me did I feel my ghost-warning headache.

"I apologize for the surprise," he said insincerely. "You know when I'm coming. Perhaps this will remind you of my power." He laughed, a deep, macabre sound. "You have good reason to be afraid. And don't be so surprised. Of course, I can read your thoughts, simple as they are. I'm not here to ask anything new of you, just what I already requested."

"But I don't know what you want." My hands trembled with fear.

"Protection, of course. The idiot patriarchs of this family defy my wishes, and the desires of all departed Bachmanns. You, however, can see us. So you know our desires."

He talked like he was a part of the family. And he looked like Gramps, from Gramps's younger days. But something clicked for me. "You're not Gramps, are you?"

"Silence. We don't have time. Only *you* can save this house and this family from destruction. For over a hundred years, we've lived in this mansion as a legacy to our glorious family past. Now, your bumbling father and idiot uncle want to allow the family power to slip away, into the hands of unappreciative outsiders who care nothing about the toil that went into building the house. You can prevent such a calamity."

If not for my continued fear, I would have laughed a little at how weird he sounded, like a gent out of a nineteenth-century novel. "No, I can't. They won't listen to a crazed teenager who claims to see spirits."

"You'll have to figure out how to change their minds. I've dropped them some hints from time to time. Otherwise, I'll hurt other people, like I did your uncle."

So the spirit confirmed he'd caused Harold's illness. He scared me more, but he also made me angry. "Who are you? How does hurting other people get you what you want?"

He glowed more red than I'd ever seen him. "You can't fool me. You want to live. And you'll do my bidding. Or perhaps I should go after the ugly cur of yours? Relieving itself all over the grounds. Or perhaps another family member?"

I glared at him. And translating his old language took me a few seconds to know what he meant by cur. *Do not threaten my dog.*

"Ah, you're not so bold now, are you?" he mocked.

I struggled to breathe and fell to my knees. *He* was attacking, strangling me. I gasped, choking, and collapsed when he released me.

"Now are you ready to believe? I can do the same to you and everyone else here. From this point forward, I'll attack one person at a time for each occasion you disobey me. Your father might need to feel what his brother is going through, don't you think?"

I coughed, trying to get my voice back. "I—I don't know what I can do for you. I don't know why you've chosen me." The ghost could not have made a worse choice, in deciding to rely on me for whatever he wanted. Me. The wussy gay boy of the family.

"Ah, yes," he snarled in disgust. "Stop your abomination. You're a man, but you cower like a girl. Embrace the power of your manhood. It's not a power to squander with another man. But if you continue down this repulsive path, I can use your inclinations against you. And I'll always know. The disgusting boy who treats you like a woman fled from you because of me."

"He never saw you."

"Do you think your mother 'happened' to see the light on in the carriage house?" He lifted a ghost's eyebrow as if amazed at his own genius. "That scares you too, doesn't it? Others finding out."

Mom already knew. But what about Dad?

"Now, will you listen? Or should I alert the entire family to your vile behavior? I'm quite sure your attractions would interest your father." He smiled in triumph.

My brash attitude evaporated, replaced by fear. He called my bluff and won for the moment because I couldn't deal with being outed to my family. Not yet.

"Listen with great care." His voice sounded smug. "Save this house. Save it for a Bachmann resident. A Bachmann must reside here. And the jewels must remain in the family's possession."

"What jewels?"

"The jewels that exemplify everything your Bachmann ancestors struggled to build for this family, and this home is their American legacy. Find the jewels. They must stay in the family. I'll give you further instructions when necessary. You needn't worry about my leaving you alone." He laughed again.

He wanted me to find the jewels. Which meant *he* didn't know where they were. Did he lock the attic because he thought they were up there? And if they were, why couldn't he take them?

"Do we have an agreement?" he asked.

"Yes," I lied. At least, I hoped I lied about working with him, more than anything to keep him from hurting anybody else.

"Good. Now go to the funeral, where our work begins."

Our work? What was he planning? Jenn thought we were safe as long as we were away from the house, but I had wondered. He sounded like he could go anywhere. Was the funeral safe, or not?

"You're never safe from me." He read my mind again, but parts of my thoughts, not all of them. Maybe I could learn to shield more from him. "Now, go. And don't ever forget I'm the one in control." He drifted away, as if evaporating from the room, but not before another show of strength. A force grabbed my balls and squeezed hard. I yelped and again collapsed onto the ground. The pain subsided with his fading laughter. How messed up was the situation? A ball-grabbing, maniacal ghost? Maybe I cracked for real.

*

But I composed myself as best I could and went down to breakfast, where I busted Dad sneaking a few bites of his roll to Darth.

"Good morning," Dad said, trying to sound pleasant.

"Yeah, glad you decided to join us." Lincoln made a face at me. He looked kind of funny, dressed in a tie instead of his usual T-shirt. "I thought you might ditch the funeral."

"Bite me. Morning, everyone."

Dad shot me a look, but I ignored him and sat down and picked a donut. We ate in silence, but I signaled to Jenn we needed to talk.

"I'll get my jacket and then we better go," Dad announced. "You boys still ready to be pallbearers?"

"Yeah." Lincoln rolled his eyes at Dad behind his back.

I nodded, though I had forgotten about my duty. Dad asked us both before we left Colorado. I agreed, not because I wanted to carry the casket, but because I had no choice. How could I say no? The obligation made me feel even more vulnerable to the ghost. I wished I could say goodbye at the funeral, without needing to carry Gramps around, without a crazy, angry spirit after me. Fuck.

While Mom cleaned up the kitchen, Dad and Lincoln hurried upstairs and I led Jenn out the front door. "We gotta talk. Listen, I almost thought I shouldn't tell you this. The spirit—the angry one—has a plan for the funeral. He told me, before breakfast, when I went back to my room to get my lapel pin. So stay close to me, okay? And don't panic. He wants us to panic, so we can't."

She stared at me, eyes wide. "What's he going to do?"

I shrugged. "Don't know. He told me to keep the house in the Bachmann family. He wants to send a message at the funeral about his desire. But I don't think he'll do anything major to us. He kept mentioning the Bachmann legacy, so the family must mean a lot to him. He won't destroy us." But he could make life pretty painful, like with Harold, but saying so would freak Jenn out.

Before I could say anything else, Mom came outside. "You two okay?" Mom wrapped an arm around each of us.

"I guess." Jenn's eyes welled with tears. "As much as possible."

Mom shook her head as she gazed at me. "I haven't handled things well. You know I still love you." The words meant everything to me, especially how she said them in front of Jenn, because I doubt she knew I told Jenn. Mom saw me shoot a look at Jenn. "I couldn't imagine you kept this from her. I hope she did better than me."

I was thankful Jenn always knew what to say because my tongue got all tied up. "Of course, Jaret told me everything. And I'm glad he did."

Mom started to continue, but the front door slammed shut, and Dad and Lincoln hurried toward the Blazer.

"Let's go," Dad yelled, and we followed.

As we climbed into the Blazer, I spotted Darth's face staring at us out the bay window. For a dog, she looked pretty upset. Anxious. I always hated to leave her, but today was harder. For one, I wanted her with me at the funeral, and I knew she hated the house. I would never forgive myself if the evil being attacked without my being there to protect her.

Please, leave her alone.

The closer we got to the cemetery, the more my headache pounded, like a drum beat. I wished the Bachmanns could be like normal people and have a church service for a funeral, rather than going to the cemetery. Maybe I'd be safer in a church. Maybe we all would.

As we approached the main road leading to the cemetery, Dad spoke. "Will you boys help me this afternoon? We need to find those jewels. I talked to Harold this morning. He feels better but Tony wants to keep him in the hospital for observation. He thought the funeral might cause a relapse. Missing the funeral is eating at Harold, but his health is more important.

Anyway, Harold says we have to find those jewels, no matter what we decide to do with the house. Gramps hid them in the attic, so we need to bust the door down."

I sat in silence. How the hell did he decide to throw such a task out there at the moment? Besides, he came up with the worst idea ever. We had no idea what latched the door shut, or why. I could guess to myself the evil ghost was behind the deed.

"Sure, Dad," Lincoln said. "I'm all for busting down a few doors."

"You with us?" Dad glanced back at me.

"Um, yeah." But I wasn't.

"Thanks. We'll get this done yet." Dad sounded too cheerful. He grated on my nerves. Why couldn't he get over logic once in a while and maybe listen to another person for a change? Like me?

Jenn and I raised our eyebrows at each other and suppressed little smiles. At least neither of us faced the crisis alone.

When a welcome hush fell over the SUV again, I gazed out at the tranquil scene of rows of houses with well-manicured lawns passing by. The morning's dew evaporated, the slight chill in the air giving way to warmth. The world was peaceful, controlled, and organized.

Until the cemetery came into view. First, I saw the iron fence surrounding the cemetery, and then the taupe stone tower in the distance, kind of a weird structure with a big stained-glass cross in the middle, and an arched stained-glass window above the building. Mom called the style gothic, a grown-up architectural idea, I think. I'd say it's strange. This tall thing stood there in the middle of the cemetery like a lighthouse. Today the structure appeared less welcoming than ever, and I rubbed my forehead as my headache increased. I never did know why the stone structure existed or what it housed. As kids living in Fremont, Jenn and I used to pretend a nice monster lived there. We always said "hello" to him when we passed and made up stories about his life and why he lived in a cemetery tower.

As Dad pulled through the gates, we all glanced in the direction of the double plot Gramps had bought when Grandma died, though we couldn't yet see the location. I hated cemeteries. Lonely and forlorn, where people buried their memories along with their loved ones. And then I noticed the air, whether a trick of my mind, a reality of the trees shading everything, or the work of the ghost, was cooler inside the cemetery gates. I didn't see any people, anywhere. Though the family restricted Bachmann funerals to the pastor and immediate family members, I figured a few visitors might be around, checking the graves of their own families. Everything seemed quiet. Too quiet. No birds, no squirrels in the big trees. Nothing.

I looked out the front window and saw a cross about five feet high at the funeral location, near a church banner, and next to the cross, a hole in the ground with a pile of dirt nearby. Aunt Alice, Tony, and Jill sat on metal folding chairs around the pit. Then I saw the jet-black hearse and almost cried because I knew Gramps's body lay inside.

Dad pulled the Blazer behind Alice's car and slammed it into park. I peered at the tower in the distance, still hovering above us and then looked at the grave, where I spotted Pastor Schmidt behind a small lectern, thumbing through his notes. He looked pretty much the same as when I was a kid. Pastor Schmidt was a big guy, and he could shut someone up with a look, which made him an effective preacher. He wore his white robe, and peeking out at the top was his white clerical collar and black shirt, again the spitting image from my memory. His shiny wingtips reflected the light like he polished them before leaving the house.

We filed out of the Blazer toward the gravesite, moving pretty slowly. Like our pace would change anything. Gramps was still dead, and we were still at his funeral. The funeral director requested we go to the hearse and get the casket, which reminded me I wanted to run as far away as I could, but I'd agreed to the task, and for Gramps, I'd do my duty.

We lined up in pairs near the back of the hearse and the funeral director motioned for us to help him pull the casket out a bit so we could get leverage. I hated being here, every minute of it. Nobody said anything as we marched across the grass, the weight of the coffin not as difficult as knowing Gramps lay inside.

At the grave, we placed the casket on metal rollers set on a frame above the hole. The pulleys and ropes to lower Gramps seemed out of place, too contemporary and sterile for a setting where we'd be saying our final goodbyes. Our task completed, I turned toward Jenn and the family with relief, but my relaxation was short-lived, because the air seemed unsettled around us. A supernatural force, though I wasn't sure what. I took a seat in the second row next to Jenn.

Pastor Schmidt watched as we settled in. I glanced around, monitoring the tower glaring down at me, though I tried to think about the invented monster Jenn and I befriended as kids.

*

It was a tower. An old, stone tower. Nothing to worry about, I told myself over and over. And my mantra worked for a few moments until a vision in the upper window appeared. *Oh, no.* I saw the source of the instability I'd felt in the air since we got here. The ghost watched over us. The spirit could not even allow us a peaceful goodbye to Gramps, who had honored the family's legacy more than the evil ghost, who chatted about Bachmann heritage all the time.

"I came *because* of the legacy," his voice said in my head.

I looked around. No one else seemed to have seen or heard him. But a piercing pain in my skull served as a warning he was going to act, in a bad way, and I possessed no way to stop him, no way to know what was going to happen or to prevent his intentions.

Pastor Schmidt's deep voice broke the silence and startled me back to the family as he began the funeral service, but I had a hard time paying attention because I knew we were in trouble. I reached over and clutched Jenn's hand, which prompted her to look up and see the ghost in the tower too.

We both clutched hands tighter at what happened next, Jenn adding a startled yelp.

The ghost floated out the tower window toward us. Not menacing or fast, but at a slow descent. He drifted to the top of the trees and circled the funeral. Jenn and I alone saw him there, until Jenn stared at me, pleading with her eyes for me to take charge. But I didn't have any clue what to do, so I sat there, waiting, frozen like an idiot.

Pastor Schmidt continued talking, a mantra in the background of loud thoughts racing through my skull.

Jenn squeezed my hand harder. What could I do? What was *he* waiting for? I wanted to think he was paying his respects but knew better. I felt stupid, sitting there without doing a thing, but felt captive to being a teenager surrounded by adults, captive to the monster floating above who controlled the scene.

We stood to sing Gramps's favorite hymn, and again I heard his voice in my head.

"Are you ready?" the spirit asked.

"Who is that?" Jenn asked me. Shit, she heard him too.

I tried to ignore him. And her. Maybe he'd go away, or at least wait until the service was over.

"My plan begins, whether or not you're ready. You failed to convince me you'll obey. So now I must get involved before this foolish family gets rid of the house and all the Bachmanns represent."

Jenn's nails dug into my hand.

"I expect you to agree." He smiled, mocking me. "Unless, of course, you want me to tell them about your disgusting habits."

I refused to answer.

"Very well. I'll tell everyone to follow my directives, which I'll have to issue through you. You must obey my commands and anyone who defies me will come to harm, as your uncle already knows." He then shaped himself into his transparent human form. He floated down from the tower as a vapor but assumed a shape before me. He wore a tailored black suit and tie, and for the first time with hands, feet, and a defined face. Most frightening, he wore his ominous smile, digging into my soul with its ridicule.

"What should we do?" Jenn whispered. She was holding my hands so tight my fingers were numb.

"I don't know." I shrugged. "Sit tight."

I stopped when Mom shot us a look to shut up.

The spirit descended a few more feet, stopped in a clearing above the trees, and sneered down at us. "I do this out of necessity," he said, his voice filling my head. "You must understand I love all of you, but no one comprehends the importance of the house, the jewels, and the legacy. Generations of Bachmanns have struggled to reach a pinnacle of existence your father and uncle threaten to destroy. I have a duty to stop them, and if I must sacrifice a few people, so be it." The ghost turned his attention to the rest of the family gathered at the grave. I glanced up to see what he might be doing when Jenn jabbed me in the side with her elbow and pointed at Gramps's casket.

Oh, my God. Fuck me. Gramps's solid form floated through the lid. Jenn saw him, too, and she was scared, her hand shaking inside mine. What frightened her gave me hope, because Gramps was spoiling for a fight, and his presence confirmed the evil spirit who attacked me did indeed differ from the loving ghost of my grandfather.

I leaned over and whispered to Jenn, "He's on our side."

Nobody else noticed what was happening. Pastor Schmidt droned on, and the rest of the family sat watching him. A ghost war broke out above their heads, and no one knew the truth, casting me back into a world of fantasy and of questioning my own sanity. Except I knew what was going on was all true, true with a terrifying reality. At least I felt better knowing for sure Gramps tried to protect us, and the evil ghost was a different person.

"Well, well, look who's here," the apparition mocked Gramps.

Could everyone hear? Or was the noise in my head alone? What about Jenn? Then I heard Gramps speak for the first time since we got to Fremont.

"You can't scare this family and win. Violence isn't the solution."

"And how would you know? Have you tried a good fight?"

"Release this family from your grasp." My grandfather spoke in his bold, reprimanding tone. "They're carrying this family forward quite well, without you. There's more than one way to honor our ancestors. Let them live in peace."

"Don't presume to tell me how to view what these cowards do. The plan existed long before even you were born. You can't reveal yourself now and dictate what happens. Go away." The evil spirit swept his hand through the air.

"Yes, I can't control what you do. But that's not the limits of my ability. I'll protect this family. Let me begin by reminding you I know the jewelry's location, unlike you."

Gramps turned to Jenn and me, his expression softening though the determination remained. "He can't find the jewels. Even if he could, the living can move them but not a ghost. Don't give in to his fear tactics. You have power over him."

The evil spirit raged, his irate voice echoing through my head. "Be careful what you ask of them. You may doom them all. You don't know anything about my power. I control forces you can't imagine. I've vanquished stronger opponents than you."

But Gramps ignored him and continued to talk to us. "The jewels are in the attic, as you suspected. Look for the trunk with the Bachmann family crest. Take the jewels. Once you control them, you command him." He smiled. "I must go, but I'll be watching over you."

Gramps's ghost disappeared.

"I'll destroy all of you if you listen to him," the spirit roared as he hovered above the funeral, his voice like a petulant child.

Jenn closed her eyes in fear, but Gramps emboldened me, and I stared him down.

He laughed. "Stare at me like an arrogant brat all you want. I *will* win this battle. You think the old fool can force me to release control of this family? Don't be absurd."

Without warning, a windstorm encircled us. The wind whipped and howled through the trees, which groaned from the strain, as everybody reacted to the weather and grabbed each other for comfort. Pastor Schmidt's notes whirled through the air like leaves caught in a storm, his hair whipped about, and a couple people screamed as everyone scrambled to their feet and ran.

The spirit glared at me as he motioned with his hand toward an enormous oak tree nearby. With his arms outstretched to command the wind, he yanked hard at the tree.

The huge oak pulled free of the ground and sailed toward us as if a giant tossed it with little effort. The log headed toward Aunt Alice, who halted and stared, frozen in terror, her eyes wide as saucers. Then another force rushed by my head, my hair flying out in all directions and blinding me. I brushed my hair out of my face to see Gramps's spirit fly between the tree and Aunt Alice. When the tree got to him, it snapped in half like a twig, Gramps's spirit acting as a buzz saw slicing through the wood, the bottom half falling at Alice's feet, the top half crashing down nearby.

"You idiot!" the angry spirit shouted in rage. The wind stopped as fast as it began, but he gathered the air again in his arms, lifted it high above his head, and sent a gale crashing onto the funeral below. Paper, flowers, and dirt flew through the air. The gust sucked the air out of my lungs for a few seconds, and when I regained my breath, I saw its worst damage: the force collapsed the lid of Gramps's coffin onto his dead body.

The ghost laughed with menace as he raced back to the tower, leaving the family standing in terror and confusion. We all stared at the horrid scene before us. The casket lay on its side, busted open with Gramps's limp body hanging half out, a macabre scene fitting of the ghost war above us.

And only Jenn and I could explain the scene.

Lincoln moved first, head down and stomping toward the cars without saying a word. Alice whimpered as she stared at the fallen tree-cum-assassin, still frozen in terror.

Pastor Schmidt took control of the situation, appearing alarmed but unsurprised, steady yet cautious. He grabbed a nearby tarp and covered the casket. "Go home," he instructed in his authoritative baritone voice. "You should leave here, and I'll handle the situation. There's nothing else to do. I'm so very sorry, but I think it best you leave and we'll take care of things. I'll be in touch."

Shocked, everyone obeyed without comment and plodded toward the cars and Lincoln. Perhaps they all felt the same relief as me to listen to instructions without the need to decipher or explain what happened.

I had no clue what to do, even if I felt for all the world as if I would need to act, and soon, because of my fucking ability to see ghosts and because I knew the jewelry's location. And Gramps had once again informed me I alone possessed the power to combat the demon.

Chapter Six

Magical Revelations

I raced inside the house the minute Dad parked the Blazer in the driveway upon our return home from the funeral-cum-nightmare. To no one's surprise, we rode home in the Bachmann tradition of total silence when faced with a crisis, even if I longed for Mom or Dad to speak, anything to indicate we could grasp the situation and survive. The quiet gave me too much time to think and come up with horrifying scenarios.

I shoved the front door open, greeted Darth with her wagging tail, and hurried for the stairs but Dad's voice halted me before I got more than three steps. "Don't go anywhere. We need to talk."

Maybe I was wrong. Maybe I didn't want him to take charge because my shoulders tensed while I thought about what may come next.

I turned around to see Jenn right behind me, stopped in her tracks too.

"Go into the living room, *now*."

Even Darth stopped halfway up the stairs and spun around at Dad's command. I followed Jenn and her into the living room, where I plopped onto the floor, leaned against a chair, and patted the ground next to me for Darth. Sitting here kept her off the furniture and gave me the comfort of her presence for whatever was about to transpire. Jenn sat in a chair next to me, and Mom and Lincoln filed in to take seats on opposite ends of the couch. Dad walked in with a frown but gave a nod toward our obedience, pulling out the piano bench for himself.

"I don't know what in the hell's going on," he spoke with calm but also conviction. "I don't know what in the hell to do. I wanted to bury my father in peace, to say goodbye in the respectable manner he deserved, but..." he trailed off and shook his head. "The last thing I need is for this family to fall apart. I mean us." He gestured around the room at each family member. "The five of us. We'd better pull together and damn quick. I've no idea what Alice and Harold or their kids will want. And we can't do anything about their decisions anyway. But everyone in this room had better come together."

Despite his tone and words, I heard a note of hesitance in Dad's voice, maybe even a glimpse of fear. Wow. Shit. I'd never seen Dad betray himself with those emotions.

"So what should we do?" Lincoln asked before the silence became too awkward.

Dad sighed and held up his hands. "No fucking clue." His hands slapped down to his lap. Something else new to me—Dad dropping the f-bomb.

"That's enough." Mom threw her hands in the air and stared at my father to shut him up. "It won't solve anything to sit there and cuss. Why don't you start by telling us what you *do* know. You've kept a secret from us. The rest of this family has. I know there is a story here. For too long, this family hid a secret. If you want us behind you, then you have to come clean too. I think we all know there's more going on than rumors and pretend fears about a ghost."

You go, Mom, I thought as I petted Darth with nervous energy.

Dad stood up and started to pace. "I've told you everything. You're not the only ones in the dark. Your Gramps argued with your Grandma about strange things happening while I was a kid. We all knew why. Their argument would come up at the dinner table or while we worked on the house. But they always left the room so we couldn't see or hear them fighting. I know Grandma thought a spirit haunted the house, and Gramps thought she allowed her imagination to run wild. Harold and Alice have said people around Fremont talk about a haunting here all the time, but I never heard any of the gossip, because I trusted Gramps. Now, I wonder. Or maybe your gramps is responsible for these weird things, going so far as to hide his power from my mom, your grandma." He sighed. "I admit the truth. Something is wrong. There *is* a haunting, even I've felt a spirit."

Without considering the consequences, I jumped in. "Gramps has nothing to do with the problem. Not how you think. Trust me. A ghost haunts this house and doesn't want you to sell the property or the jewels. And Gramps hid the gems from this ghost in the attic." With all the crap going on, everything we witnessed, I made a mistake in thinking I was safe with telling them the truth. My parents' expressions told me a different story. Fuck me.

"We know you mean well." Mom sounded calm, but her tightened posture indicated she was anything but. "But this isn't the time for us to talk about the things you think you see."

"You don't know anything about what I see," I retorted, trying not to get hysterical but, nevertheless, getting hysterical. "This evil spirit talks to me. He lets me see him, here, in this house. But we can fight him because Gramps wants to help. You have to believe me."

The room fell silent. I should have kept my mouth shut.

"I believe Jaret," Jenn said so softly I strained to hear her.

The awkward silence returned. Darth shot me a dirty glance because I bobbed my leg up and down when she wanted to use me as a pillow.

Mom and Dad gave each other an odd glance, a secret parent communication. Their looks seemed to calm Dad because he sat back down on a bench. "Let's take a break. We all need rest. Mom and I will talk about what to do. I don't need you three worried about this."

"You admitted it's true, and now we can't talk about the haunting?" I almost shouted my question.

Dad glared at me. "We're trying to protect you."

I almost shot back at them again but held my tongue. Seriously, it was a little late to keep from worrying us. A shitstorm blasted apart Gramps's casket as an oak tree tried to murder my aunt. Who wouldn't worry? I suppose they meant well, even if they made no sense. Of course, no doubt they thought one of their sons was crazy, and their daughter was going along with her brother for support or because he influenced her. Instead I got up to leave, followed by Lincoln and Jenn.

Before we got out of the room, though, Mom called us back. "Wait. Jenn, will you help me? I need to go to the store."

"Do I have to?"

"Yes, please." Mom was trying to be all nonchalant, but I knew she wanted to separate Jenn and me. Jenn looked at me and rolled her eyes but followed Mom out the door with slumped body language. When they left, Dad asked me to sit back down with him but let Lincoln leave. I bit back a groan.

"Don't get your sister worked up about what you think you see. I don't know what's going on, but I want to help you. The stress is hard to deal with. And the sadness. And whatever else is going on."

Hurt that neither Mom nor Dad believed me, I stayed quiet and fought against either crying or lashing out.

Blowing out a breath of frustration, Dad asked, "Do you understand?"

"Sure. Whatever." My self-control escaped as fast as his patience, but after waiting a few seconds for the backlash that never occurred, I left and went upstairs.

*

At first I headed for my room but decided to take a detour to Gramps's office and the phone. "Fucking ridiculous," I whispered to myself, again reminded about my lack of a cell phone. I wanted to hear Steve's voice, to replace the churning in my stomach with butterflies of anticipation.

I pushed the door to the study open, worried a ghost might be in there, but when Darth shoved past me into the room without pausing, I knew I could enter without worry. I followed her in and sank into the big leather chair near the fireplace and picked up the phone.

"Yo," Steve answered. Such a jock thing to say. He made me warm inside.

"It's me. Jaret."

"I figured, babe. I know your Gramps's number and doubted your mom called to chat. What's up?"

"Sorry I called your phone. Will your Dad find out? You said he monitors everything."

"Relax. It's cool. One call won't hurt. He checks my texts more than the calls." He laughed. "Keeps worrying I'll start sexting with a girl."

I laughed too. "Yeah, well, we don't want to put anything on the phone to let him know there will be no girls, but boys might be a different story. Anyway, do you think you can come over?"

"What's up? Is something wrong?"

"I don't want to talk on the phone. But the funeral was a disaster."

"I'm on my way. Where should we meet?"

"The back door," I said. "Only my dad and brother are here. We can sneak upstairs."

"Are we safe? I don't want you to have to deal with your folks again."

"Yeah, we're fine. Hurry."

"Give me ten," he said and hung up.

I placed the phone back in its old-school, huge cradle, feeling more relaxed with Steve on the way. Chilled enough to giggle a little at the ancient phone. And Steve believed me, at least, unlike my parents.

Realizing I might look a fright from the wind and chaos of the funeral, I pushed out of the chair, hurried down the hall, and checked myself out in the bathroom mirror, where I primped and gave up because the elements had frizzed my hair. Then it was down to the kitchen to wait.

I passed Dad and Lincoln, watching TV in the side parlor, doing their Bachmann thing of blocking out negative emotion and stress by flipping through channels as if experiencing another normal day.

What a whacked family, I decided. But I was the one who could talk to ghosts. And one of those ghosts had sent me on a mission to discover a hidden family treasure and do a marvelous but unexplained trick with them. No wonder Dad thought I was nuts. Lost in my mind, I jumped when a being moved out of the corner of my eye through the screen door window on the back porch.

Steve giggled at me.

My heart pounding a little from the scare, I smiled at him. "Come in," I whispered.

He stepped inside, tiptoeing I presumed for the sake of quiet. "I can't believe I get to enter the haunted house." Steve wiggled his eyebrows.

"Get your ass inside." I covered my mouth to stifle a giggle. "The haunted house isn't so funny when you meet the ghost."

Steve surveyed the room. "I do feel creepy in here. Knowing what you told me, I mean."

"Let's go." I motioned with my head for him to follow me.

Darth had planted herself in front of my father, who was eating potato chips and throwing her one at times, which left Steve and me alone, so we sneaked by and headed up the stairs.

I glanced behind me to make sure nothing, ghost or human, followed us before I locked my bedroom door. I turned around when Steve grabbed me by both arms and kissed me, his tongue jamming into my mouth as I pressed back against him. All the tension, fear, and anxiety flooded out of me when I felt his strong arms embrace me, his lips against mine, his tongue sliding across my teeth. In seconds, we ended up on the bed making out.

"I missed you." Steve blew in my ear. "I couldn't wait for this."

The wind blowing and rattling the window startled us, but we both laughed after we realized the source of the noise and our tension dissipated. "We better separate, in case someone wanders up here," I recommended, though I felt Steve's hard chest under my hand with renewed lust. We sat near each other on the bed, despite moving a little apart.

"So, your mom didn't kill you after I left?"

I laughed. "No. No death sentence, yet." I patted his thigh. "She was all right, I guess. Not happy. But she wanted me to keep what happened from Dad. And she was a lot better today, even after she found out I'd already told Jenn. It's the best I can expect. Mom'll be okay. I think she'll be better once we tell Dad. I think he'll be pretty cool with the truth."

"Then why not tell him now?"

I sighed. "It's complicated. I promised Mom I wouldn't. She thinks telling him would be too stressful, even though I think it'd be better to get my sexuality out there." My stomach ached from thinking about my talk with Mom earlier in the morning. I laughed a little. "I suppose the way she found out didn't help anything."

Steve laughed too. "I can't imagine my mom finding out. She'd freak. I don't know if I'll ever tell my dad or brother."

"Can you at least tell any of your friends? It's not good to have to keep stress inside."

"Hey, don't worry about me. You've got enough on your mind. Worry more about being so hot." He leaned over and pecked me on the cheek. "I never intended to tell anyone in Fremont. When we go far away for college, I'll tell more people. Less than a year away. Besides, I have *you* now."

I bobbed my leg up and down. "We'll keep in touch, won't we? I mean, sure, we want to go to the same college. And that's half a year away. But I mean, before then?"

"I already figured out what we can do." Steve held my hand. "Of course, we'll talk on the phone. We can use those calling cards to hide the numbers, because my Dad checks my cell phone records. He's a snoop."

I worried about how much he feared telling his parents. What would they do to him? Could he ever accept being out enough for our relationship to flourish? But these thoughts seemed too grown up, too distant to consume me.

"Hey, don't worry." He gripped my hand tighter. "I'll be outta here soon enough. So what else is going on?"

I fidgeted. Did I want to tell him more and get him all worried? Or further tempt him into thinking I was a loon bird? "Um—"

"You don't have to talk about what's up if you don't want."

I sighed and snuggled back against him. "I *do* want to talk."

"Okay, babe. Let it out."

"The whole scene was bizarre." I took a deep breath. "So we went to the cemetery for the service. We don't do the church thing. And the bad spirit showed up."

Steve stared at me with wide eyes. "No way. The thing from when your mom found us?"

"Yep, the one and only." I told him about my confrontation with the spirit before the service, the chill in the air at the cemetery combined with the eerie quiet, and how the ghost was hiding in the tower. "He warned me this morning to obey him. Even threatened to out me to everyone if I failed. Then he told me he planned to come to Gramps's funeral. And he did, but Gramps fought him off."

"Your grandpa showed up? As a ghost?"

"Yeah." I nodded, half convinced I sounded nuts, half imploring Steve to believe the bizarre tale. "I know the story sounds fucking insane. But Jenn saw him too. And experiencing the moment was so awful and so scary." In my mind, the trees shook with violence, Gramps rose out of the coffin, and the cosmic collision between two forces took place again.

"Go ahead. It's okay." Steve rubbed my back.

"They kinda fought. Gramps and the spirit, I mean. I don't know how else to describe the battle. At the end, the spirit sort of heaved the wind at Gramps's casket and blew it apart. The scene was so horrible. Then everybody left, because Pastor Schmidt told us to go. And we came back here, and my dad had a hissy fit. So I told him there's a bad spirit here, and Gramps told me about the jewels."

"Oh, no. How'd he take the news?"

"Bad." But I laughed a little at the absurd memory. "My parents think I'm crazy again. And that's about it."

Steve ran his fingers through my hair for a moment before speaking. "What a terrible story. But I believe you. I don't know what else to say." He shrugged. "I want to help because I don't think you should try to fight this on your own. But I have no idea what to do."

"Stay with me. Support me. Promise not to disappear when things get weird."

"Oh, you mean things aren't already weird?" he teased.

"Good point." We laughed, though I clutched him tight to me.

"I'm not going to run away. Never. Hey, how did Pastor Schmidt react?"

"I'm not sure. He took charge after the spirit exploded the casket and made everyone go home, like I said. He seemed okay, in a weird way. I thought a few times he felt a spirit around, like he knew about the bad ghost hung in the air. But he didn't say anything. I think Jenn and I saw the actual ghost war but no one else. Pastor Schmidt did not act like anyone else. Like, he accepted the wild shit was happening. He wasn't afraid, but he didn't fight the forces either."

"I wondered because of all the things he used to say during confirmation. I thought maybe he performed an exorcism in the cemetery."

"Maybe he should have." I nuzzled Steve's neck. He believed me. I never thought anyone but Jenn would believe me.

The doorknob rattled, causing us to leap away from one another and for my heart to pound in my chest.

"Shit," I muttered. Steve pushed himself off the bed and put more distance between us. Then Darth whined and scratched the door. We burst out laughing.

"Fucking dog!" I yelled through my laughter.

"Fucking scared the shit out of me." Steve flopped onto the floor.

"Sorry. She does that all the time because she hates being locked out." I opened the door and she bounded in, proud of herself.

He raised his head to look at me. "You gotta chill. I'm not mad. No apology necessary." He jumped off the floor and hugged me. "I won't turn on you all of a sudden." He kissed me and I got turned on again; when he pulled me harder against him and I felt his crotch against mine, I wanted to explode.

*

Too late to flee, I recognized the telltale pounding in my head. An invisible force hurled us apart, slamming me against the door and throwing Steve onto the bed. We both gasped for air, his eyes wide with fear, mine searching the room to find the ghost. The room's temperature dropped, and I stumbled to get up and go to Steve. He regained control of himself and moved toward me, only to fly through the air in the opposite direction and smash into a standing mirror. The mirror remained upright, but I saw blood on Steve's cheek when he stood up. We froze in place, afraid to move, unable to speak, and waited.

The spirit materialized before us, the spitting image of my younger grandpa but transparent, not solid. "What vile behavior is this?" the ghost roared. "I allowed this abomination in the guest house, but not under this roof. Not so long as I control this house. You will obey," he pointed at me, "which from this point forward includes admonitions against such things as this." He waved his hand in the air, as if the motion explained what he meant.

While he always appeared pissed off, I'd never seen him so enraged, without even the hint of his typical sinister smile. Nor was the air around him ever so cold. "I thought we spoke about this proclivity," the spirit continued. "I thought we came to an understanding about who you obeyed. But you did nothing at the funeral to protect my interests." He flew around the room, agitated, then floated in front of me. I saw Steve through the spirit, staring at me with worry. "I suppose you think your grandfather's little display buttressed your cause. It didn't." Then he whirled around and glared at Steve.

"Such a pretty little boy," he said, sarcastic. "Did you want to protect your prized possession?" He floated behind Steve, who turned around and backed closer to me.

"Leave here and never return," the spirit said to Steve, who glanced at me for an answer, and I shook my head. *Please don't go.* Steve inched closer to me and stood his ground.

"Aren't you afraid I'll hurt your little boy thing?" The spirit glared at Steve as he pointed at me.

"He won't listen to your threats," I said, trying to distract the spirit from Steve. "Besides, you need me." Despite my defiant tone, my knees shook as I confronted him and my voice quivered.

The spirit failed to respond but instead glared to the side and behind Steve and me. I glanced back to see Gramps standing in the corner, arms crossed over his chest, with a stern look on his face.

"I refuse to engage your nonsense." The spirit talked to Gramps. "You may control them for now, but I won't relinquish my power to you. Your pitiful knowledge about what I can and cannot do will not stop me. You'll learn the wisdom of what I demand."

Gramps waited, without saying anything.

And then the spirit vanished. My headache, too, was gone. I grabbed Steve's hand, and he looked around in awe and trembled a little when he turned to see Gramps, but I had no time to explain anything because Gramps motioned for us to follow him as he floated through the door, so I pulled Steve along, opened the door, and we left the room.

"Come on, Darth," I called and patted my thigh. "It's safe."

*

Gramps led us to the attic door, which he opened with ease. A stream of light cut through the dust stirring beneath our feet as Gramps floated up the stairs. The attic appeared as if no one had been up there in years. Our footprints were visible in the dust as we walked and cobwebs hung from the ceiling. Which was weird, because when I was last up here, the attic looked neat and organized, making it clear Gramps even cleaned up here. But the scene came right out of a horror movie.

Darth scampered around to inspect the corners while Steve stayed close to me, holding my hand in a vise.

Gramps smiled at us, a warm face to express his sorrow at our being in the middle of the chaos but an acknowledgment we were trapped.

"What's going on?" Steve whispered.

"Gramps wants to help. We can trust him."

"I'm not sure what to do."

"Wait. Watch."

I found Gramps's total silence odd. He'd spoken at the funeral, so I thought perhaps we ended the confusing and frustrating attempts at silent communication, but here they were again.

Gramps stood about three feet away and waited. When Steve glanced over, Gramps smiled, and whatever dread I'd felt around the other spirit seemed to flow out of me. "See, even Darth is cool with him." I pointed to where she sat at my feet and patted her head.

"Okay. I'll follow your lead." Steve squeezed my hand.

Gramps shushed us by putting his finger to his lips. I so wished he could at least explain the reason for needing total quiet. Who could have heard, and why did he worry about making noise? The other spirit came and went as he pleased, hearing everything that took place in the house, anyway.

Gramps walked to a pile of trunks lining one side of the attic, stacked to the roof, and pointed to one on the bottom, indicating for us to get it.

When I got to them, I wondered how to reach the tallest one and already knew they were heavy. Thank God for Steve, who reached up and grabbed the high one, not even straining as he set the trunk on the ground. "I think I'm supposed to handle this part." Steve winked at me and patted my cheek. "I don't want you hurting yourself." Steve grabbed another trunk and brought it down.

Darth sniffed each trunk as it hit the floor, like our personal TSA inspector. As Steve got to the last one, I was pretty sure what Gramps was about to reveal to us inside. But as he uncovered the bottom trunk, my headache intensified and my fear increased—the evil spirit had to be around.

The last trunk, about five-feet long and three-feet deep, appeared older, with worn leather and a more meticulous craftsmanship. Despite its age, the iron hinges and wood were firm and looked almost new, well cared for. The Bachmann family crest was painted in detail on its lid.

As Steve and I gazed in awe at the old trunk, Gramps floated to the opposite side. I knew—sensed—before he indicated anything, or we opened the lid, that the jewels were inside, and a sudden tingle ran down my spine, as if the gems called to me. I wondered if these jewels could assist us in combatting the ghost but kept my thoughts to myself, because that sounded crazy even for all the crazy going on around us.

Gramps nodded to me and pointed to the trunk, so I reached for the handle with my free hand, when wild laughter filled the attic, and Steve was ripped from my grasp, and sent flying through the air toward the rows of boxes on the other side of the room. When he crashed into them, Darth barked and growled nonstop. A headache blinded me to the point I could make out nothing but vague shapes in front of me. I couldn't get to Steve. I couldn't do anything. All I knew was he was lying among the scattered boxes, injured. What the fuck? The headache subsided, and I looked at Gramps, who stood grimacing.

He spoke to the spirit in a defeated tone. "I'll go. Don't hurt them."

I heard his voice above Darth's persistent howling when as fast as Gramps appeared in the bedroom, he turned to wink at me then vanished.

*

"Fool," the spirit said and waved his hand in the air, as if his swipe eliminated Gramps. "You can't trust your grandfather." He rolled his eyes. "He's a coward. He thought he could hide his plans from me. I knew he hid them here. Did you think I didn't watch his every move while he lived? Did you think I couldn't hear him tell you where to find them at his funeral?"

Again, I wondered if I had gone fucking nuts, chatting with an evil ghost and thinking I could control anything. Still, despite his bold words, something bugged him about the jewels. He feared them.

"Open it, if you're so excited about them," the spirit said as he motioned at the trunk. "Take a look at the legacy

I want you to uphold. Power and glory, right at your fingertips."

I shook again with fear and shot a look toward Steve, who lay motionless.

"Ignore your sin! Open the chest."

I warred between running to Steve and obeying the demon, fearing what he would do next if I defied him. My hands trembling, I fumbled with the latch and got it loose so I could lift the lid. Inside, I found a series of organized containers and opened a few, only to find them empty. Tins held odd trinkets like a small iron box or old coins, and a box contained clothes. However, a gold-trimmed jewelry box at the bottom of everything was heavier and more ornately decorated than anything else, so I pulled the chest out.

"Open it," the spirit said, sounding almost reverent.

I did, and caught my breath at the sight of the Bachmann jewels. They sparkled, even in the dim light, all different colors, many in settings even I knew were of excellent craftsmanship, without my having any idea about jewelry or its value. Again my spine tingled in excitement, an electric current of anticipation. What the hell?

"You see? I promised you a special surprise."

I picked one of the jewels up. Okay, so they were pretty. So what? What did these have to do with the spirit's wishes? But then my fingers buzzed with energy.

"You're such a simpleton," the spirit spat in frustration. "Male Bachmanns haven't chosen their wives well so have diluted the stock. We'll correct the problem with *your* wife. These aren't pretty things to admire. The strength of future generations rests in what they represent, and in this house."

The spirit made no sense. Jewels? Wives? Me with a wife, seriously? What did future generations have to do with a bunch of gemstones? I glanced again at Steve and my heart sank.

"Dammit!" he shrieked and Darth whimpered. "Stop looking at him! How did the Bachmanns come to this? How has the future of our proud legacy, a legacy built over centuries, fallen into the lap of an imbecile and sodomite? We're a noble kin, banished from the Old World but rising from the ashes in America. Here, in this house, is the foundation for all you possess, all you represent. But you trod upon our history." Scared for Steve and bewildered, I still stifled a little grin because of his old school language. Trod? Who says that? He paused and glared. "You're not amusing. And you must erase the abominable feelings in your mind. You can't lie with other men and achieve the heights you must. In your hands lies the future. You can see me, so you know I watch over this family. Your brother can't lead us because he fails to see. It's time for you to be a man, not a child. And not a sick demented sodomite."

Sodomite—another ancient term. But no smile came because I was terrified, for Steve, for me, about the whole fucking situation.

"Stop your foul language and the ridiculous fear. So childish. Soon, I'll show you how to grow strong, using the blood coursing through your veins."

I patted Darth on the head, as she leaned into me and growled at the spirit. Glancing at Steve, I prayed, *Please get up. Please.*

"Stop looking at him!" the spirit roared. "You are an abomination!" As he grew angrier, he faded but soon regained control and solidified. "Very well. I see what I must do. In order for you to fulfill our destiny, I shall remove the source of your abomination."

I gasped in terror.

"Relax the theatrics. Go to him." The spirit waved his hands in Steve's direction. "Wake him. He's alive and unharmed. Well, for the most part. I'm not so stupid as to cause a death in this house. But you haven't seen the last of me." He chuckled and vanished.

*

I rushed over and knelt next to Steve. The blood on his cheek from the bedroom episode had dried—the wound was a scratch, not serious. And I didn't see any other visible injuries, but what the hell did I know? He could be internally bleeding or have a broken bone I couldn't see. Feeling helpless and bewildered, I started to get up when he stirred.

"Steve?" I touched his shoulder.

He grimaced, and then a slight smile turned at the corners of his mouth. "I guess you weren't lying about ghosts, huh?"

"How can you joke right now? Are you okay?"

"Fine. Well, sore. But fine. I'm a wide receiver, remember? I fly through the air and get hit all the time, and by much bigger things than boxes." Steve rubbed his head and sat up. "Does this shit happen in here all the time?"

He prompted me to laugh. "No." I shook my head. "Never this bad. And I still don't know what the hell he wants me to do. I'm thinking he might be kind of crazy."

"Might be?" Steve laughed and grabbed his side from pain.

"See, it's not a time for laughing. Anyway, he doesn't like us being together. He's got a serious issue with the gay thing."

"Are you worried because a ghost hates us?" Steve grabbed my hand and sat up with care, looking more himself. "We'll handle him."

"So you're okay?"

"Yeah. It hurts like a motherfucker to fly through the air and crash into shit, but I'll live. You seem more scared than me."

"I am. He trapped me. I couldn't get to you."

Darth calmed down, too, and sat between Steve and me on the floor. Steve patted her on the head before reaching over to grip me by the wrist.

"Where do we go from here?" he asked. "I can help. We have to figure out what your grandpa's trying to tell you. Maybe we need someone else involved."

I rolled my eyes. "Like I haven't tried to find that my entire life. No one believes this shit." I waved my hand in the air, as if the magical weirdness hovered before us. "Unless the spirit pops them in the head, too, they won't believe. Even after what my family saw at the funeral, they're trying to ignore the haunting."

"Settle down." Steve cupped my face with his hands and stared at me. "You sure get worked up fast. So what if everyone rejected the ghosts before? I didn't. And you can't stop trying. You gotta let me help. Jenn too. Let's find people who'll listen so you're not alone." He pulled me close to him, squeezing Darth between us, so she jumped up and lay on my other side.

I put my head on his chest. "Okay. I'll try. I'll let you help. But I still don't know what to do."

"What about the jewels? The spirit wants them bad. And your grandpa showed you them. Whatever the hell they mean, they're important. So take them."

I crawled over to the jewelry box and opened it again, marveling at their beauty. Steve followed and looked over my shoulder. "Shit. They look expensive. And old."

"My family brought them from Europe. I didn't know about them until Dad and Uncle Harold explained about the family gems the other day. They want to sell them. Gramps hid them for years, and I don't think anyone ever wore them. They always sat in this box, I guess." I shook the box a little to mix the jewels up and see more of them. They sparkled with different colors, sizes, and gems right out of a fairy tale.

"Pretty cool."

"Yeah. They are." I reached into the box and ran my fingers over the surface of the jewels on top. The second I touched one my fingertips tingled, like when the blood starts to circulate in your leg after it falls asleep. I picked up a handful but dropped most of them when my whole hand buzzed. But I held tight to a ruby necklace that attracted me. The longer I held the gem, the more the prickling subsided into a feeling of power.

"What is going on?" Steve placed his hand on my shoulder.

"They—there's a weird force around them. They have magic." I closed my eyes and concentrated. Supernatural energy emanated from these gems, and I knew I could control unknown forces. I don't know how I knew, I just did. These jewels were important to the family because of magic or other worldly control, not because of a monetary value.

To test my theory, I focused on the gems and channeled their energy into my mind. I scanned the attic and the fallen boxes, including their spilled contents where Steve crashed into them, then visualized repacking the stuff and restacking the boxes in neat rows. As the thought popped into my mind, the idea became a reality, with unseen forces picking up the mess, repacking the boxes, and restoring order. The chests beside us alone remained scattered.

"What the fuck?" Steve whispered.

I dropped the necklace back into the jewelry box, exhilarated and scared. Could anyone do magic with the jewels? Or was the power about me?

"You okay?" Steve asked.

"I've never done magic." I stared at the jewels with awe.

"Me, neither." Steve giggled. "So weird. And if it's new to you, it's new to me." He pulled me close. "Kinda freaky, but at least you're a hot warlock. Do you think you're a witch?"

"No." I scrunched my brow, still confused by the whole episode. "Of course not. Witches don't exist. Do they?"

"Kidding. But this *is* pretty fucked."

"Yeah, fucked."

Steve ran his fingers along my cheek, back and forth. "A few days ago, I never dreamed I'd have a hot guy in my arms. Let alone a hot magician." Then he grinned. "I mean, I grew up with a serious crush on Harry Potter but never thought he'd sit in my lap."

I grinned. "Quit making me laugh! This is serious shit. And I'm not a wizard either." To shut him up, I kissed him and wanted him all over again, until I heard a bad sound. I jerked away, alarmed. "Shh!"

*

Footsteps echoed up the attic stairs. I held my breath until Mom turned the corner on the landing. I slumped in relief.

"Jaret?"

"Who else?"

Steve stepped out of her view.

"Oh, it's you." She clutched her necklace and let out a nervous laugh. "Thank God. With the sun behind you, I had no idea who you were. How did you get this door open?"

Darth greeted her with a lick of her hand. Mom returned the welcome by scratching her behind the ears. "Are you protecting Jaret? Good girl. So what's going on?"

Before I could answer, she saw Steve. "You're in the house together?" She looked first at him, then at me. I swallowed hard, waiting for her to start yelling or scolding us. She took a deep breath instead and smiled. "I don't think I know your name," she held out her hand to Steve.

"Steve." He stepped toward her and shook her hand.

"I'm Beth. It's nice to meet you." An awkward silence ensued before she continued. "I'm sorry for throwing you out the other night. I handled things poorly."

"It wasn't the best of circumstances."

I stared at Steve. He was smooth, for sure. I think his being hot helped with Mom too.

"I'm not trying to keep you from seeing each other. I don't know how to feel about the two of you, but I'm not trying to control you. Could you at least be more careful in the house?"

"Sorry," I said. "I was scared to come up here alone. We'll be careful." Lame. If Steve was a girl, nobody would have said anything about us, but I also didn't want to create another argument with her.

"I hate to do this, Jaret, but we need to talk. Can you come to the living room for a couple minutes?" She spun around but paused and turned back to us. "It was nice to meet you."

"Likewise." Steve smiled.

She continued down the stairs.

"Your mom seems pretty nice when she doesn't catch us with my tongue down your throat." Steve said.

"Stop! And, yeah, she's pretty cool under normal circumstances. You know, nonsexual situations."

He laughed again. "It's a little weird she knows. Not sure how I feel about other people knowing."

"Won't people know?" I worried about his comment.

He shrugged. "Maybe. Anyway, I'd better leave so you can go talk. Wish I could stay for moral support."

"I'm sure we're heading for another family freak-out. You don't want to see one of those."

"If I could help, I would." He pulled me toward the stairs.

"Can I call you later?" I asked.

"You'd better." He stopped, smiled, and squeezed my hand. "Let me know what happens." He kissed me on the forehead and started down the stairs.

Before we got to the hallway, though, I yanked him back to me.

"Hold up. I need to put the jewelry back."

Only then did I think Mom either missed them in the middle of the room or ignored them. Maybe Steve distracted her. I ran up and locked the box, then put it back in the trunk and latched the chest shut. But beforehand I grabbed the ruby necklace and a ring, I think a sapphire, and put them in my pocket. I hurried down the stairs, making sure Darth followed, the force of the gems in my jeans warming my thigh and sending another tingle through my body.

Steve and I made it to the kitchen and onto the back porch without anyone noticing. "Okay, hot stuff. Call me." He slapped my ass, kissed me, and darted away.

I took a deep breath and turned around toward the back door, getting ready for the family conference, and rubbed my pants to feel the jewels in there, calling to me. I wondered what the Bachmann meeting would entail, glad to know at least Mom wouldn't bring up my sexuality.

"Why would she? You're vile. She's ashamed of you."

I jumped a foot in the air at the spirit's voice, cried out, and almost tumbled down the back steps. I noticed the warning headache too late, so numb from the pain happening around Gramps's all the time I had ignored the warning, allowing him to sneak up on me.

"Don't speak," he said. "Lest they hear you talking to yourself."

I realized his voice sounded in my head, not aloud. My stomach hurt.

"Did your mother's visit to the attic surprise you?"

"You seem to know whatever I think," I thought back. "Answer for yourself."

"Your haughty attitude doesn't become you." He paced in front of the door, a transparent apparition but fading in and out, seeming to struggle to maintain his form. Why? "Do you have any guesses as to how your mother knew to find you up there?"

It dawned on me. We had closed the attic door so no one could find us. She either tried the door herself, doubtful given how everyone believed the attic locked shut, or a ghost opened the door for her.

"Ah, there's a bright boy. I'm proud of you," he mocked. "Your mother was in the hallway. I thought perhaps she might need to see her son and his abomination hiding in the attic. I gave her another fright along the way, since we have her believing." He paused and circled, looking me up and down. "She disappointed me."

"Why?"

"I needed anger. I wanted her to remove the sinner from the house and forbid the two of you from meeting. She did once, after all."

"She loves me."

"How quaint." He rolled his eyes. "And how useless. I assume you deduced how I locked the attic door against the family? That's *my* decision, whether anyone goes up there. Not your grandfather's."

"Yeah, I figured. Except he got us up there."

"I've resealed the door." He spat the words at me. "You'll never play with the jewels again."

"Unless Gramps takes me up there."

"Don't be so sure he or those jewels can save you."

I glared at him, finding resolve to challenge him. "You're afraid of the jewels."

He smiled and laughed. "Of course not. The jewels represent a grand legacy and must remain in this family. I'll do whatever I must to ensure the tradition."

My hand shaking, I reached into my pocket and felt the rubies. Their energy grew in his presence, pulsating through my body, though nothing came to me about how to use them or to make them perform my bidding. Still, a force lurked beneath the surface, pointing me to a future where I controlled them.

"Did you take them?" His eyes flashed with rage.

As I pulled out the ruby necklace, his eyes grew wide, and he recoiled a few steps.

"Very well." He fought to regain composure. "I hope you noticed their beauty."

"Powerful too." As I spoke, an energy attempted to pull the necklace out of my hand so I clutched tighter against its strength. The necklace started to slip away from my grasp, but I focused my eyes on the rubies and commanded the necklace to stay. The jewelry stopped moving.

"Bravo. You can play with necklaces. I'm so impressed." The countering force stopped tugging at the necklace.

I heard a loud crack behind me and spun around to see a tree branch hurling through the air toward my head. An instinct shot through my body and caused me to toss the ruby necklace toward the projectile. The branch halted in midair in front of the gems, which also floated in the air. I commanded the wood to fall to the ground with my thoughts. The object obeyed and the necklace returned to my hand. Whoa. Fuck me. They did give me a magical witchy fucking power.

"Idiot!" The spirit came around to the yard and hovered before me, more furious than ever before. But the angrier he became, the less solid his form. I could barely see him. Over time nothing but a glowing head hovered before me though his voice came through loud and clear. "You and your stupid, dead grandfather don't have as much control as you think. You can't fight me so easily. For decades, I've maintained power over this family. Decades. Nothing will stop me. Don't be foolish." He jeered. "You're a novice and can't comprehend what you have. I, after all, control people's thoughts. So you've forced my hand. I warned you. You chose your fate." His anger dissipated and he materialized more solid before me. "Best not to keep your parents waiting." His maniacal laughter filled the air as he faded away.

I stared after him, trembling with both fear of him and excitement about the gems. I controlled a power over him through the jewels, I was a witch or some crazy shit. But I was also still a teenager, so went back inside to head toward the meeting. I grabbed a Pepsi out of the fridge, stalling to calm down and think for a minute. The ghost wanted the jewels, and he wanted me, but why? Why didn't Gramps explain more to me? I wasn't any closer to a concrete answer.

"Jaret, are you coming?" Mom called from the living room.

"Be right there. I'm getting a pop." I looked at Darth. "See, even you don't want to go in there." I cracked the can open and took a sip. "Should we run away?"

She perked up her ears and tilted her head at me.

"We could escape from the crazy people and go eat Snausages forever."

Darth wagged her tail as I gave her a few pats.

We headed for the living room, where Mom and Dad sat in silence.

"Okay," I tried to sound unconcerned. "What's up?"

"Sit down. We need to talk," Dad instructed.

Classic Dad, quick and to the point. My heart sank. They had the look again: I was insane.

Chapter Seven

Insanity Runs in the Family

The three of us sat without speaking in the living room for a minute. I had followed Dad's command to sit, but I sure didn't want to start talking, because anything I said they'd take as more evidence I was crazy. Instead, I called Darth over and pulled her onto my lap. My heart beat faster with every silent second ticking by in slow motion as I petted Darth and kissed the top of her head, all while shaking my leg up and down and staring at the fireplace instead of looking at my parents. They sat opposite on an antique couch, not moving. I even wondered if they'd stopped breathing.

Mom and Dad glanced at each other, so I shifted in my seat and pulled Darth closer. Her ears were back, as if she sensed the tension too. Every second felt like ten years. I'd already lived through the longest day of my life, and we were at midafternoon.

"Your father's worried about you." Classic Mom, break the silence and move us along but deflecting at the same time.

"Why?" The bitterness came out before I could regulate my tone.

Dad sighed. "These things you claim to see. Do you realize they always come when you're under stress? I believe you think they're real." He held his hands up toward me, as if warding off my anticipated anger. "I hoped this had passed, because you haven't mentioned them in a long time, but since we got to Fremont you're acting like when you used to tell us you saw things." Dad wiped his forehead. Mom sat staring at the carpet as Dad continued, "You and Gramps were so close. This must be hard for you. We want to help. You're not alone."

Great. I was right. They thought I was loony again. Their fucking insane son. What shrink would they send me to? I remained silent because my thoughts would make things worse and blow up an already tense situation. And I was pissed beyond belief. The spirit haunted them too; they were at the funeral when he went all apeshit. But we repressed that to go back to crazy Jaret mode because thinking I was off-kilter was easier or something. How could they ignore what they'd experienced? Adults were fucking nuts.

Dad began rambling various ideas—about Gramps, the family, and me, but I stopped listening, instead hearing his voice like the cartoon honking noise they used for adults in the Charlie Brown cartoons.

"Anyway," I heard when I tuned back to him, "I want to help you see how you see things when you get emotional. We can make this go away again for you."

"We want you to feel safe." Mom leaned toward me. "This isn't negative."

Whatever. I believed they thought they were helping, which made my anger toward them more difficult to process. Because they weren't. At all. Like always, they were patronizing me and treating me like I was five years old. Nothing I could say would matter.

I sighed, no longer able to hold my tongue. "I know you think I'm bonkers."

"That's not true." Mom shook her head.

"Then why are you talking to me like a couple of psychiatrists?"

Dad shook his head and grimaced. "No one said you were crazy—"

I cut him off. "Whatever. I do see ghosts. I've seen them all my life. It's not like I *want* to. Who would want to be able to do this? My ability sucks. It sucks seeing them, and it sucks more you don't believe me. I don't know how to convince you. If you think I see things because of the stress or my imagination without listening to anything I say, we're done. Leave me alone then. We won't talk about the truth, so no one feels bad, and you can quit thinking I'm fucking nuts. We'll all pretend like the funeral was normal. Who doesn't see their dead grandpa spring out of the casket with one final goodbye?"

"This attitude bugs me." Dad jabbed his finger in my direction. "You shut us out and don't listen."

"Because you don't listen either. You tell me I'm wrong. But you know I'm right."

"Dammit—" Dad said, but Mom cut him off.

"Stop. Both of you. What good does yelling do?"

The room plunged into an awkward silence for several minutes. Mom's leg bobbed up and down, and Dad's face turned bright red as I stared at the floor and held Darth.

"What do you want us to hear?" Mom folded her arms across her chest but spoke in a level tone.

"Promise not to interrupt?"

"Just tell us." Dad clenched his jaw.

Unconvinced talking was a good idea, I launched ahead because no other option existed. "Do you remember the fight you told us about between Gramps and Grandma?" I looked at Dad. "You said Gramps was right. But remember Uncle Harold and Aunt Alice weren't as sure as you? I'm trying to say I think you need to take Grandma more seriously. I mean, I think Grandma was right, not Gramps. She saw hauntings in this house, and I see them too. The spirit is protecting a Bachmann legacy I don't understand. Something to do with the jewels and keeping them in this house—"

"For God's sake," Dad erupted, "what are you talking about? The jewels are lost in the attic, and your aunt and uncle are under a lot of stress. It's not about a damned ghost." But he glanced around the room, as if looking to see if one would materialize to contradict him.

I bit my tongue, frustrated and humiliated. Dad's rational, businesslike approach to everything never allowed me to contradict him. And then he wondered why I didn't tell him anything.

The silence unnerved me into answering, again against my better judgment. "This is why I didn't want to say anything to you. You decide I'm wrong without thinking about what I say."

"That's not true." Dad shook his head. "But you want us to agree with you and not have our own opinions."

"How can you ignore the other people who agree with me? Grandma said the same things. Even Uncle Harold and Aunt Alice know. And you were at the funeral too."

"You explain the events in a different way." Dad folded his hands in his lap. "Like you *know* about ghosts and spirits. They all talked about the house and things going on here, but not with the same conviction. And you've made these claims for years, in other places where no one else saw anything."

"And Gramps's funeral?" I asked. "You can't tell me those crazy winds were natural. What weather could focus on a casket alone? Why did Gramps's casket shatter into pieces? Why did the wind blow right around us but nowhere else? Other trees in the cemetery did not move. The spirit was angry with Gramps and trying to send us a message. He attacked Uncle Harold, which is why he's in the hospital. Plus, he locked the attic door. How else can you explain how the door won't budge, even with all the tools in the world?"

"I was afraid of this." Dad looked at Mom. "He's worked up again. When he gets this way, he won't listen to anyone."

"Hello? I'm still sitting right here." If he wanted to act like an ass, then I got to use sarcasm and annoy him right back.

Mom stared forward in silence.

"Your mom and I think you should see someone about this, right away. You're trying to deal with too much emotion by yourself."

Yep. On cue. The conversation went to the same place as every one before it: the part I dreaded most of all, when Mom and Dad walked away without listening and proclaimed I needed professional help. They kept saying they didn't think I was insane, but their solution sent me to the shrink again.

I wasn't ready to give up, yet. "Mom, tell Dad about the attic." Mom shot me a look of alarm. "Tell him how you found Darth and me up there." Of course, I left Steve out, avoiding stirring another explosive into the pot.

Dad tilted his head in question. "Is that true?"

"Yes." Mom nodded. "When I went to find him, he and Darth were in the attic."

"How did you get up there?" Dad asked me.

"You won't believe me even if I tell you."

"Quit playing your damn game."

"Gramps took me up there." I shrugged. "He and the other ghost can go anywhere they want in the house, including through locked doors and into the attic. The other one, the one who hates Gramps, acted to keep us out. But Gramps can get through the door. So go on and get the straitjacket now. We'll bypass the shrink and send me right to the asylum."

But Dad ignored my smart-ass comment because my getting into the attic bewildered him. "You got into the attic by using the doorknob?" he asked.

"No. Gramps opened the door, and I walked in."

"What did you find?"

"The jewels. Gramps hid them in an old chest, a cool one with the family crest on the lid. This trunk was at the bottom of a pile of other trunks. Then he showed me the jewels in it. But I don't know if we can get back up there without him. I think the spirit locked the door again."

Dad sat stunned, I think believing me. He ran his hand through his hair then patted his cheeks and tapped his foot, more lost than I had ever seen him.

*

A piercing headache shot through my skull as a familiar voice within my head broke the silence. I leaned over and grabbed my forehead, peeking to see if Mom and Dad heard, too, but their befuddled expressions remained as before.

Leave me alone, I chanted in my mind. Darth struggled out of my grasp and ran around the room, barking as if a burglar entered the room. I fought to lift my head and appear normal.

Darth's behavior got my parent's attention. "Darth," Dad asked, "what's gotten into you?"

"You're not behaving," the spirit spat into my brain. "We agreed on what to do. I don't like this conversation." I felt the ghost's presence wrap around me, but he remained invisible.

Pissed off, I decided to fight back. "I think I know why the jewels are so important." I talked to Mom and Dad without a hint of the pain smashing through my brain or the voice talking in my head, or the loud piercing sound of Darth barking.

"Silence," the spirit commanded—aloud.

"What?" Dad looked at me.

Mom and Dad spun around where they sat, startled, trying to see who was with us.

"Your son's a sodomite," he said.

I gasped, "Ignore him. He's trying to fight me. Don't listen!"

The spirit raged on. "Ask him about his wretched habits. The boy strayed from your upbringing. You should be ashamed." He roared a last laugh into my head, so loud the sound felt like a person turned a stereo up full blast and sat me in front of the speaker. "Still doubt my power?"

Dad looked at me with a mix of frustration, hurt, and anger. "What's going on? Did you speak? Are you gay? Why didn't you tell us?"

"I'm sorry," I whispered. "I didn't know how."

"Did you speak?" Dad continued scanning the room for an intruder. "Who talked?"

"You wouldn't believe me." I sighed.

Mom was staring straight at me. "Was that—"

I nodded. "Him. The bad spirit." I was miserable. I had forgotten about the jewels I possessed and thought about getting them out as proof when Dad threw me off with his next question.

"Are you being careful? With your health?"

I stared at Dad in confusion when I realized he was talking to me. He'd experienced a supernatural event, but his anger evaporated, and he turned all his attention to me with a concerned expression.

"Uh, yeah."

"You use protection, so you won't get ill?"

"Dad. Stop." But my heart lifted a thousand feet off the ground because he handled the news by first and foremost worrying about my safety.

"I want to know you're protected," he persisted.

"Everything's fine. I promise." Despite his good intentions, getting so close to talking about sex made me way too uncomfortable. I'd rather go back to the ghosts.

"Does your sister know?" he asked.

"Yeah, she figured me out." My leg bobbed up and down again.

"What about Lincoln?"

"No."

Dad turned to Mom. "Did you know?"

"I—suspected," Mom evaded the question.

He looked hurt. "What will this mean, in terms of who you plan to tell?"

Lost, I said nothing. I didn't know. I was so tired. Drained.

"We know he'll be careful," Mom answered for me. "He promised."

Darth returned to my side, pushing against my leg. I petted her, more to calm me than her. At least they hadn't thrown me out of the house—just back into the closet.

"Can I go now?"

Dad ignored me. "At least this explains a few things to me. This is why you see things. All these years I wondered what caused your problems, and here's the answer. Do you think you hide behind these ghosts to protect yourself?"

Dad sounded like a lunatic, chatting away to no one in particular and reaching ludicrous conclusions. Why would being gay make me see ghosts? Or seeing ghosts help me cope with being gay? Did he even listen to himself? Yet we returned to the familiar territory of thinking I belonged in the loony bin.

"Maybe the visions will dissipate as we address your being gay," Dad declared.

I stared back in disbelief. "The spirit doesn't have anything to do with my being gay. And why are you trying to deny what you heard? How could you think I said those things? I'm not a ventriloquist."

"We know you well," he said, bumbling on. "Maybe you should consider my idea when you get stressed out. There's a natural connection."

"Do all gay people see ghosts? Why didn't anyone ever teach me this idea?" I knew being snotty hurt my cause, but I was on a roll. "And who the hell says 'sodomite'? Not me. Ancient ghosts use outdated words."

Dad got more frustrated and a flush crept up his neck. I stared back and my own face felt hot. My shaking leg prompted Darth to jump off my lap and lay at my feet.

Without warning, Dad stood and shouted at me at the top of his lungs, "What was going on up in the attic? Did *you* lock the door?"

His tone scared the shit out of me. I reached down and picked Darth up, refusing to look at Dad. He blamed me for everything wrong in the house, even the attic door.

I suppose being gay came with a habit of locking doors at random. What did he think I did up there? To keep my anger under control and because nothing I could say would make any difference, I glared at the floor.

Mom, having kept an odd silence through the diatribe, spoke, "Jesus Christ, what in the hell are you saying?" So she agreed with my assessment, at least.

Dad's face reddened more. "I don't know. Hell, I wish I did. I want to know why he kept us in the dark about the attic, when we've been trying so hard to get up there. He's hiding stuff from us."

I launched out of the chair, set Darth down, and marched out of the room.

*

"Please come back," I heard Mom plead from behind me.

I stopped and turned around.

"And you," Mom pointed at Dad. "Shut up." I stood frozen in stunned silence, never having heard my mother sound so angry and stern toward my father. "You're both saying things you don't mean because you're angry. Calm down and stop it. Please come back." She motioned me into the room, and I obeyed.

I did not need any more drama, but no sooner did I get into the living room than the spirit drifted in front of me wearing his usual, sadistic grin. He winked. I gritted my teeth, but no one else seemed to spot him, so I sat back down in the returned silence. Mom wiped at her teary eyes, Dad twitched his leg, and I picked up Darth and held her on my lap. At least the spirit had vanished.

I almost jumped out of my seat and screamed, though, when Aunt Alice stepped out from a side room without a warning.

"I'm glad you came back," she said to me, "because I need your help. So does your sister."

Oh, God. She'd heard everything.

Alice came into the room and went straight for the bar. Only then did I see the empty glass in her hand, which she filled with whiskey, I guessed. She added an ice cube, then grabbed her cigarettes and lit one with a shaking hand.

"Please remain seated," Aunt Alice commanded, sounding like the elementary school teacher she used to be.

Aunt Alice eased herself into a chair and took a swig of her drink before she leaned over and set the glass on a table. She puffed at her cigarette and blew smoke into the air above her head.

"Jenn, it's okay," Alice called.

On command, my sister appeared from within the alcove and walked into the room with wary glances toward our parents. Crossing in front of me with her back to everyone else, she grinned and made a funny face, causing me to smile in return. Jenn took a seat nearby.

"Where's Lincoln?" Alice picked her glass up for another drink.

"Lincoln?" Mom yelled.

Jenn and I laughed, because our family never went to get anybody, we yelled for them like barbarians. Our laughing eased the tension because Mom chuckled and even Dad grinned at the unexplained family joke. Alice sat there as stoic as before, drinking and smoking.

Like a dog called to dinner, Lincoln sprinted down the stairs and skidded into the living room, halting with surprise when he saw everyone.

"Good. You're here too. You need to hear this," Alice said.

Lincoln took a seat and flopped his leg over the chair's arm.

With our full attention, Alice took another drink, puffed on her cigarette, and began talking. "You'll also need one of these, when I'm finished." She held her glass up to Mom and Dad. "The kids may need a shot too. Tony and Jill already know all this. So does Harold. Tony doesn't believe though." She shrugged. "Not his fault. The men in the family almost never do. Jill was more open to the idea, but she tries to ignore the rumors. No one wants to do anything. Not Jill, Tony, or Harold, and he treated me the same way Gramps treated Grandma." She took another pull on her cigarette. "Harold said the haunting was nonsense, until Gramps died. Over the next couple days, he started to wonder too. He decided not to move into this house because he wasn't so sure anymore. Now he believes me. I wanted him to tell you this. But Tony says we have to keep him calm. So the explanation fell to me." She drained her glass and got up to refill it, talking as she did. "After the funeral, I told Harold what happened. That's when he insisted I sit down with all of you. Today. So here we are."

She dragged at her cigarette then extinguished it in an ashtray. Her glass filled with more alcohol, she returned to her chair. "Before we start, I'll warn you I'm in no mood for the Bachman stubbornness from any of you. Including you," she said to my father. "Got it?"

"I'm listening," Dad answered, sounding like a contrite school kid.

"Where to begin? I suppose the story starts for me with your grandmother," she said to me. "After we married, Harold kept me in the dark about all this, and

I'm sure your grandfather wanted him to. When she tried to bring the ghost up, they silenced her. And they made sure we were never alone. Yet in the few comments she got in before they shut her up, I knew she was indicating a spirit she thought was in the house.

"At first, I thought she wasn't quite right, especially after they found cancer. I wondered if the tumors affected her thinking, maybe the disease prompted her seeing ghosts. With Harold's stubbornness, I knew not to ask him about the rumor, even at our own house. I worried about her. I did. But I didn't think there was anything I could do, and there was no one I felt comfortable talking to about the issue.

"Things changed as she got sicker." Aunt Alice's eyes teared up and she clutched her drink for comfort. "For the first time, I visited her alone. I was struck at how I was married to her son for ten years and never had a moment alone with her before. As she declined, and she deteriorated pretty fast, there was no choice but for us to take turns taking care of her. I came over almost every day to help clean the house and do laundry. Tony and Jill were little, so they came along. Your grandmother liked having them around because their being here cheered her up. She fed off their energy. I don't know if they stopped on purpose or not, but Gramps and Harold stopped monitoring what she said around me. I mean, Harold was at work, Gramps puttered around the house, mowing the lawn and such, and he needed someone to watch her. One day, she told me to sit with her, so I did."

I glanced at Dad to see his reaction to Alice so far. To my surprise, tears filled his eyes. Everyone else sat enraptured because none of us, even Mom, had ever met my grandmother. When I looked back at Alice, a tear trickled down her cheek.

"Before this day, we chatted about ordinary things, but I worked most of the time while she talked to the kids or watched them play. I wasn't even in her room very often. But this time, she looked around, told me to sit with her, then asked, 'Is he outside?' I nodded so she started her story, the side they never let her tell. She told me Harold, Dan, and Gramps didn't believe her. They didn't think these things were possible. So she warned me not to tell them, even pleaded with me to make this our secret. She was sure they'd scold her if they found out. So I promised. She had a hard time breathing during her illness, but she found the energy to get this out."

Aunt Alice paused and looked around, as if searching for an idea she could not see. She drained her glass and crushed out another cigarette. Thankfully, she did not light another one because the smoke got to me, but she did walk across to the bar and pour a fourth drink. I was worried she'd be plastered before the story ended.

"Anyone else?" she asked.

"I'll take one." Dad raised his finger.

Alice made him a drink, then got one ready for Mom without asking. At least I had grabbed a Pepsi beforehand. Poor Lincoln and Jenn sat empty-handed.

"Now, where was I?" She swirled her drink. "I was sitting on the edge of her bed, right next to her, but your grandma started to whisper. I could almost hear the mower outside better than her. I'll never forget her face. She was scared. Like a demon might attack her at any minute. Yet she was determined to get this out. And I'll admit, at first I thought maybe the cancer attacked her brain and she was losing her mind. But the more she spoke, the more I believed. Her eyes weren't the eyes of a crazy woman, but rather of a frightened one. They pierced right through me and in her eyes, I saw she told the truth.

"Your grandma," Alice continued, looking at me again, "first emphasized the rumors floating around Fremont about a ghost in the Bachmann house were not myths, but true. Something *did* haunt the house. She said a spirit watched over the Bachmann legacy. Then she explained how, while she'd raised Harold and Dan, she'd felt a presence in the room that never threatened her but made the hair on her neck stand straight up."

Another gulp of alcohol, another boost to Alice's courage and the rest of the story.

"Dan, you know this. Your mother was a strong Christian. So this feeling of a spirit terrified her because she felt the presence went against God's will. She was disturbed at how she also sensed the spirit protected her. The ghost meant no harm. But she also thought there was evil afoot. At the very moment she spoke those words, I detected a presence in the house like never before. Not because of what she said, but because my senses alerted to an unnatural force. She continued to tell me this spirit also protected the kids. She knew the ghost moved things out of their way and one time threw a pillow to the ground when Harold rolled off his changing table when she turned her back. She had no other way to explain where the pillow came from.

"Before she got to the next part, she started to cry. She said she knew the demon was evil because it killed Gramps's brother and one of her babies. Well, of course, I was stunned. I knew Gramps's brother died in his twenties, and they'd lost a baby as an infant. I wanted to ask how she knew this, but she plowed through her story without any more explanation.

"She asked me what I thought, and what I intended to do. Her question caught me off guard. What did she think I *could* do? Why was I any different from her? I didn't say anything, and she leaned toward me and in a scolding tone said the last thing I ever heard from her. 'Listen to me. Protect your babies. This thing haunts the house. The ghost doesn't harm most Bachmanns and won't threaten you. But it's evil. Pure evil. I tried to protect my boys. And my grandkids. Except my little one. I couldn't protect him. And the men won't believe the ghost exists. They ignore all the signs. Harold, Dan, and my husband. I need you to guard those grandkids for me. Tony and Jill need you now more than ever.'

"Then she stopped talking and grabbed my hand. Tony and Jill were her grandchildren. You guys weren't around yet." The ice in Aunt Alice's glass clinked as her hand trembled. "Well, you can imagine I was scared. But I never got to say anything to her because Gramps came into the house. So I hurried about my business while she pretended to sleep. I never told Gramps or Harold about the conversation. And I never knew what to do. I thought about what she said all the time, but I ended up feeling lost and alone. I never talked to her again because she died.

"Even before this, the house always felt big and old to me. I can't say I ever thought a spirit hovered around here. I had an uncomfortable feeling. I was a visitor, nothing else. I figured being at my in-laws made me uncomfortable, but after she talked to me, I realized a deeper fear created these feelings. From that day forward, when I entered this house, I noticed the aura didn't feel right." She took another drink. "This sounds crazy, I guess. How in the hell do you describe these sensations?"

She stared at the floor then looked up again. "Eerie. Like something watches me. Ever since my conversation with Grandma, I feel eerie when I walk into this place."

She looked up at us and smiled. "I sure am glad you're here with me right now. Oh, I forgot. She mentioned one other thing during our chat. She told me her new pastor, Pastor Schmidt—this was his first year in Fremont— agreed to perform an exorcism."

Dad opened his mouth but then closed it just as quick.

"She'd been meeting with him for a few weeks," Alice continued, "ever since he arrived, and he claimed to see the ghost too."

Pastor Schmidt could see the spirit? I glanced at Jenn, but couldn't read her expression.

"He tried a couple things to get rid of the haunting but failed. He told her about doing an exorcism, and she wanted me to promise to get him to do the ritual. But I never did. I was afraid Gramps and Harold would be angry, and I never even mentioned a word to Pastor Schmidt. I suppose he gave up on us, because he didn't know if anyone else in the family knew about Grandma's wishes. You don't hear about Lutherans running around doing exorcisms very often." Alice shook her head. "I sure was a coward."

Dad got another drink and brought the bottle over to refill Alice's glass. The farther my aunt got into her story, the more her words slurred, but the drinks also seemed to give her courage to continue.

"What else do I need to tell you? Well, I knew a devil haunted this place. The ghost protects the Bachmanns, but in other ways, maybe not. That's about all I can tell you. Why is the spirit here? I don't even know whether she was right the demon killed Gramps's brother or her child. I mean, I believe her about the spirit. But who knows if a ghost was responsible for the deaths? More than anything, I feel evil in these walls now the minute I walk into the house. I'd always sensed something, but her confirmation of a spirit brought reality home for me." She took another sip. "Strange, though, I never feel threatened. At the same time, I don't like what goes on. I think there's something wrong in this house." She looked over at Dad. "Now, you can decide what you think about the legend. You can think I'm off my rocker or a drunk. But I've said my peace, and I want you all to help me if you think you can. You won't hurt my feelings. I hid from Harold and Gramps for too long, and I won't take a passive stance anymore." She looked around, as if challenging anyone to disagree with her. Nobody said anything.

"I'm not moving into this house. Harold and I made a decision, and of course, he thought I was being ridiculous, but I reminded him of things happening, things even he couldn't deny. So he agreed we wouldn't move in and even started to think there was truth to the ghost rumors. I don't know if he'll admit it to everyone, but he's starting to think the ghost caused his health problems. Who knows? Maybe. But he and I both know without question a ghost is in this house." She began to sound like a repetitive drunk, forgetting she said the same things already.

"And I'll tell all of you another thing," she added. "Once I got my nerve up to tell him, I told myself I wouldn't hide my feelings from anyone anymore. No more. The Bachmann men have ruled the roost for too long." She nodded once to emphasize her point. "I may have taken too long, but I'm doing what your grandmother told me to do a long time ago."

We all sat there looking at each other and then at her. She didn't need to tell me these things. I'd been trying to get people to listen to me all day, after all. Alice then stared hard at me.

"I'm sorry if this gets you into trouble. But you know the ghost is here, in this house. I can see in your eyes you know about the demon. You always have, haven't you? Well, you're not alone anymore. Jenn told me everything. As for the rest of you, it's time to change your tune. No more Bachmann denial. Ignorance won't work anymore. Silence is too dangerous." She sat back in her chair.

After a long silence, Dad sighed. "I don't know what to say. I always believed Gramps. I can't explain this stuff. I can't see a ghost like you." He paused. "But I've seen weird stuff. Unexplainable. So what do we do?"

Wow. Even though he couldn't see the spirit, he was admitting the ghost might exist. A pretty quick turnaround.

"Do you believe?" Alice asked.

Dad tilted his head and stared a moment in silence. "Like I said, I don't feel anything. I grew up in this house and never felt anything like what you said. It doesn't mean I don't believe you though," he added with a grudge. "I mean I've never experienced anything until recently. What am I supposed to do?"

"Start by listening to your son." Alice gestured toward me, much like I thought my grandmother must have done to her so long ago. "He knows everything. He has an ability none of us can comprehend. Listen to him, because no one else can help. Your grandmother said the same thing about Gramps's brother. She said before he died, he agreed with her and saw things in this house."

Gramps's brother, again. Who was he? How did he die? I waited for her to fill us in on him, but she didn't.

"You communicate with the ghost." Aunt Alice got up and came across the room to kneel in front of me, spilling her drink as she went. Some of the alcohol splashed onto my pant leg. "Why did I take so long to see? Your grandmother told me a few Bachmanns could talk to this thing. So you're the one, now. Like Gramps's brother. There's one every generation, she promised, and told me to watch for him." She slapped me on the leg. "How could I have missed your ability? I knew you saw things, but why didn't I make the connection to the ghost in this house?" Then she dropped her voice to a whisper I alone could hear. "Gramps's brother liked the boys too. Or at least they always rumored as much."

Alice got up with effort and wove back to her chair, leaving me stunned. Liked boys? Again, nobody said anything. Alice looked around, like she expected someone else to speak or take charge. Part of me wondered if I should step up, but I was too nervous. Too locked into being one of the kids under the firm control of adults.

*

"All right." Dad stretched his arms above his head. "I'm sorry about what I said earlier." He directed his comment at me, and his eyes teared. "I don't understand everything, and I've never seen a ghost. So I'm not sure what to believe. But I let my doubt affect too much how I acted. Today's made me realize how much I do trust you. I believe you." A tear trickled down his cheek. Like Alice, he took a big swallow of his whiskey when he finished. "I love each of you. I love you so much." He looked from me to Jenn, then to Lincoln. "I never want to hurt any of you. I'm very proud of all three of you."

In that moment, I forgave Dad for everything. Tense energy flooded out of my body, to the point my muscles twitched.

"Good, good," Alice said. "Forget being angry with each other." She laughed and shook her head. "A tradition of a gay one who talks to the ghost."

Boy, did the alcohol loosen her lips. Lincoln shot me a glance, but I avoided his gaze. Aunt Alice outed me.

"I believe Jaret and Alice," Mom said. "We should listen to them." Everyone turned to her, knowing she seldom spoke when the Bachmanns convened, but when she did, people listened. "I don't feel any of this either. I don't see anything. But we know strange things have happened here, today even more than normal. How else can we explain the funeral? We need to think in a different way for a change."

"Can I talk?" Jenn raised her hand, as if in school, speaking above a whisper.

"Yes. And I was wrong about what I said earlier to you," Mom replied. She left the statement hanging in the air, I presume because she referred to instructing Jenn to ignore me or avoid my hysterics.

"I see the ghosts too." Jenn's hand shook as she put it down. "And I know they talk to Jaret. I never saw them before when we visited Gramps. But I see them now, in this house. You all need to know the spirit scares me, but Jaret keeps me safe."

My heart melted from her support, though I wished I trusted myself as much as she trusted me.

Dad cleared his throat. "So this is what happened at the funeral?"

"Of course." Alice sounded even drunker. "Death upsets the balance. The spirit tries to protect the house and legacy when the family leader dies. I don't know why he wanted me dead, but it's pretty clear he did. You saw the tree. Could be simple as the fact I know about him." She looked up at the ceiling. "Angels saved my life. It was angels, I tell you." She pointed at me for emphasis. "And I have no doubt the ghost is even angrier he failed to get me. I bet he's listening right now, getting more and more angry. What I want to know, is why other Bachmanns aren't helping out? The dead ones, I mean. Why does this spirit get away with what he does?" She made a *humph* noise.

Dad put his head in his hands. Then he looked up and rubbed his eyes. "So my father is haunting us? He destroyed his own funeral?"

"I wish I knew," Aunt Alice slurred.

"Um," I hesitated to insert myself but took a deep breath and plowed ahead. "Gramps has nothing to do with this. He didn't ruin the funeral. He was trying to help, because the bad spirit was attacking. Gramps protects us."

"How do you know?" Dad asked.

"I saw what happened. Gramps confronted the bad spirit, and he kept Aunt Alice from getting hit by the tree. And remember how Mom found me in the attic? After all the trouble we had getting up there? Well, Gramps led me up there to show me the jewels. And those jewels can fight the spirit. They have power in them. If Gramps was against us, he wouldn't have shown me the jewels."

"You've seen them?" Dad's eyes widened with astonishment.

"I told you already." I reached into my pocket and showed him the necklace.

His eyes grew wide. "We need the rest of them," he asserted. "We need to get into the attic."

"I think I can open the door with this." But my sentence ended in a raised voice question because I still doubted myself, even as I held up the jewel in my hand.

"Put that away!" Dad shouted. "We don't want to harm any of the jewels. Let me get the tools." Dad clapped his hands together and started to get up.

"Stop!" I half shouted. "Listen to me. We don't need them. If you don't trust me with the necklace, then trust Gramps. He'll help us. He'll take me up there." I was actually kind of glad he halted my attempt to use the magic, because I still didn't trust myself. And it would be a complete disaster if I made a big show of commanding the gems to open the door and nothing fucking happened.

Dad pondered a second before he spoke. "Until we know more, you need to be more careful. Especially with that." He pointed to the necklace. "We can't trust anything. Even Gramps. We'll have to fix this ourselves."

I sighed and looked to Alice for support, but she'd had a little too much to drink and stared into oblivion. Jenn sympathized and rolled her eyes.

"I know what I'm talking about," I offered in a lame whisper.

"And I need to protect you." Dad came over and placed a hand on my shoulder. "So I'll grab the tools. Meet me upstairs in a couple minutes." Without waiting for a response, Dad walked out.

Typical Dad. Trying to avoid issues through action. Whatever. Fuck it. Maybe I needed to follow along and take a break, even if my inaction allowed for a futile effort with tools on the attic door.

"I'm getting a drink first," Jenn said.

"I gotta hit the bathroom," Lincoln announced, so while Jenn headed for the kitchen, I called Darth and went upstairs to wait in my room. As Darth and I walked by the attic door, she hugged the opposite wall and growled.

"This whole situation has me freaked too," I told her. At least she understood. We both knew the spirit was angry. And a little frustrated his plan wasn't working. More than ever before, I grasped my ability to sense disturbances and interpret them. Great. I intuited everything was fucked up but nothing came to me about how to fix the problem. Lovely.

I hurried to my room, glad nothing attacked me in the hall or lurked on my bed. I flung myself onto the mattress, needing a few minutes of peace. But ten seconds later, Lincoln barged in.

"What in the hell?" he asked.

"Sorry." I scrambled to a sitting position. "I wanted to tell you. It's hard."

"We're brothers," he said, pointing first at himself and then at me. "How could you keep a secret from me? When did you plan to tell me?"

I held up my hands. "I don't know. It's not easy. I don't know how to explain my feelings." I sounded like an idiot, but I was exhausted from all the emotion and shit swirling around me.

"That's bullshit."

"Whatever. Like you make telling you anything easy. What about the other day with Jenn? She tried to tell you about the ghosts, but you blew her off. If you listened, maybe I would have told you then."

"You didn't say shit the whole time. How was I supposed to know you agreed with her?" He threw his hands up in the air.

Well, he made a good point there. "All right. I fucked it up." I shrugged. "Both of us fucked up. I'll tell you whatever you want to know. No more secrets. Can we move on?"

"Okay. But be honest with me. Quit hiding things."

"I'll try, but if you start acting like Mom and Dad and thinking I'm crazy, then I won't." Lincoln sat on the end of the bed and patted Darth on the head.

"Where should we start?" I asked him. "I mean, do you believe me? About the ghosts?"

"What you said downstairs?"

"Yeah."

He frowned. "I guess. I'm kinda like Dad. I don't see any ghosts myself. But the funeral freaked me out. I know a strange thing happened there I can't otherwise explain."

"That was the spirit Aunt Alice was talking about. He was there. And pissed."

"I believe you." He petted Darth in silence for a few seconds. "Do you think Dad knows what he's doing? I think he's overreacting."

I laughed. "You know Dad. He has to be in charge. I don't think he has a clue what he's doing. He won't listen either. So I guess we have to go along, as usual."

"Is that a good idea?" Lincoln raised his eyebrow.

"Uh, no. Not at all."

"Are you being serious or sarcastic?"

"Both." I smiled.

"So are you going to try to tell him?"

"Nope."

Lincoln smirked but dropped the topic and moved from the bed to sit in a rocker near the window, fiddling with the curtain and twitching his leg. I was nervous too. "So, the other thing Aunt Alice mentioned?"

"Yeah?" I tried to stall.

"You know, about you."

I fidgeted. I decided I hated coming out. But Lincoln was my brother, and I guessed he needed to know. "Yeah, I'm gay." My voice fell to a whisper. "I should have told you."

"I wish you had." But Lincoln still refused to look at me.

"I started telling people. Please don't be hurt. I didn't tell Jenn until we got to Fremont, and she was the first to know. Dad found out about ten minutes before you. I didn't know how to tell people." I shrugged. "I was scared. It's not like gay people are the most popular in the world, you know."

He dropped the curtain cord and stood up. "If it helps, or whatever, I don't mind. You don't need my approval, of course. I want you to know I'm cool with who you are. Like the ghost thing. I don't understand or relate. But you're my little brother."

I relaxed, tension pouring out of my body as my muscles untightened. "Thanks."

The awkwardness broke when Lincoln laughed with a sudden snort. "Dad's a maniac. What's he going to do with tools? I mean, what's he thinking?"

I laughed too. I was going to either laugh or cry.

"Did I tell you about when he and Uncle Harold tried to open the attic door?" Lincoln asked.

"No. What happened?"

"They kept getting madder and madder at the door. They spent about fifteen minutes pulling on the handle, like the knob would budge. Then they took hammers, crow bars, and other stuff to pry open the door. Of course, they didn't want to damage the door or the frame either. It was so ridiculous. I tried to help but left before I laughed in front of them. Dad was bright red."

I laughed too. I knew how Dad could get.

"I'd better get going. I'll see you at the attic door. No getting out of the fun this time."

"I'll be there." I smirked. "But it's not like this is a good idea."

Lincoln laughed and shut the door behind him, leaving Darth and me alone.

Chapter Eight

A Ghostly Confrontation

Lying on my bed, I tickled Darth's stomach and hugged her as I waited for Dad to appear with his tools so he could begin his latest crusade against the attic door. I must have dozed off because the next thing I knew, I jerked awake, and there was Jenn, standing at the foot of my bed.

"Shit. You scared me! This is not the time to sneak around."

Jenn laughed hard. "Oops, didn't mean to. It's not like I floated in. And I knocked, but you were too conked out to hear. Darth answered the door for you."

I looked at my dog, who stood next to Jenn wagging her tail. "Traitor." I sat up and stretched, noticing the setting sun through the window as it disappeared behind the trees lining Gramps's property. Darkness already shadowed parts of the house and yard. I'd been asleep a while, then.

"What's got you so jumpy?"

"The spirit keeps visiting." I shrugged, as if she didn't need any more explanation. "How are you, anyway? We haven't talked since Mom and Dad separated us."

"I'm okay." She sounded less than convincing. "Mom made me promise not to listen to you because she said you upset me. As usual, when they try to make me act a certain way, their orders make me want to talk to you right away. But I thought I should wait for a better time. Parents suck. Then I was on the sun porch listening to music when Aunt Alice came in." Jenn smiled. "I felt safe with her, so I told her everything. Like, I knew she would understand, and I needed to talk. We were finishing up when we heard everyone in the living room. I started to go in, but she stopped me so we could listen for a while. I tried so hard not to laugh, with Aunt Alice and me spying on you guys." She grinned, which made me laugh a little. "She said we had to help you, and so we barged in. I think she was already drunk when she got to the porch. But not sloppy drunk or irrational, like she needed to chill and get the truth out."

"And whatever her state, she was on our side," I added. "Mom and Dad trusted her. Mom most of all. Without her, they'd still think we were nuts."

"Yeah. I was glad she knew about the ghost too. She's the first person to believe us. I think she realizes her experiences really were ghosts."

Jenn sighed. Despite our hopeful conversation, she frowned and seemed bothered. "What else?" I asked.

Jenn twiddled her fingers. "I didn't want to worry you anymore. But I'm scared. Since we talked, I saw him a few more times. The bad spirit. He looks at me. Like he's telling me, he knows I know."

"Does he talk?"

"No. I'd freak. He just looks at me."

"I think he's letting you know he's there. He likes to make people believe he controls everything."

"He can control me if he wants. I'm not going to make him mad at me."

"You might not have a choice. Are you sure you want to do this attic thing with us?"

"Why not? I can't hide from him anymore. Sitting down there with Mom and Aunt Alice would make me even more loony. I don't wanna be like them, and let the boys do everything since I see the ghost too."

"Don't worry, you're nothing like them. This all scares me too. I don't want you doing this because you think you have to."

"I'm already scared. If I went somewhere else or stayed downstairs, I'd be just as nervous but in the dark about what's going on. That'd be worse."

I smiled. So logical and adult already. "You realize Dad's acting like a lunatic, right?" A half joke, but laughing made me feel better.

Jenn giggled. "Not anything new."

"And we know we can't stop him," I added.

"Did you figure anything out? Anything new?"

"You don't know about the jewels!" I slapped my head for forgetting to tell her.

"You said they're in the attic."

"There's more." I motioned her onto the bed and sat next to her. "They'll get here soon, so I have to hurry. Yeah, Gramps showed me the jewels in the attic. Remember how he said I could control the ghost with the jewels? Well, when I held them I felt a kind of energy or power. They're a lot more than just valuable family treasure. Here, watch this." I pulled the ruby necklace out of my pocket.

"Beautiful." Jenn smiled.

I tossed the necklace in the air and commanded the jewelry with my mind to float. The gems did. Then I told the necklace to lift my suitcase off the ground, and it did. Three feet in the air. After a few seconds, I pictured the suitcase returning to the floor and the necklace to my hand, and both happened.

"Did you control the magic?" Jenn's eyes grew wide. "Because this is a lot different than knowing you see ghosts. It's almost creepy."

"Tell me about it." I floated the necklace to Jenn, and she grabbed the jewelry. "Once I touched the jewels, I experienced a weird sensation. I knew I could do this. I even tested them against the spirit and my power worked. We were outside the kitchen and he started flinging shit at me, but the jewels stopped anything he tried." I took out the sapphire ring to show her too.

"Is this safe? I mean, do you know what to do against him?"

"Not for sure, but I'll be careful." I started to explain more when we heard footsteps on the stairs.

Jenn got up and peeked down the hall. "It's Dad and Lincoln."

I stashed the jewels back in my pocket, and we joined them in the hallway. Dad was acting all confident, his usual in-control self, seeming to be happy to have a task to do instead of sitting there bewildered.

"What should we try first?" Dad asked. "We might have to damage the wall or frame to get this done."

Unless you were a ghost, but I kept the thought to myself.

Jenn, Lincoln, and I watched in silence as Dad opened the tool box and rummaged through various things.

I wondered if, like the ghosts' power, the jewels could open the door? Might as well try. I reached into my pocket and grabbed the sapphire ring, commanding the stone with my mind to unlock the door. I heard the lock click open but kept my mouth shut to avoid having to explain my magic. Instead, I watched Dad select a couple tools.

Dad grabbed a screwdriver and pliers and stood up. "I'm so glad we found the jewels!" Dad smiled. I choked on a retort about how *I* located them, not we. Sometimes I knew when to stifle the snottiness. "No more guessing where Gramps hid them."

Lost in the happy moment, I almost tumbled to the ground when pain slammed through my head, beating hammers against my temples, as Dad moved toward the door. The jewels in my pocket tingled with electricity. I regained my equilibrium and rubbed my temples, but my effort didn't stop the pain. When I could focus, Jenn was staring at me. She knew, too, something was up.

"Here goes," Dad announced.

Though the pain in my head remained, I commanded the necklace and ring to make sure the lock was still disengaged as Dad began unscrewing one screw that held the doorknob in place. When he grabbed the knob for leverage, I ordered the sapphire to open the door. It did, and the intense pounding in my head multiplied. Dust swirled through the air, once again making the area look like no one had come into the attic in years, despite my earlier adventure up there. Even my father paused. I was pretty thrilled with how I used the magic to do my bidding, even if I kept my success a secret.

"Wow." Dad picked at the faded wallpaper, and it flickered to the floor. "Last time I came up here, the attic was still pretty nice." He ventured a step up, followed by Lincoln, then Darth, me, and Jenn, who grabbed onto my belt. With each step, dust whooshed into the air.

"Was this dust here last time?" Jenn whispered as we climbed the stairs.

"Yeah, but it's worse. And the footprints and stuff are gone from when I was here. Not good."

*

The scene at the top had reverted to its previous gloom and mustiness too. A thick layer of dust covered everything, and the boxes and trunks had returned to their ordered stacks and rows. Everything but the jewels' trunk. That chest had been relocated to the center of the room, though the trunks sitting on top of it were restacked in their appropriate places. The trunk with the family crest also glistened in the sun as if polished and without a trace of grime. Even the worn leather reflected light, the aged cracks gone.

"This trunk's been up here for as long as I can remember. Look at the crest." Dad launched into a story about the emblem, but I stopped listening too in awe of what I saw around me, too distracted by the continued pounding in my head. Every bit of air seemed to tingle with a disturbance more powerful than anything I had ever experienced. *He* was watching our every move. *He* was getting angrier with each second, and he wanted me to feel his rage.

Jenn grabbed tighter to my belt and pulled closer to me, hiding behind my back. I also looked at Darth to see her reaction because last time up here she darted around the room sniffing. She stood next to me, her hair on end, her ears perked in anticipation. She also kept whining.

"Hey," Lincoln said, "Are the jewels in there?"

"Dad, did you ever see them before?" Jenn added.

"A few times. Gramps's brother showed me once before he died. And Gramps showed us a couple times as kids. Then, when Mom died, Gramps told us he hid them in the house, and we should leave them alone until he passed away."

"Are you going to open the trunk?" Lincoln wiped his hands on his pants.

Without answering, Dad leaned toward the chest.

Anticipating a bad reaction but without knowing what, I reached in my pocket and grabbed the ruby necklace, concentrating on its energy.

As Dad opened the trunk lid, the hallway door slammed shut, shaking the entire attic. My heart pounded, knowing *he* approached before I saw him or felt his presence.

"What was that?" Dad jerked his head around, scanning the attic.

"The door," I said, stating the obvious.

My father shrugged and looked in the trunk.

"Which container has the jewels?" Jenn asked.

"The pretty box." I pointed to it. "In the middle." My head ached and I was holding onto the necklace so hard my fingers hurt.

"Oh, yeah, I remember." Dad smiled as he reached for the container, and then Jenn grabbed my arm and pointed at the stairs.

Fuck me. The bad spirit sauntered up the last few stairs as if he had to walk up like a living person. He sure liked drama—so much of what he did was for show, but his efforts worked in scaring the shit out of me every time. Still, I sensed his anger, almost palpable in the air, as if he struggled to control his ire and maintain his form at the same time.

Oblivious to the newcomer, Dad opened the jewelry box. "Wow, look at these. Even more beautiful than I remembered."

My head snapped back and forth from Dad to the spirit, not sure where to concentrate, except to clutch the necklace for protection.

"I'll succeed without you," the spirit growled into my head. I couldn't tell if he let Jenn hear, too, but Darth turned her whine into a guttural growl.

Dad looked over at Darth with concern but returned his attention to the gems.

"Um, Dad—" Jenn said but was interrupted when the chest's lid crashed down with a boom to shake the room yet again.

"What the—?" Dad stood up and tightened his fists at his side. "What the hell's going on?"

"The ghost." I jerked my head toward him. "The bad one. He doesn't want us up here."

"What do you mean? Where is he?" Dad glanced to where I gestured but saw nothing.

The spirit walked to the other side of the chest where he stood glaring at all of us.

"Jaret?" Dad said. "Can you see something?"

"Yes." Yep. Whether I wanted to or not.

"Where?"

"Crap," Lincoln added, crouching a little like he was getting ready for a fight.

"Uh," I managed. Should I tell them the spirit was right next to them? "We need to leave," I said instead.

"Why?" Dad glanced all around. "What is the demon?"

Before I could answer, the spirit took control. Boxes started flying around and Jenn buried her face against my back. The boxes smashed against the wall, onto the floor, and contents poured out all over the place. Pieces of glass fell to the floor, too, and the windows rattled as old trunks burst open.

Paper, Christmas ornaments, and clothes fluttered everywhere, whirling into tornado-like frenzies wrapping around boxes. Everyone ducked and dodged and Lincoln was yelling at the top of his lungs while Darth barked herself into a frenzy.

"Now do you understand my power?" the spirit asked me, as casual as if we chatted about the weather. "You can't control me. And now I'll crush you. I'll crush your family. Stupid boy." He seethed more with each word, like no creature or being I had ever seen. Irate. The jewels tingled, in part in alarm but I sensed also as a message, signaling his anger worked to our advantage. If I knew what the fuck I was doing.

"Jaret, can you help?" Jenn shouted through her tears. She dropped to the floor to avoid another box, and Darth yapped next to her. Lincoln and Dad were standing and trying to bat the boxes and debris down with their arms. Finally, Dad was able to push all of us toward the stairs.

"Wait!" I turned back for the rest of the jewels and a box whizzed past my head. The ghost's force prevented me from lifting the entire jewelry box, but I concentrated on the necklace's power in my pocket to enable me to grab another batch of gems. The spirit howled in rage and directed all his energy at me, throwing everything toward my head. In desperation, I commanded the gems in my hands to halt the explosion of material heading toward me.

Everything dropped to the ground.

"*No!*" the spirit screamed. I felt the crackling of unseen forces in the air, but the boxes and debris stayed in their places.

I bolted down the stairs but stopped on the landing, where I found Jenn watching Dad and Lincoln pound on the attic door—again sealed tight. Learning to trust my instinct, I threw a piece of jewelry at the door—a ring—and it burst open, flinging Dad and Lincoln onto the hallway floor. Jenn jumped over both of them on her way out, followed by Darth, who stopped and came back into the stairway, looking for me. Then she ran out again.

I threw myself down the stairs and lunged for the opening. Too late. The door slammed shut in my face. "Shit!" I smacked the wood with my hand and then turned to look back up the stairs. A stillness enveloped me. I saw dust in the dim light settling from above and tense silence fell upon the stairwell as the spirit drifted down toward me. Air so cold it chilled me to the bone encircled me.

The momentary silence was broken by a violent scratching sound on the other side of the door, followed by Darth's howl as she tried to dig through the wood. Next, Dad shouted for Lincoln to go get the Blazer and load everyone into it, then Dad pounded on the door.

"Jaret! Jaret! Goddamn it, answer me."

"I'm here," I called back.

The doorknob rattled as he yanked on it. "Son of bitch," Dad yelled. "Hang in there. We'll get you out."

I knew his efforts were useless.

"Stupid boy." The spirit feigned a yawn of boredom. "You dared to challenge me?"

I reached in my pocket and asked the jewels to open the door. Nothing happened, and the spirit laughed.

"They aren't as powerful as you thought. They may have worked for a moment, but I'm still in command here."

I strained my neck to look up at him, still lording over me a few steps above. But his form wavered, as if he fought to maintain his presence, as if his anger sucked up too much energy.

"Although I'm surprised to see this much fight in you. Pansies don't tend toward bravery. The last one who tried was your great-uncle."

Gramps's brother?

"Of course, your asinine grandpa's brother. He had your ability. He could see me. And he liked to play games with me, like you. He died a tragic death." The spirit shook his head in mock grief. "No one believed him either. And his abominable attractions forced my hand. Would you like me to tell you how he died?" He floated back and forth on his step, pacing and anxious, still glaring down at me.

"Yeah. Sure." Maybe I could get him riled up and distract him.

"Perhaps I will, since the same fate awaits you."

And then I lost my shit. Totally lost control. "What the fuck do you want?" I shouted. "Tell me. What the fuck is it? Fine. Take me. Leave my family alone and don't hurt them. And tell me what the hell you want."

"Now, there's a reasonable boy. But what a foul mouth." He slowed and solidified a bit, though still transparent. "You already know what I want. Bachmanns must stay in this house and so must the jewels."

"Okay. Fine. But how should I get such a thing done? You see they don't listen to me."

"You figure out how. You think you're so clever, get the job done. I might suggest, perhaps your father should return to Fremont." He paused and looked thoughtful, as if contemplating the answer.

I hoped his theatrics offered a window of opportunity, so I clutched an emerald locket and flung it at the door, commanding the knob to turn. The panel swung into the hallway and slammed against the wall. I launched myself through the air, and barely avoided getting hit as the door ricocheted back toward me. I rammed into Darth, who had stood vigil the entire time. She yelped and stumbled but regained her balance and then we both raced for the stairs, almost knocking over my father as he hurried back with a chainsaw. I almost laughed. A chainsaw! Shit. "Run!" I yelled as Darth and I barreled past him.

*

The three of us bolted down the stairs and out the front door. Lincoln had pulled the SUV around, and he was in driver's seat, waiting for us, with Alice and Mom in the back seat. Wait. Where was Jenn? Oh, there. Sitting in the cargo hold. Dad jumped into the back next to Mom and I started to get into the passenger seat.

"Where's Darth?"

"Get in," shouted Dad.

"I can't leave her." I sprinted back, opened the door, and Darth raced toward the Blazer with me. She bounded onto the seat and I pushed her aside so we both fit. The second I closed my door, Dad yelled at Lincoln.

"Gun it! Get us out of here!"

Lincoln jammed the SUV into drive, and then my headache came back with a vengeance. Damn it, he wasn't going to let us leave with such ease. Darth started growling, and then she barked as the Blazer lurched forward and the tires squealed toward the end of the driveway. I looked everywhere for him, but saw nothing until Jenn started screaming in the back. She was staring out the back window, tears streaming down her face.

I looked up at the house to see the attic window blast open and glass crash onto the roof and sidewalk next to us. The spirit flew out the opening and came straight for the Blazer, almost invisible. The mere outline of his form plummeted toward the SUV.

I witnessed the next moment, a couple of seconds, as if in slow motion, every detail seared into my mind. The Blazer sped toward the street, but the spirit plunged in front of the vehicle. And then he smashed into the windshield, shattering the glass into a thousand pieces, debris flying everywhere.

"Fuck!" Lincoln shouted as he covered his face. I heard whimpering and crying from behind me.

As I closed my eyes to avoid the glass shards, I noticed the spirit's features were twisted with rage. The Blazer stopped, still in the driveway, though Lincoln pressed down hard on the gas pedal, revving the engine.

"It won't go," he yelled. "Shit." He jerked the shifting lever and kept pressing the gas before pounding his fists on the steering wheel.

I opened my eyes to see the spirit, more transparent than ever, pacing back and forth in front of the SUV. We were frozen in fear except for Darth, who launched herself out of my lap and onto the Blazer's hood. She bared her fangs and growled and then jumped to the ground and circled him, barking with madness.

He ignored her and stroked his chin as he continued back and forth, growing more and more solid, his self-righteous demeanor returning. Uh-oh. He was getting control of himself.

"Oh, my God," Mom whispered. "That's him, isn't it?"

"Jesus," Dad said.

"I told you." Alice chuckled an inappropriate laugh.

He appeared to all of us for the first time. His grand finale? Dusk added an eerie glow to the scene, portending total darkness around the corner. I had to fight him. I grabbed as many jewels out of my pockets as I could hold in my hands.

"What should we do?" Jenn's voice quavered as she spoke. "Jaret, tell him to leave us alone."

"Gramps," my father yelled, "it's us. Your family. Don't hurt us."

"Dad, listen." I fought to keep the fear out of my voice. "He's not Gramps. I know the ghost looks like him. But you have to trust me."

Dad shut up, and then Jenn said, "That's him. The one I see."

"I know. We're okay." I wish I believed my own words. "Stay in the car," I told everyone as I jumped out.

"Jaret," Mom screeched after me, but I slammed the door, hoping everyone would obey.

Darth ran to me, then spun around to keep herself between me and the ghost. A low growl came from deep within her throat.

"So you've decided to join me. Is your head empty as usual?" he asked.

"This is the big plan, huh? You're holding us hostage? What do you want? A ransom?"

"Oh, going for the smart-ass approach again, are you? Don't think you control this conversation. You're expendable, remember?" He started to fade. Good. I'd pissed him off a little. He paced a bit then glared at me when he at last stood still. I held the jewelry, which was giving off so much energy my hands were numb.

"I never wanted our relationship to come to this," he said.

"What are you talking about? This is all your doing."

He faded a little, then returned to a more solid form. "You've shunned me. You've ignored my authority. So you must go. All of you. None of you has done a thing for our Bachmann heritage."

"What heritage? A crazy spirit who goes around hurting people?"

"Silence! Never before has one person poisoned the entire family against me. I should have dispensed with you much earlier, like I did your grandfather's brother. The minute he started to tell people things. The second they believed his nonsense. I should have killed him then. Or when you were but an infant. I should not have let you live, as I did to your grandfather's son. No wasted time. No games. I tried to believe the best of you. To reset the storyline. Stupid of me, I realize. Now I must get rid of you all."

"Fine. So what are you waiting for?" I gripped the jewels even harder.

He laughed. "You're still naïve. Foolish. I'll destroy those of you who refuse to live in the house. In such a way no one will ever know what happened."

Maybe I was nervous. Maybe I was so tired and pumped on adrenaline I couldn't help myself, but I laughed at him. "You're the lamest thing I've ever heard. How can you get rid of half the family and make the carnage look normal? How can you off everyone and still keep your Bachmann legacy? With zombies?"

"Your snide attitude is why you're in this predicament," he snarled. "And you wonder why you have to die." But once again his anger got the better of him. His form dissipated to almost nothing. He spun around, and a tornado of wind close to as strong as the one he'd whipped up at the funeral whirled around us. I grabbed onto the door handle of the Blazer, and Darth got under the car for cover. As the SUV rocked back and forth, I realized he so lost control he wanted to flip the vehicle over with everyone in it, to hell with how the disaster appeared to the outside world. Everybody inside screamed and then an ancient oak tree in the front yard crashed down in front of us while other branches rained down everywhere. A little more than a shadow, he raced back and forth through the air in a vortex of energy. Out of nowhere, rain pelted my face. Then almost every window in the house shattered outward and a blast of thunder shook the ground under my feet.

*

Lincoln and Jenn jumped out of the Blazer but everyone else sat paralyzed inside. With every ounce of calm I could muster, I let go of the SUV and used the jewels' energy to walk me to the middle of the driveway despite the fierce rain stinging my face.

An innate knowledge guided my actions. I put my hands together and rubbed all the jewels within them. "Stop," I ordered. "Stop the car from moving." I tossed a couple of them in the air and guided them into the front seat, and the Blazer stopped rocking despite the chaos outside.

"Lincoln, Jenn, get back in the car. Now." They obeyed as I asked the jewels what to do next.

A familiar voice yelled at me from the porch, above the commotion and cracking of branches and creaking of the house. "At last. You're ready."

Gramps? I turned to see him standing on the porch steps. Unlike the maniac spirit, he appeared as solid as a human. I could even see the raindrops hitting his clothes and leaving a wet imprint. I wanted to reach out and grab him.

"What do I do?" I pleaded.

"He can't control the jewels. You have to be alive. Those gems contain more power than you, or he, can imagine. You can counteract him. You're in control, Jaret. *You're* in control. They'll obey you. Believe." He stepped down and walked toward me.

"The spirit told you about my brother," Gramps said, his voice loud enough to hear above the spirit's anger. "He killed him, though we thought he died of natural causes. And he killed my son. He *knew*, Jaret. He knew my brother and my son possessed your gift. I can't do much from this realm, but you can from yours. Protect your family. Stop him."

I closed my eyes and concentrated on hearing Gramps's voice and feeling the energy of the jewels in my hands. Then I threw them all into the air and commanded them to retake control of nature. They jumped out of my grasp and hovered before me before flying through the air. The rain stopped and the wind subsided. Everything calmed in an instant. And the spirit was gone.

"They won." I almost didn't believe what I saw, let alone how I had anything to do with their success.

"No, *you* won," Gramps corrected. "I have to go. Others are coming. Remember this isn't finished. Keep learning and fighting." He vanished.

I stood dumbfounded for a second, listening to the silence. Baffled. Exhilarated. Shaking.

I took a deep breath and turned toward the SUV. "Okay, come on out." They all obeyed without a word.

"Was that Gramps?" Jenn asked.

"Yeah. He's on our side."

"He looked so much like the other spirit." Jenn pulled at her hair. "And he looked alive."

"I know. I've noticed too. I think it's because Gramps's spirit isn't angry, like the other one. I don't know why, but I think the angrier the bad spirit gets, the harder it is for him to appear. Remember, Gramps loves us. He's not mad. So I think his feelings help him become more solid."

"Who is the other spirit?" Jenn asked.

"And why doesn't he go, well, wherever he's supposed to go?" Mom moved close to me.

"I wish I knew. I think Gramps stays around to protect us. But I don't know about the other one."

"What are you talking about?" Dad put his arm around Jenn. "Two ghosts? Where?"

He sounded like he never saw Gramps, though I knew he could see the evil ghost. "Wow. You can't see Gramps? Jenn can." Why couldn't Gramps make others see him, like the bad spirit?

"You saw Gramps?" Dad asked. "You and Jenn both?"

"Yes!" We nodded for emphasis.

I continued, since we had gotten Dad's attention, "The spirit you saw, he's not Gramps. The one who attacked us? I don't know anything about him. He talks about protecting a Bachmann legacy and knows all about the family. But that's not Gramps. They look a lot alike, but they're different. The second ghost *was* Gramps. He came to tell me I could stop the storm with the jewels."

"This is weird." Lincoln was still pale. "Is he done now?" Lincoln asked me.

"I wish. But I doubt he's appeased. He's pretty pissed."

"Hey, look at the tree," Dad said.

The spirit had ripped an enormous old oak tree from the ground, crashing the trunk to the earth, exposing the tree roots, and leaving an enormous hole where it stood moments ago.

Everyone walked over to the hole, glancing down into the abyss. Jenn held onto Dad as he leaned over to see. Alice and Mom peered down then stepped back, still not speaking, though Alice rested against Mom.

I turned to see Mom burst into tears and hurry over to me. "I was so worried about you." Mom put her head on my chest, crying. "I was so afraid. Are you okay? Is he going to hurt you?" The wall of anger and suspicion standing between us since we arrived in Fremont came tumbling down.

I wrapped my arms around her. "I'm okay. We can handle this."

Weird, how the family looked to me for answers, using the ability they used to say was all in my head. And weirder, my ability to see ghosts *did* come in handy. We all stood staring at the tree when I heard a car coming down the street.

"I hope it's not the neighbors," Mom said as she wiped her face with the bottom of her shirt. "How are we going to explain this?"

"It's not." Gramps told me someone was coming. And we were about to find out who.

Chapter Nine

Pastor Schmidt

I moved away from the gaping hole, and my family, toward the other side of the tree to see who drove up. Through the branches and leaves I spotted a dark figure get out of the vehicle after the car was parked near the curb. Still jumpy, I was nervous until I spotted Steve. Despite the circumstances, a big goofy grin spread across my face.

He trotted over to me. "Hey sweetie. How's it going?" he whispered. He also surveyed the downed tree and squinted toward my family on the other side. "I guess things escalated a little."

I blushed. "No. Not at all. This tree is half the story. What are you doing here? I'm not used to seeing you before midnight."

He smiled. "True, but I'm not a vampire. I can come out in the sun. Unless you like that kind of stuff."

"Maybe I would with you." I smiled back, and he took a turn at becoming bright red.

"Seriously, I brought help." He pulled himself together and glanced back toward the car. "I couldn't stop thinking about you and this house all day. I worried so much my stomach hurt. So I went to the one person I could think of."

"Other people believe now. The spirit attacked everyone. God, I don't even know where to start." I kicked at dirt in front of me. "And the jewels. I know how to use them now."

"Whoa, slow down."

I wanted to kiss him but knew any physical affection was a bad idea, so close to the street and my family.

"Listen to me." Steve grabbed my arm. "Before you tell me anything else, you need to meet someone. You already know him." As if on cue, the driver's side door opened and an older man got out of the car. He carried a large black briefcase and wore all black, except for a small piece of white at his throat. His clerical collar. Pastor Schmidt.

"I asked him to come because my grandmother told me he helped your grandma," Steve whispered in my ear as Pastor Schmidt plodded toward us. "I told him everything and asked about the house. He wants to fight the demon. He believes you."

"You told him *everything*?"

"Everything about the *ghost*. I said we were friends because you wandered downtown one night."

"Jaret!" Pastor Schmidt extended his hand and smiled. "It's good to see you." His booming voice had not changed from my childhood memory of a deep and authoritative baritone. But I detected the sincerity in his words. "I wanted to speak with you this morning at the funeral. Circumstances prevented our discussion." He motioned for us to continue along the tree and around toward my family. "I want to speak with your whole family. I can help. I promised as much to your grandmother before she died when she requested an exorcism. Perhaps I'll at long last fulfill my pledge."

I wondered if Pastor Schmidt could help. His low voice, clerical garb, and self-confidence made him look the part, as if straight out of a movie. Substitute a Lutheran minister for the Catholic priest and we were headed toward a scene from *The Exorcist*. But could succeeding be so easy against the spirit haunting the Bachmanns? Victory sounded too simple for a man of the cloth to walk in and reverse a century of hauntings.

"Um, Pastor Schmidt," I said.

"Yes?"

"More happened at the house today." I unleashed the entire episode on him and Steve from start to finish. Both Steve and the pastor listened as we walked toward my family, still gawking at the tree. Glancing upward, the pastor frowned at the sight of the broken windows above. Steve was horrified. He kept looking at me and I figured he wished we were alone so he could ask me more questions. I wanted to be alone with him, too, but that's not how things were working out so far. As I finished the story, we joined my family.

"Frank." My father extended his hand to him.

"My condolences. And also my sympathies about this morning's, uh, situation." They shook hands, and then the pastor began going to each family member in greeting. "If there's anything I can do, please let me know. Beth, Alice." He nodded. "And look at your kids. They were little ones when you left Fremont." Jenn and Lincoln smiled in an awkward way. Darth found a stick for Steve to toss for her, which reminded me to introduce him.

"Everyone, this is Steve," I said. I tried to hide my nervousness but a slight embarrassment came through, nonetheless, and my voice cracked. Shit. "He goes to Pastor Schmidt's church too," I added and felt my face burn red.

Jenn stifled a giggle next to me, but everyone greeted him like they would anyone else.

My stomach churned when I heard Mom address him, wondering how she would react in a different setting. Without her son's tongue down the guy's throat. "How are you?" Her voice sounded kind. Normal. Only I was freaking out.

"Fine, Mrs. Bachmann."

"Call me Beth. I'm glad you're here."

"All right," Pastor Schmidt said. He always liked to take charge. "Jaret told me what happened today after the funeral. I know a sinister being haunts this family and has for a long time. I doubt we need to worry about anyone in the family disbelieving anymore. While I know few Lutheran pastors who study exorcism, unlike those in the Catholic Church who have kept the old practices alive, I learned from a priest about the ritual. I believe exorcisms work. Sometimes the Enlightenment and modern thinking don't have what it takes to address certain things."

"Can you do anything here?" Dad asked.

"I believe so. I can perform an exorcism. The Catholic rituals have had a great deal of success, and still do today."

I wanted to believe him. Because a pastor swooping in and fixing the whole mess sounded like heaven. But I had doubts. Serious doubts. I thought he already tried to intervene with my grandma. Did his effort fail? Or did he have a new trick to try?

My father invited everyone inside, and Mom offered refreshments, which I thought was kind of funny. I mean, we were gearing up to fight a ghost, and she's serving tea and crumpets? Jenn, Lincoln, Steve, and I brought up the rear.

"This sounds kind of weird," my sister blurted what was already on my mind.

"I agree." I smiled. "But weird is what this family does well. At least they believe us about the ghosts. And we're not charging up the stairs with a toolbox to attack a door."

"Maybe you should take control," Lincoln said.

I shook my head. "Uh, no. But thanks."

"You know more than them." Lincoln pointed toward the door.

"And I'm still a kid to them. I'll do what I can. Pastor Schmidt seems in charge." I stopped at the top of the porch. "Shit. I forgot one of the jewels. You go on ahead." But I signaled to Steve to stay with me, so we returned to the Blazer and went around to the street side, between the SUV and the fallen tree but out of everyone's view from the house.

"You gotta be more careful with those things if they hold so much power." Steve raised his eyebrows.

"I didn't forget one. I wanted to see you alone."

He grinned and took my hand, leaning in for a quick kiss.

"Is everything okay?" My heart pounded hard as I waited for an answer.

Steve laughed. "Well, for the most part, yeah. I mean, you can't say it's cool. This house freaks me out. It's kinda ironic, you know? I find a boyfriend, and he comes with a gang of ghosts."

My heart sank. I sighed and nodded while staring at the ground and stepping away. But he grabbed me by the waist with both hands and pulled me back.

"The ghosts are a problem." He kissed me on the nose. "Not you."

I grinned. "I was worried—"

He put his fingers on my lips to stop me. "I know. Don't be. Except about the ghosts. We'll worry about them together."

I pulled away but didn't want to. "As much as I want to stay out here or run away, we better get back."

"Yeah. To ghost hunting."

He gave me a last quick kiss and we went back to the house, where we found everyone assembled in the living room. Pastor Schmidt's tough persona contrasted with the plush pink chair in which he sat and the cup and saucer in his hands. Others had various drinks and sat around in a circle. Only Aunt Alice drank liquor, sloshing out of a glass she held at a forty-five degree angle. I sat on the floor next to Jenn and called Darth next to me, where she curled up and put her head on my knee while Steve sat on her other side.

"If you'll indulge me." Pastor Schmidt cleared his throat. "I'll explain my methods."

"Please, do." My father nodded, too excited, too convinced we found the solution.

Pastor Schmidt launched into a dry and detailed history of exorcisms, ancient Christian rituals, and why they disappeared. He droned on, sounding worse than the most boring lecture I ever heard in school, so I zoned out. History wasn't going to fight the ghost. I wasn't even sure a Bible or holy water would do the trick either. The fucking ghost could rip trees out of the ground and change the weather. I saw visions of a bad horror movie where the priest gets offed by the spirit in the middle of the ritual. Pastor Schmidt wanted to throw baptismal water in various rooms, call the hosts of heaven, and declare how God sanctified these premises. Why would the spirit give a crap about that? His plan, I decided, was a bad idea.

Pastor Schmidt opened his briefcase and pulled out an old, tattered Bible and several books on demonology. The books creeped me out a little, when he showed us pictures and read passages about what he was going to do. Yep, I thought again. A *very* bad idea. My eyes glazed over. I shifted around, trying to get comfortable, and glanced over at the sun porch.

*

And there was Gramps. He walked into the room, circled everyone, then stopped and beckoned at me from the other side. I looked around. Everybody else seemed interested in the pastor's monologue—even Steve. I got up, figuring they'd think I was going to the bathroom, and followed Gramps into the foyer and toward the stairs.

When we got to the second floor, Gramps turned the corner toward his office. He remained silent as he walked past the shelves and shelves of books dominating the room. When I closed the door behind me, a fire burst to life in the fireplace, adding a nice warm glow, even in the spring heat.

Gramps went to a glass-enclosed bookshelf behind his desk. All the other books sat on dark-cherry shelves, accessible to anyone. But a very few old and delicate manuscripts were lined up in a neat row and locked in the case. Those old texts always fascinated me, but Gramps would never explain them beyond dismissing them as old family histories. Not anymore, because Gramps motioned for me to open one of his desk drawers. I did and found a small key hidden inside a compartment he pointed out.

I unlocked the case and opened the glass door. Most of the stuff in the cabinet was old and written in German. I ran my finger across the leather bindings and touched the golden embossing of words on the side covers. As my finger reached the last book, Gramps touched it, too, to tell me to open the cover. I grabbed the text and sat in his big leather desk chair, then looked around for Gramps.

He'd vanished. The fire had gone out, too, and the room went still.

I placed the volume on his desk and pulled myself forward to examine the cover. The binding looked even older than the other books and more tattered. I glanced through the first few pages, all in German, without any clue as to what they said. I took German in high school so recognized the language, but not enough to translate because the book didn't say anything about asking to go to the bathroom or greeting a stranger. I could, however, decipher the Bachmann family trees and read enough to figure out I looked at a family history, dating back a number of centuries. Holy Shit. As in, literal centuries.

I flipped through the pages with more reverence. The volume was not a typewritten manuscript or published book. Someone handwrote each chapter. And different people, from the look of the handwriting changes. The volume also contained pictures, inlaid or glued in. I went through the whole thing, happy to find the last two chapters written in English. The first English sentence explained how the next chapter was written in English and German, alternating from one paragraph to the next, but both languages containing the same information.

The very last chapter was in English and typed. I thumbed to the end, and there was Gramps's signature to a chapter he'd added on the family history after his father died. So my great-grandfather wrote the combined English/German chapter. Most of Gramps's chapter cataloged names, births, deaths, and weddings, along with an updated family tree. I found Lincoln's name, followed my mine and Jenn's.

Cool, to find an ancient family document, except the tome left me wondering why Gramps wanted me to see the book amid the fight against a pissed-off ghost. I turned to the last page and found loose-leaf papers tucked into the back. I pulled them out. Gramps typed them, too, but as a separate entry from the book.

I read the first paragraph.

The following is a brief summary of parts of the family history contained in this book but written in German, aspects of which are much disputed among the family. I do not believe the magical enchantments described herein. Rather, I type this to outline my understanding of what these pages say. I, in no way, endorse these beliefs. This is my grappling with the information. I hope my thoughts will assist future generations if these matters arise, and so I include my ideas in this family history that contains hundreds of years of records, both of a genealogical nature and of a magical character.

*

I blew out a huge breath and my hands trembled, as I was convinced my secret ability was tied to a hidden family history. I wasn't demented or fucked-up. Cursed, maybe, by the family past. But one paragraph alone had already validated my own history with seeing ghosts and shit.

From the date, I could tell Gramps must have written this right after Grandma died. Despite expressing misgivings in what he wrote, I suspected Gramps's ghost changed his mind. I scanned the document, astonished. No way. I wasn't the only gay guy in the family. And I wasn't the only one who could see ghosts. I looked up from the book, tingling with excitement. Everyone needed to read the book. Even if the content made them uncomfortable. I ran downstairs, clutching the tome tight to my chest, and into the living room. Pastor Schmidt was still talking, but I interrupted. Lincoln jumped at the sound of my voice when he woke up.

I set the book on a table but held up the separate, typed pages. "Everyone, listen." The adults stared at me like I'd lost my mind again.

"Can this wait?" Pastor Schmidt frowned. "I was about to begin the process."

"No. You need to hear this first."

"Jaret," Dad said in his scolding tone.

"C'mon, Dan. Let him talk," Aunt Alice slurred, holding yet another drink. "Remember what I told you?" She glared at my father, who shut up.

"Okay." I took a deep breath. "I found this book in Gramps's study." I pointed to the book on the table. Waving the loose sheets in the air, I continued. "Gramps wrote this part after Grandma died. At the time, I don't think he believed the story, but you'll see what he wrote *is* true. It's about the Bachmann family history." I sat next to Darth, who put her head on my leg. I ran my fingers through my hair, surprised no one raised further objections to my latest comment, and hurried ahead.

I read fast, because the tale was pretty dry and talked about our lineage, like being nobility in Prussia—we used to be rich! And Gramps's entry included crap like establishing successful businesses in Fremont, and why my relatives came to America to escape military service.

But for the most important part, I slowed way down. When I stopped, I looked up to see everyone staring at me.

"So this Henrik Bachmann," Mom said. "He was the one who immigrated from Germany and built this house in the late 1800s?"

"Gramps's grandpa." I nodded.

"Sounds to me like he had major issues," Lincoln announced from his chair. "I mean, look at him. He's married with a kid, and he falls for another guy. That sucks in the 1800s."

"Right. And then the guy he loved killed him," I chimed in. "Henrik came to America, built the house, then went back to Germany. He sends his wife and kid ahead with the family stuff, then goes to meet the guy he was in love with at the inn—"

Lincoln jumped in again. "And the guy goes nuts because he's about to go into the ministry, and he feels all guilty, so he kills a bunch of people at the inn, including Henrik." Lincoln whistled and shook his head. "That sucks. It'd make a good movie though. On the cool side, we're a family with a bunch of Harry Potters. Including you." Lincoln stared at me.

"Who's Harry Potter?" my aunt asked, making everyone laugh.

"It's a bunch of books and then movies," Jenn answered. "He's a wizard. Like Jaret."

"Like all the wizards the family history told us about." Alice pointed at the book. "Centuries of wizards. And all of them liked the boys."

"Like Jaret too," Lincoln added. His words made me feel good, to hear him acknowledge and affirm my being gay. My big, macho brother was willing to think outside the box.

I nodded agreement before continuing the story, "After he was murdered, his wife shipped his body to Fremont to bury, and to start the Bachmann legacy in America. His ghost must have hitched a ride here, too, so Henrik could do his haunting thing and watch over the gems."

"So Henrik was the one who protected the jewels," Dad said. "And those jewels are tied to certain men in the family." He gave me a look.

Aunt Alice contributed to our summary. "Gramps's brother, who died of sorrow after Gramps's son died. He could see things. He was the one from his generation."

"But what happened to Gramps's son?" Lincoln asked. "Why did he die so young?"

"Well—" I lowered my head. "—I think Henrik killed him. Because he threatened Henrik. Henrik figured out the legacy and knew which son threatened him, so he wanted to preempt the problem. And I'm not convinced Gramps's brother died of sorrow at losing this nephew. I bet Henrik killed him too. So all of this explains a lot," I said in a soft voice. And the explanation included the inference about my being my generation's warlock, but without benefit of anyone before me being alive to teach me.

"What has been explained?" Pastor Schmidt's expression was a mixture of confusion and maybe a little bit of discomfort. *The gay thing*, I guessed. *Or the ghosts? I bet both.*

"The myth, the ghost, why the spirit haunts the Bachmanns," I answered, impatient. "Gramps wrote all this without believing the truth. Yet he laid out the story we need to know, almost like he disagreed with his own dismissal of the legend."

*

Pastor Schmidt cleared his throat. "With all due respect to the Bachmann history, what Jaret read to us does not help with our problem." He stood and put his hands on his hips. "If I may proceed?"

"Can't you see?" I asked. I ignored the pastor, which made me nervous, but my idea was important. "We all know a ghost haunts the house. Grandma and Gramps's brother knew about the ghost too. You saw the spirit today with your own eyes. And I know Gramps was skeptical when he wrote this." I reached over and jabbed the book with my finger. "But he nailed what's going on here."

"What are you trying to say?" Dad asked.

"The jewels possess magic. They manipulate forces we can't understand. And one Bachmann per generation controls them. Maybe the situation *is* like Harry Potter." I wanted to add the Bachmann edition was like the gay version of Harry Potter but thought better of popping the joke at the moment. "I know it's true. I just do."

Jenn nodded. Maybe her younger mind allowed her to process the fantastic faster than adults. "*You're* Harry Potter. The Bachmann one. You used the jewels in the driveway to protect us. I mean, you stopped the storm. You're a witch. Your whole life, you saw ghosts and supernatural stuff, all leading to now."

"My God," Mom said. "I understand. All this time, we wanted to help you, but instead we did the opposite. Because your uncle died as a little baby. He would have watched over you. He would have explained your power to you. But we didn't know. We tried to protect you. Thought someone could fix you."

I choked back tears. I didn't want to get all emotional here, but Mom's words touched me. She believed me. After all these years, she believed me.

"If only we had known," she whispered.

"We do now," I said.

"So what would you like me to do?" Pastor Schmidt broke the moment. "Shall we proceed?"

Of course he took charge again. "I'm sure you can help," I said without believing my words. "But I have to be involved."

"Is that wise?" He lifted an eyebrow at me. "I'm not sure you understand the magnitude of—"

"Wait a minute!" Jenn exclaimed and interrupted him. Pastor Schmidt took a deep breath of annoyance as Jenn continued. "There's more to the story. You kept part from us. What else?"

I scratched Darth behind the ears, stalling for time and nervous. I could have hidden my omission from everyone else, but never Jenn. "Well, yeah. I mean. Uh, I think—the story seems to—" I hesitated.

"Tell us." Unlike before, Dad sounded sincere, not annoyed or questioning. "We want to know what you think."

"Okay." I blew out a breath. "Gramps's story explains the ghost's identity. His writing tells us why he haunts this house. The story makes sense for why the ghost is angry. Pissed. But also why he's so protective. It all makes sense." I winced during the last words because my head pounded with pain. The spirit was back, and he was not happy.

Steve glanced up, worried, and even put a hand on my foot in front of the whole family.

"So who is the spirit?" Lincoln asked.

The name caught in my throat as a red glow materialized before the fireplace, hazy but visible. A chill filled the room as the red fog formed itself into a definable shape. I worried blood would seep out of my ears from the pain in my head when the ghost became a more definable entity.

"Yes, Jaret," the ghost stated. "Tell them who I am. Tell them why I command this household and their futures. Tell them why I control you. Explain why you fear me. Tell them of my *power*." He clenched his jaw, venom dripping from each word. Our final confrontation had arrived.

Chapter Ten

Final Confrontation

Everyone in the living room turned to stare at the figure, who materialized before them in front of the fireplace. For the first time, he manifested himself to the entire Bachmann family and even our guests. His face showed more anger than ever before and was more sinister and maniacal. Yet he fought to maintain his form, which fluctuated between almost solid to almost transparent, and I had never seen him glow blood red.

"Well, Jaret?" He grinned at me, like a villain from a superhero movie. "Why don't you tell them about my power? Explain how I control you."

I returned his glare without answering. I understood what was going on, I recognized my own power, but I was still scared of him. After all, he killed Gramps's brother, who must also have controlled the jewels.

A sudden crash and shattering of glass made me jump a foot in the air. I whirled around to see Aunt Alice had dropped her drink on a table, sending the crystal glass to the floor where it burst apart. She gasped in horror. "That's him. He's the one." She pointed at him. "He haunts us. As your grandmother always said." My aunt stumbled out of her chair and over to the bar. She grabbed the bottle of scotch, opened it, and took a swig before carrying her liquor with her back to her seat.

Pastor Schmidt backed away toward the door, making the sign of the cross. His face contorted with complete dread.

The spirit laughed. "A man of the cloth has no reason to fear a simple demon such as myself. Don't worry. We're on the same side."

A vase flew across the room and smashed into Pastor Schmidt's forehead. He fell to the floor unconscious, shards of colored glass all around him. I fumbled to get my hand in my pocket, to get the jewels ready before he tried another stunt against my loved ones.

"That's better." The spirit smiled. "His tricks would interrupt our business. This is a private Bachmann affair."

Other than Alice, who was busy sucking down more scotch, everyone in the room seemed paralyzed, staring at the spirit. I got up from the floor and motioned for Steve to stand behind me.

"Except you're not a Bachmann." The spirit glared at Steve. "Jaret and I established a mutual respect until you came along. But don't worry. I'll deal with you."

"Cut the crap." My hand clutched the jewels in my pocket. "What do you want? What are you going to do?"

"Oh, listen to you. Such assertiveness." He pretended to shake in fear. "Don't think those stones can match *my* power." He pointed at my pocket. "I had more training with those jewels than you could ever dream of." He started pacing before us but kept his glare on me. "Let's go back to my original question. You know so much, why don't you tell them about me? Or are you afraid telling them will solidify my authority?"

"Jaret, who is he?" Dad asked.

"Would you prefer if I called you Great-Great-Grandpa, or by your name?" I asked with sarcasm.

"Watch your tongue. Answer your father."

"It's Henrik." I gestured at him, as if introducing a king or queen who entered the room. "Everyone, Henrik Bachmann haunts this home, the very one he designed and built, on the property he selected on his first visit to Fremont."

He did look like a younger Gramps, almost identical to the wedding pictures of my grandfather. But, when coming to me, Gramps always took the form I remembered best—an older, loving man. Henrik, however, was locked to the age at which he died. As I introduced him, he bowed in mock deference to my family, but his scarlet aura remained, flickering a little from his effort.

"Let me explain further." The weird grin remained plastered on his face. "My death showed me the true path. My beloved wife returned my body, and therein my spirit, to Fremont after my assassination. Doing so allowed me to possess this house and ensure the viability of the Bachmanns for years to come. My soul was trapped in the coffin while in Europe, but at the viewing in Fremont, right in this room—" He waved his arms to indicate the space. "—I was freed. I was able to occupy this house. I can move about Fremont at will, though I'm most comfortable right here because I protect the family."

I coughed. "No, you stay because your anger keeps you from moving on and leaving us alone."

"Shut your mouth! Sodomite!" He pointed at me. "I had the same vile and despicable sexual urges infecting me. Like you, I could not resist acting upon them. My actions were a sin. The rest of the world disdains these proclivities. But the Bachmanns—generation after generation—have accepted the behavior. A few even thought the situation normal and anointed these heretics to a higher position in the family. I acquiesced to this drivel and it led to my death. So I vowed to protect future generations. I wanted the Bachmanns to succeed in this country, to establish and grow the legacy I fought to preserve. But the wretched behavior stood in my way. My duty has been to purge the perversion from the family. It's why so many people reviled and attacked us in the Old Country. We could have rid ourselves of this filth in the United States."

"No." I shook my head, done with his issues. "Your anger keeps you here. You're not doing anybody any favors. You're angry and stuck. Nothing else. This isn't about noble protection of the family. You got stabbed to death by a man you thought loved you, and you felt all guilty because of your wife and kids. And you couldn't do anything to help them, nor could you even help yourself, and you're so angry your spirit can't move on."

His form wavered. "You're wrong. I promote righteous living in order to preserve the Bachmann heritage. What you do threatens this family. I eliminate sodomites because my action protects our family from the sickness and evil their behavior encourages."

"But the family's legacy is more powerful than you. That's why I'm here—to combat you. You didn't accomplish your goal last time, even though you killed two family members. So what makes you think you can succeed this time?"

"Don't you dare underestimate me." He seethed with each word. "I have killed. I'll kill again."

"Yeah, you're so brave to take out a baby," I goaded him.

"Silence! I destroyed your grandfather's brother. The death of his nephew was meant as a warning, but he failed to heed my omen. I had no choice but to execute him. How much good did those precious jewels do in his case?" He smirked. "I'll make sure you meet a similar fate." He was fading in and out, incensed, maybe out of control.

"You can't kill all of us and still preserve the family." I rolled my eyes. "Your plan makes no sense, to kill the family in order to save us."

"Don't presume to tell me what I can and can't do. Ask Uncle Harold about my abilities."

An image of Uncle Harold in the hospital flashed into my mind, but if the spirit thought to scare me, he screwed up. The vision made me angrier. I wouldn't let fear keep me from stopping him. "So what's your plan?" I asked. "Are you going to murder everyone? And then expect the rest of the family will trip over themselves to move into this death trap? No one will live in a house where all their relatives met a horrid demise in the living room. Doesn't sound like a great plan to me. Nobody already wants to live here because you're such an asshole."

"You little—" he started but almost faded out of sight before steadying himself. He paced again, but his form kept sputtering in and out.

With deliberate effort, he stopped, closed his eyes, and gathered himself. His form became more solid. "This family has existed for centuries. The noble blood coursing through your veins deserves a rich legacy. Not a—a sodomite. Each generation must honor this exalted tradition and ensure its continuity. I built this home for our legacy. I built the financial empire to make the Bachmanns comfortable for the first few decades they were here in this country. I can rebuild the legacy again. How dare you sweep this legacy away without thinking."

He flickered again, gritting his teeth. "How can you throw the Bachmann legacy away? I spilled blood to build this house," he screamed. "I promised future generations our monument would stand forever!" He was shouting so loudly the volume hurt my ears. Then he softened his tone. "That's why people must die. Maybe most of them," he said, engaged in a conversation with himself. "But Tony. I'll convince him to move into the house. We'll start anew, he and I. He doesn't believe, and he won't know the truth. And I'll make sure this bane of the Bachmanns—these sodomite warlocks—never live past infancy. So, how shall I proceed?" Henrik asked. He looked back to us, grinning. "Do any of you want a say in your demise?"

I wanted to blurt out how I thought he'd lost his marbles for good, but better judgment guided me. "Aren't you better off if you keep more of us alive?" I wanted to distract him and keep him thinking he held the upper hand. "Not me. I get it. But more Bachmanns alive would help carry on your legacy, right? Do you want everyone here to die?"

"Yes," he answered. "Everyone here must die."

"But you're planning to use fear to get Tony to move into the house. You said so yourself. Don't you think everyone in this room is afraid too? So use fear against them."

His eyes narrowed as he regarded me. "What are you suggesting?"

"You said one warlock in each generation screws up your plans. So take me. I think we both know I'm the one this time around. Gay. Sees ghosts. Controls the jewels. So take me, and let them live. They'll obey you. They're scared. Look at them."

"No!" Mom burst out.

"That's insane. I won't allow him to take you." Dad jumped to his feet.

I held my hands up to stop them. "You have to let me. There's no other way."

Mom started crying, and Dad dropped his arms to his sides. His shoulders drooped.

I turned back to Henrik. "Leave them alone. Take me."

"Perhaps you have a point. And as long as they promise to do my bidding, no further harm will come to them."

"They'll obey. They already seem pretty compliant." I hoped they would remain as such, at least until I could move against him.

He turned on me, moving forward at a slow walk, the maniacal smile still plastered on his face.

I grimaced. "Don't kill me in front of them."

"Upstairs, then."

The attic, I guessed. "Lincoln, hold Darth." A lump stuck in my throat, because I wanted her by my side, but I had to keep her safe too. I followed Henrik toward the stairs.

*

"Wait," Jenn called after me. I stopped. "I can help you. I see everything too."

I whipped around and walked over to her. "Listen to me." I grabbed both of her shoulders and stared into her eyes. "I know you care. It means a lot you'd go. But if something happens to me, we need a person left who sees this stuff. We can't both face the same danger, in case he wins. You have to stay here to protect everyone," I said to make her feel a little better. No way would Henrik leave them alone if he managed to get rid of me.

Her eyes welled with tears as she embraced me in a smothering hug.

"I know you can fight him," she whispered in my ear. "And I know you can beat him."

I hugged her, then turned toward the stairs and attic above. Halfway up, however, I heard a person following me and glanced over my shoulder to see Steve.

"Go back. You can't do anything but put yourself in danger."

"I won't let you go alone." Unlike Jenn, his clenched jaw and icy stare told me it was useless to argue with him.

"I don't want to be responsible—"

"I'm going because I want to. Not because you told me to." And he followed me upstairs.

The darkened hallway smelled musty, and the attic door stood open. One shaft of light came down through the attic doorway from above. The jewels in my pocket seemed to heat up, and a jolt of confidence raced up my back. I could stop him. I had won outside, so I could stop him again. Even without any special warlock training or whatever he said downstairs, I possessed power.

Steve grabbed me from behind before I stepped onto the stairs. "Are you sure you have to do this? Are you sure it's all up to you?"

"He'll kill everyone if I don't."

"What about the jewels? I thought they could fight him off."

"With my help. I control them, which levels the playing field against him. But they don't do anything by themselves."

"You've seen what he can do. How can you beat him?"

"If you think this is a suicide mission, then stay with them," I snapped and pointed back toward the stairs. I spun around to continue, but Steve grabbed me from behind with a tight grip. He pulled me to his chest, his face against my hair, his lips touching the back of my neck. "It took too long to find you. I can't stand to see you hurt. I always wanted to be the big bad football player guarding his boyfriend. But I'm scared."

I reached behind and hugged him harder into my back. "I can do this. I'll need your protection in the future. But let me lead this time." I turned my head and kissed his cheek; then he looked at me and we kissed.

"Stop that and get up here," Henrik's voice roared from the attic.

I plodded up the stairs, feeling behind to make sure Steve followed, at the same time reaching into my pocket to get out the jewels with my other hand. At the top of the stairs, I once again absorbed the all too familiar venue, with its dust, ordered boxes, and the strange way the space returned to a normalcy after the earlier destruction. A single bulb dangled from the ceiling, and the dim light cast creepy shadows around the room.

In the middle of everything, Henrik fought to materialize in a crimson blur.

"I must be nuts, negotiating with a ghost who lost his mind centuries ago." So much for holding my tongue. "You're so pissed you can't stay in any form."

Henrik smirked. "Do you question me? You promised yourself in exchange for their lives. So as long as you submit, I'll honor my end of the bargain. You and I both know it's your unique ability I need to suppress, not their helplessness. You got one thing correct, to my surprise. I can use all of them to rebuild the Bachmann legacy."

"So what's next?" I asked, hoping to buy a little more time. "I don't suppose you'd give me a second chance?"

"You seek a compromise. Too late. You passed up the chance when you refused to cooperate with me. Like your great-uncle, you thought you could control me."

"Tell me the whole story." I kept up the conversation, though I'd started shaking, my confidence wavering in and out like his form.

"The past no longer matters. Face your sentence."

"Which is what?"

"I'll let you choose." He smiled, again with the nasty villain smirk.

"You want me to choose my own death?"

"Would you rather I give you options?"

"It's a little weird. Why haven't you moved to the next realm? You suffer over and over again by sticking around here."

"I've heard enough from you." He started gathering himself, and the air turned cold as the wind swirled around me.

"Shit," Steve whispered.

"Wait!" I yelled. "I have another question!" I spotted the ancient chest, the one housing the jewels, sitting open and out of place. The gems called to me, an image of an iron box with a golden key in the lock popping into my head.

Henrik paused. "I'll grant you another question before you expire."

"How can you kill the warlock born to every generation? You tried infanticide once. But killing Gramps's brother and then his son didn't stop the legacy, since I'm here. So you'll have to keep killing and killing. Right? And one may sneak through anyway, like me." I rubbed the stones in my hand as I spoke.

"Those won't help you," he scoffed and motioned toward them.

"They have so far."

"You haven't learned everything yet. And you never will. Besides, you've already forgotten important details."

More distraction, good. Again he mimicked the dumbass superhero villains who get distracted as they drone on about their stories. "Like what?"

"You feel the stones' power and learned to use them, but to stop what I begin, not to initiate action. But I know about them. I know everything they can do. I started out like you, as the family witch. I used them in my life too. Did you forget? I'm the one who made sure they got to America with the family. I put them in the chest right there."

"And yet they failed to save your life."

"Shut up and listen." He swirled into red vapors of anger. "I know about everything in the trunk. The magic was mine before the power was yours. You can't hide anything from me."

"So impressive. You remember what these things can do." I understood part of my strategy must include pissing him off because his rage weakened his power. "You're so superior, with your lofty goals and all. But you said you'd answer my question. Are you going to keep killing people? A witch will appear generation after generation to confront you. So you'll kill all of them? How noble. So brave and honorable to whack a baby off every ten years or so."

"I'll deal with you and the mess you've created. Such unpleasantness will wait for later."

Steve inched toward me.

"Rather crass of you, when you think about it. Pretending to be so noble and in control. But no solution but killing a teenager comes into your head. Must have always had limited intellect, even in life. Nothing in your noggin but brute force." I sensed the power of the jewels running up my hands and arms and an image of the iron box and golden key appeared in my mind again. The box. Henrik belonged in the box.

"You sound so bold and smart. If fixing the problem were as simple as killing you," Henrik said, "things would be easy. I could get rid of you and frighten your family into obeying me in the process. But you dragged this—this *concubine* into my plan." He jabbed a finger in Steve's direction. "As even you pointed out, I can't risk bringing others into this house. The pastor and this boy threaten the family. They could start spinning tales to the outside world."

"So you're scared of me?" Steve asked.

"Protecting your little sissy boy, are you? So you can defile him again?"

"Fuck off. You'll have to kill me, too, to get to him."

"Such bravery," Henrik said with a snort, but his form started to fade in and out.

"Leave him out of this." I put myself between Henrik and Steve, but Steve pushed my arm aside and stood next to me.

"He got himself into the situation," Henrik retorted. "I gave him the option to leave, and he refused. I can kill him too. His wouldn't be the first body I've hidden. I think a nice mystery makes a good story to tell people, about how two sick sodomites ran away together."

"Fuck you," Steve spat.

Henrik roared with laughter. "Charming, masculine façade. How many men would you like to bend you over a chair so you can take a dick like a woman should? You're a sodomite. A perversion of nature."

Steve lunged at Henrik but fell through him and crashed to the floor on the other side.

"Steve, stop!" I yelled as the situation got out of control.

Steve scrambled to his feet but went flying through the air across the attic, the same as last time he and I were up here. I launched a handful of diamonds, emeralds, and rubies at Steve, a little too late to keep him from smashing against a window, but they slowed him down enough to keep him from flying through the glass and landing three stories down on the driveway. He hit the wooden frame and collapsed to the floor, unconscious.

*

I ran over and knelt beside him. He was breathing, but out cold.

"Ah, how tragic. Your perversion in ruins."

Tears streamed down my face, and my courage faltered as I clutched Steve close to me.

"Even as you face your end, even after I've shown you how useless this boy was to you, you still have to sicken me as you fawn over another male. It's wrong. You can't procreate. How dare you violate this home's sanctity?"

I stared at Henrik as he paced before us.

"Not such a man after all, was he?"

I refused to say anything, taking a moment to pull myself together.

"He deserved this fate." Henrik said. "Deep within, you know the wickedness of what you do. It's not too late.

We can heal these wounds between us. Think of our combined power."

Luke! Come to the dark side! Together we can rule the galaxy. Great. Even in the face of extreme danger, stupid movie lines popped into my head to humor me. And then I smirked at him.

"Don't ridicule me," he shouted.

"What kind of weird alliance would we enter?"

"When death brings sanctification, the end of life upholds what is good. We can rid the world of this sodomite; then I can help change you for the better. We can transform your soul in life as mine was transformed in death."

"I can't murder a person I care about." Whoa. Where did *these strong feelings* come from?

"Men can't love each other. What did he ever do for you? He can't even protect you, like a proper man should." Henrik returned to flickering.

"So when someone dies, they lose every feeling and emotion they ever had? Then you're an empty portal. There's nothing there but despair, anger, and sadness. What happened to you?"

"I care about this family. I love them. How dare you?"

"Then why are you spending all these years running around scaring everybody? Is this how you were when you were alive? Were you always a big asshole? Because honestly, learning the truth bums me out—one of my ancestors was such a prick." And then I braced for his freak-out, but he surprised me. He slowed his movements and solidified, becoming less hostile.

"I treated everyone with love and compassion. Those closest to me most of all. I never raised my voice at my wife, but she suffered because of my sexual transgressions. She deserved so much more, though I treated her like the honorable woman she was. I honored my parents. I was a respected and loved person."

"So why not treat the family the same way now? Why not let me be like you were?"

"Because I learned from my sins. I'm trying to prevent you from doing the same thing. You can't do with men what men should do with women and honor the Bachmann legacy."

"Except men loving men is part of the Bachmann legacy. For as far back as we know. You mean you never loved any of the men you went to bed with? Was your urge an animal instinct to fuck?" Oops. Too far? My potty mouth often got me in trouble.

"What do you expect me to say?" he growled. "Of course, I felt for him. And, of course, I loved him. But my actions were wrong. *Wrong*. I had no idea what our relationship did to him or my family. I died because of this sin. I earned that death. I'm here now to protect the family from suffering from this type of failure in the future. Don't you see? That's the love I have for you. I didn't have any idea what I was doing to him or anyone else in the family. Instead of sneaking away to be with him I should've been with my wife and child. Bedding another man can't make you happy." His rage returned as he shimmered again, solid and then not.

I held Steve's limp body for comfort, yelping in fear when he gasped for air. Henrik was hurting him, and panic shot through me.

"I understand what feelings drive you," Henrik said. "I shared the same ones. Learn from me of their evil. I can prevent you from suffering my fate."

An idea dawned on me. Gramps wrote how Henrik went with a number of partners, but Henrik talked about one. "Your meeting wasn't by chance, was it?" I asked.

He regarded me, wary. "What do you mean?"

Steve stopped struggling to breathe as Henrik calmed down.

"The man who killed you. You knew him."

"Of course." He sounded sad.

"I mean, you were lovers. It wasn't just sex."

He stopped moving. The red rage of his glow softened to pink as he gained control of his manifestation and looked more human, still transparent but without the awful blood tint.

"If you must know, yes. I knew him."

"How?" So he did have a nice side.

"He lived in my family's village. We knew each other all our lives. And you were heading down the same, dangerous path."

"What do you mean? What was his name?"

"Josef. I can't describe how much time he and I spent together. Taking walks. Exploring. Catching secret moments in each other's arms. But know, I never went to bed with anyone but my wife and Josef. My dear Josef." With each word Henrik became more solid. "Perhaps you understand. Like you, I saw nothing wrong with these desires. I married a woman because society expected such behavior, and all my brothers were dead. I had to ensure the Bachmann legacy. And don't forget how much my wife meant to me, how much I cared for her. But my passion I reserved for Josef. I protected him, ensured his security, and provided him with luxuries few could afford. I loved him. We loved each other.

"But before you become too sentimental," he warned, "listen to the end of my story. There was so much political turmoil then, the politics necessitated my moving the family to America. I was devastated, but I had no choice. What would this mean for Josef and me?

"I told him, of course. I explained the whole situation and offered to pay his passage. I promised him work in my new ventures." He paused and faded for a moment. "My plan seemed perfect. But he refused. I was stunned. He said he was afraid and unwilling to leave his parents. He wanted a religious life and knew nothing of seminaries here, and he feared being in America, away from me and alone if he ever left Fremont. I tried for weeks to change his mind. I couldn't envision leaving without him. I sailed to and from America, made all the arrangements, and never once acknowledged I may fail to persuade him."

His story softened my hatred, but not my resolve to defeat him and protect those I loved from his warped reality as a ghost.

Lost in the past, he continued. "The evening of my death, my world all came crashing down. We met at an inn, in the port where I was to sail back to America the next day. I remember crying together all evening. I pleaded with him one last time to come with me. But what I wanted to be a touching, sentimental moment, turned ugly. We argued and shouted, neither giving in to the other.

"The innkeeper heard, and he came to quiet us. He knocked but then forced his way in without waiting. He saw what was going on and threatened us with exposure. I attempted to buy his silence, gave him a large sum of money, and promised to double the amount before leaving in the morning. He left, quite pleased with himself, and I don't think he ever intended to tell anyone. He wanted money and got his reward. So I thought nothing more of his threat."

Steve moaned, at least signaling he was alive.

"Josef, however, feared the problem remained. He thought someone would come for him after I left, but he wouldn't have means to pay for their silence. He accused me of being selfish and of leaving him for no reason. He said I ruined his hope of becoming a minister, and the Church would find him out. He ran from me, sobbing and yelling."

Henrik stopped and was quiet for a long moment. After one hundred years, he was still in love with the man who'd killed him. "I cried too. I lay on the bed and wept until exhausted. I slept once I exhausted the tears, thinking I would never again see Josef. I was wrong. Very wrong."

He smirked, the hate and anger reflected once again in his eyes. The anger boiling inside him anew. "In the middle of the night, I woke because I heard a noise in the room. I listened but decided the sound wasn't anything and shut my eyes again. But then I heard what were footsteps, and I sat up. A man. There was a man in my room. I didn't know it was Josef yet. I tried to get out of bed, but he stabbed me. Excruciating pain. My throat. There was blood everywhere. I leapt out of bed to fight this unknown assailant and managed, despite my increasing weakness, to throw him against a dresser. He charged back at me, and I prepared to resist, but then I saw Josef in the moonlight. I couldn't raise my hands to him. I let him finish the deed. Unlike the wound across my throat, I felt nothing as the dagger plunged into my chest. In my final living seconds, I watched his face. He wept. And when I fell to the floor, he knelt beside me and whispered, 'I love you.'"

I held Steve tighter. How could Josef have killed the man he loved?

"I had no idea what to expect in death." Henrik seemed lost in his story. "But I was shocked when, even after my body no longer lived, my soul stayed in the room and my mind worked as before. I could still exist in this world in another realm. I died because of my sin, because I fell in love with another man. I could not let what happened to me happen to future generations in the family. God wielded His power and showed my soul the truth. Josef, the person I trusted beyond all others, had killed me. To atone, I became the guardian angel of this family."

Henrik maintained his solid form, and he glared once again in determination. "I speak the truth. Defying God and lying with other men brings tragedy."

*

I sensed the moment to attack. Despite the sad story, Henrik intended to kill me. I set Steve's body on the floor, stood up, and clutched as many gems as possible within my pockets as I inched toward the open trunk.

"I'm glad you told me about your past," I said, still moving closer to the chest. Almost there. And then I knew what to do. I rubbed the gems between my fingers, energizing them.

"Then you'll help me? You'll follow my will?"

"No." I shook my head as he stared at me in shock.

I threw all the gems at his face, then grabbed the jewelry box from the trunk and flung the rest of the gems at him too. The stones whirled around Henrik, moving so fast I saw nothing but colored lines spinning around his head.

He lashed at them, screaming. I leaned over and grabbed the iron box. *Come here*, I ordered the jewels. They did, and Henrik had no choice but to come with them. The stones trapped him inside their magical portal. They spun faster and faster, and he started to shrink, until he was nothing more than a tiny red ball of light. *Into the box*, I ordered, and the stones coiled around the iron box, pushing Henrik inside. I slammed the lid and turned the golden key, which I took out and put into my pocket. And then the jewels placed themselves back inside the jewelry case.

I stood still, listening for signs of Henrik, but heard nothing. Complete silence. I didn't feel anything either. No creepy presences. No weird energy. Nothing. The attic looked, sounded, and felt like any other attic in America. Nothing haunted the place. Not anymore. I touched the cover of the iron box and felt a little bit of him, but we were safe. I blew out a huge breath of relief.

I rushed over to Steve, who moved a little when I touched him. I lifted his head so my lap became a pillow and surveyed the scratches on his body and face, including a pretty deep gash on his forehead. Otherwise, he seemed okay.

I kissed his cheek, and his eyes blinked open.

"Ah, an angel." He smiled.

"Hardly. You're having delusions from hitting your head. How do you feel?"

Steve grabbed for my hand. "A little sore." He sat up and jerked his head around, which made him wince. "Where he is? What happened?"

I pointed toward the iron box next to the family trunk. "In there. Don't ask me to explain. But we're safe."

"You sure?"

"Pretty sure. I can't feel him in the house anymore." For the first time since the day I heard Gramps had died, I was safe. No spirits haunted me. No premonitions. My headache was gone. I got up and knelt next to the box. I placed my hands on the lid and closed my eyes, feeling the cold black metal become fiery hot, scorching my nerves but also telling me Henrik was trapped inside. Pissed off, but trapped. I jerked my hands away and sat back. The brief touch also taught me about the box: it belonged to generation after generation of Bachmann warlocks and contained mystical capabilities to capture evil spirits and perform other magic. Nothing could escape without the golden key. I could never explain how the magic worked.

Steve crawled over to me and hugged me around my waist. I leaned back against his chest.

"He's in there." I pointed to the iron box.

"A little weird. But I learned with this shit to trust you."

"You sure you're okay?" The blood on his forehead had dried, and I saw a couple of bruises forming.

"Sore. Very sore. Like I got tackled a hundred times in a row during a game. But I'll be okay. I mean, we're safe, right?"

"Do you have a concussion?" His eyes looked a little funny.

"I don't think so. I feel better than when I got one during a game and they took me to the hospital. Answer me, are we safe?"

"He can't get out of the box. I know he's trapped. I sense the control I have. Or the gems reveal the power to me. But we need to make sure no one ever opens the fucking box. Otherwise, I'm serious. It's over."

"What did you put in there?"

"I think his soul. Sounds awful, doesn't it? But he won't move to the next realm because he's so pissed. So I trapped him in there. He can never come out, because now he's angrier than ever."

"Well, I won't be the one to open the box. I'm not going anywhere close."

I laughed, then turned and kissed him.

"What's this about?" he asked.

"Thought I would let you know how much I like you."

He pulled my head down and kissed me again. "Same here. But you don't have to say how you feel, if you're not ready yet."

We fell back on the floor and lay together, listening to the complete silence around us.

Chapter Eleven

Departure

I slammed my suitcase shut, with the iron box on the bed next to it. Henrik had resided in there a week already, and everything indicated he was locked up for good–unless a fool released him. Which would never be me.

I was glad we were heading back to Colorado. Fremont wasn't for me, at least on a permanent basis. I liked to visit but not stay. Good thing Aunt Alice and Uncle Harold decided to move into the family home after all. So Dad had been fixing the place all up, after the mess Henrik made. I smiled and wrapped the iron box in a towel, not wanting to feel Henrik's pissed off aura while I carried him around. I held the box in one hand and picked the suitcase up in my other and headed downstairs to the living room.

"Come in." Harold waved at me from where he sat next to Alice. He looked a lot better since he got back from the hospital. "I wanted to say thanks one more time. I know you said you understand, but really. What you did for me, for us. I can never repay you."

I fidgeted, uncomfortable with the compliment. "You're welcome. It's my family job."

"You remind me so much of Gramps's brother," Alice said. "And you have the same gifts."

"Your support meant a lot to me when no one else believed." I wiped a tear from my eye. "Both of you. Thanks. I wish I could have stopped all this sooner. But I don't know if I ever would've gotten here without both of you." I turned around, grabbed my suitcase and the towel-wrapped box, and started toward the front door but paused before going outside and turned back to them.

"You're safe here. You know? In this house."

"We know." Harold nodded. "And if anything happens, we know who to call. You'd better get your suitcase outside before your dad has a fit." He chuckled.

I reached the front door, and Dad smiled at me from the driveway. "There you are." He grabbed my suitcase. "I made sure Darth has her spot in back. You ready?"

"Yeah. Time to get back to Colorado."

"Yep. And to work for me."

"Plus, I have to get my college applications ready."

"Well, Gramps left all of you plenty for college tuition. So you can go wherever you want."

"You made room for my new trunk, too, right?"

"Of course. And for the, uh, box." He pointed to Henrik. "You're sure that's safe?"

"You gotta trust me. He can't get out unless some nut unlocks the box with the key." I patted my pocket. "I also learned no one can use the key without magic. It'd be worse to leave this in Fremont, where no one knows what to do with the magic. Same with the jewels and other stuff in the trunk. I need to learn more about all of my abilities."

"It doesn't hurt to reassure me from time to time. But you'd better go get the trunk. I made a special spot because it's so big."

"Okay."

I jumped the stairs two at a time, with Darth close at my heels, almost tripping me in our race to the second floor. She hated coming in second and never did unless I could block her path. I almost slammed into the back of Jenn, who stood with Mom and Lincoln in the middle of the hallway.

"Hey, I hope you packed already," Lincoln said. "Last again."

"Not fair. I have an extra trunk to worry about."

"Be sure everything's locked tight. We don't need spirits and stuff flying around the Blazer while Dad tries to drive. That'd be messed up." Lincoln headed downstairs and left Jenn, Mom, and me laughing.

Mom touched my arm. "I've got to pack lunch. All we have is peanut butter and jelly. Okay?"

"Sounds good."

Before she got to the stairs, Mom turned and looked at me. "You okay?"

"How many times are you going to ask me? I'm fine."

"I know, I know. Moms are allowed to worry. So is Steve coming over to say goodbye?"

"Yeah, he said he'd stop by soon."

"Have him come say hello," she said and descended the stairs.

"Mom *loves* to worry." Jenn rolled her eyes but smiled.

"She thrives on fretting. Can you help me carry this trunk?"

Jenn followed me back to my room. "It's weird Aunt Alice and Uncle Harold will live here. I mean, I'm glad. Especially since we won't have to sell the house and never visit again. But the change reminds me Gramps is gone."

"Yeah, kinda like this room. It was always my room. No one else ever slept here. But Alice and Harold can do something different with the space, if they want. I miss Gramps too."

Jenn fell silent and glanced around the room. "Why do you think Henrik appeared to me?"

"Not sure." I shook my head.

"I wondered for a while if I had the same visions as you. Like, maybe I was a witch. But I don't think so. Because magic never happened before or since. Plus, you saw a lot more than I did."

"I don't think you're a witch, but I do think you're right. Henrik wanted to scare you, more than anything because he knew going after you got me upset. He also hoped you'd get other people involved against me. But I think he knew how much you mean to me. You got caught in the middle."

"I kind of figured. I thought about my part while you and Steve were up there. Doing nothing was hard, because I wanted to go with you and protect you. That's what made me realize I had no idea what to do to help. If I were a witch, I think I would've. Like all the jewelry. The gems look pretty to me. But they fly through the air for you. So I figured out he wanted to mess with me."

"You okay?" I asked.

"Of course. Don't take this the wrong way, but I don't want to be a witch. I like *you* being a witch."

"Promise me again you'll always come to me if anything happens. Ghosts or whatever shit. I know I told everyone, but you have to promise me."

"I promise. You know I would."

"Cool. Now, help me carry this thing."

We lifted the trunk and started out. Heading down the hall, I took a deep breath to hold back the tears, because each step took me away from Gramps. I missed him, and for the first time could concentrate on my grief and not visions or ghosts or premonitions.

Before we got to the stairs, I saw a warm glow out of the corner of my eye coming from his study. Then I felt his presence. "Hold up. Put this down and come here with me." I walked toward the study, with Jenn following.

"What?" Jenn grabbed my arm.

"Nothing bad. Come on."

*

The moment we walked through the door, the fire's warmth hit my face. Its light and a few rays of sun illuminated the bookshelves lining the room. Darth bolted in and ran to the hearth, where she threw herself on a rug and rolled on her back. Gramps sat in his usual chair, waiting.

"Come in," he said. Aloud. The sound hit me: he spoke in a normal voice.

"Sit down, please. Don't be scared. It's safe," he assured us.

I sat opposite him on a leather ottoman, while Jenn eased herself into a nearby rocker.

"It's over," I told him.

"I know. You did a wonderful job."

"I thought we wouldn't see you again."

"I wanted to clarify a couple of things. For my own sake. For my own soul's peace." He leaned forward and looked at both of us. "You're my sweethearts. Nothing meant more to me in life than my grandchildren."

My eyes welled with tears. I thought about the day we had moved to Colorado and how sad leaving had made Gramps. He told my parents our departure hurt so much to see his precious sweethearts being taken away. Jenn wiped at tears too.

"Don't cry. Both of you and Lincoln—all my grandchildren—gave me so much joy. My memory will always be with you. Until we meet again. And we will." He reached out and patted both of us on the knee. "But I want to talk to you. After my heart attack, everything was so clear to me in death. I knew Henrik intended to act against you, though I didn't know how. I saw him haunting this house and realized your grandmother was right about a presence.

"Then I saw your grandma for the first time since she died. She waited in this house all these years, avoiding Henrik and afraid but wanting to protect us. You can't imagine how guilty I felt for not having believed her while she lived." He shook his head, sad. "It didn't take much imagination to see Henrik was trapped on earth because of his anger. Your grandmother and I wanted to move to the next realm and wait for all of you to join us there. But I couldn't, knowing he threatened you here. I also learned Henrik murdered my brother and son. Jaret, I knew he would do the same to you. I had to stop him, to try to help you.

"The Bachmann warlock tradition made so much more sense then. And I could see you were the next one. That's why I appeared to you. I was so afraid of Henrik and for your safety I tried to get you to stay in Colorado. When you came anyway, I changed my strategy to help you as best I could.

"Henrik and I couldn't communicate without the presence of an intermediary, like you. Don't ask me why. I can't explain the reason. So I wandered around the house, waiting for him to confront you. Even then, I was powerless at times. He could block me if he controlled his temper enough. That's also why I could never speak to you aloud. The instant I did, he could find you and me together. Once he learned I wanted to help you against him, I feared he would move into his final attack against you. I danced with Grandma before you to let you see I intended you no harm. I showed you the jewels when he backed us into a corner. Letting you find them was my last effort to protect you."

"I knew you were always on my side."

He smiled. "The biggest problem was getting you the jewels without Henrik knowing. I'd always known my brother cherished those gems, more than because of their actual value. I dismissed the truth until I died, when I saw things from a different perspective and recognized their power. Henrik could only find them through a person who was alive, and not on his own. He watched me put them in the attic but either forgot where they were, or he couldn't see them anymore. Maybe because of his anger. I also think the forces in those stones can cloak themselves. I tried to let you know this, and help you find them without his knowledge. I failed. But you beat him, anyway. Strange, because in life he would have controlled all these things—the gems, the chest, even the iron box, because he was the warlock of his generation. I'm so impressed with how you learned about your power and overcame him."

I blushed and looked at my shoes, embarrassed.

"And Jenn, please forgive me for not doing more to comfort you." Gramps turned in his chair to look at her. "I knew what he was doing to you and hated every minute of his torture. But I didn't want to scare you anymore or play into his hands by making you react more than you already did. I figured it'd be best for you to see me with Jaret, when he could explain things to you."

Jenn continued to cry as she nodded. "I knew you wanted to help us. Especially when I saw you at the funeral."

"Ah, yes. My funeral." Gramps sighed. "I came to the cemetery because I knew he plotted. Believe me, I had no desire to see my mortal body or frighten my family. But Jaret, you still didn't know how to use your power."

He shrugged. "Well, you both realize I made mistakes. Maybe I could have done more, sooner. I want you to know I did my best and loved you the whole time. I'm so proud of both of you." Gramps leaned back in his chair and looked at Jenn again. "Goodbye. No matter how big you get, you'll always be my little sweetheart. I love you."

"I love you, too, Gramps."

Jenn got up to leave, wiping away another tear but smiling toward Gramps. She waved before she left.

Gramps and I waited until she closed the door. After a quiet moment, he stood and walked to my side, smiled, and then knelt on one knee in front of me.

"Knowing you control Henrik has put me at peace. For the first time, I understand what comes after death. I can be with your grandmother. I missed her so much. Nothing disturbs our sleep anymore."

More tears streamed down my face. I knew what he needed to tell me before he said the words.

"We're going on. I'm leaving the family in your hands, for the present and future. I love you. And know we're waiting to see you when it's time." Gramps stood up and walked toward the fireplace.

"Gramps," I half-shouted. "One more thing." He turned and looked at me. "I love you too."

He smiled again. Then he nodded, winked, and blew me a kiss.

*

The fire went out after he disappeared, and a chill swept through the room. I cried by myself for a few minutes. Not for Gramps, who went to a better place, but because no matter how much I understood, I missed him. I crawled over to Darth and held her in my arms. When I left, Jenn surprised me because she'd waited in the hall. She got up and hugged me as tears streamed once again for both of us.

"All right, we have to get the trunk to the Blazer before Dad has a stroke," I said. "He's already worried the chest won't fit with all the rest of our stuff. We didn't plan to bring back an ancient trunk full of magic."

Jenn laughed as we picked up the trunk and headed down the stairs, Darth taking the lead. We set the trunk behind the Blazer so Dad couldn't miss it and pack it according to his liking. "Where's Dad?" she asked.

"Must be inside."

"I'm going to say goodbye to Uncle Harold and Aunt Alice." Jenn started inside. "Tell Dad when he gets back."

I moved to take Darth to the backyard when I saw Steve's Jeep pull into the driveway. As much as I had hurt to say goodbye to Gramps yet again, the thought of the next farewell opened an even larger pit in my stomach.

"Hey, babes," Steve called from his window.

I smiled and got all fluttery inside. "Coming in?"

He got out and followed me inside. Before we got to the living room and other people, I yanked him aside, onto a small enclosed porch, where I wrapped my arms around him and kissed his neck.

"We don't have much time. Dad wants to leave soon."

"So you're getting me all hot and bothered for no reason?" He kissed my nose and ran his fingers through my hair. "Remember, you have my cell number. I'll figure something to tell my father about the call."

"I know."

"And you'll call when you get to Estes Park?"

"Yes."

"And you have the list of colleges?"

"Right here." I patted my pocket.

He pulled me into his arms and kissed the top of my head. "You're the best thing to ever happen to me. Sounds lame. But I mean it. I want to go to the same place and be together. It's all I'll think about this spring." Steve sounded even more insecure about our separation than me. At least my family knew I was gay. I was leaving him alone in Fremont, where no one knew. He decided not to tell his parents yet. Fremont was too small and conservative, his parents too afraid of what others might think to make coming out safe for him. But at least we could talk to each other. And he could look forward to being himself when we went away next fall.

"I'll be thinking about you all the time too." I leaned closer to him, smelling his presence next to me. "Plus, we're coming back in a couple months to help with Gramps's stuff. There are things Dad wants to take back to Colorado. So we'll see each other then." We clung to each other for a few moments. My stomach ached even when we pulled apart and the pit inside got a lot bigger.

"All right, mister. You're getting me excited again. You better get going."

I gave him one last kiss, and we headed to the living room, where another round of goodbyes waited.

After what seemed like hours of hugs and chatting, I walked Steve to his Jeep. We hugged and kissed once more, and my eyes filled with tears. When I turned to go inside and heard his Jeep backing away, I couldn't look back and watch him go.

A couple of minutes later, Mom, Dad, Lincoln, Jenn, and I got into the Blazer behind Darth, who insisted on being first for everything. Aunt Alice and Uncle Harold waved from the porch as we drove away, the new windshield on the Blazer sparkling in the sunlight. I watched Gramps's house drift away. The mansion didn't feel scary anymore, and I could hold on to the good memories I thought I'd lost in all the chaos.

Jenn and Lincoln joked around beside me as the house became a small dot and disappeared. I half listened but thought more about Steve and about the events of the last few days. I was confident. Spirits and ghosts had always appeared to me, but the jewels and other stuff in the trunk were a way for me to control them. I wasn't a victim anymore, which felt pretty good.

I reached back and scratched Darth behind her ears. Poor thing. She was hot, even in the air-conditioning. "You're a good girl," I said. "My best bud." She gave me a big kiss on the cheek, and I offered her an awkward one-armed hug around her neck, given my position.

While petting Darth, I glanced at the iron box next to my trunk. Henrik was my constant companion. As a warlock, I could control him. Though I had a lot to learn, I understood my power against him already.

I also contemplated my immense responsibility. Only I could protect my family. No matter where I went or what I wanted to do, Henrik, and maybe other forces, were my responsibility. I gave Darth a final pet, then turned around to face front. Inside my pocket, the golden key dug into my thigh, like Henrik, another eternal companion.

About the Author

Damian Serbu lives in the Chicago area with his husband and two dogs, Akasha and Chewbacca. The dogs control his life, tell him what to write, and threaten to eat him in the middle of the night if he disobeys. He has published The Vampire's Angel, The Vampire's Quest, and The Vampire's Protégé, as well as Santa's Kinky Elf, Simon and Santa Is a Vampire with NineStar Press. Keep up to date with him on Facebook, Twitter, or at www.DamianSerbu.com.

Facebook: www.facebook.com/Damian-Serbu

Twitter: @damianserbu

Website: www.damianserbu.com

Other NineStar books by this author

The Vampire's Angel

The Vampire's Quest

The Vampire's Protégé

Santa's Kinky Elf Simon

Santa is a Vampire

Also Available from NineStar Press

Connect with NineStar Press

www.ninestarpress.com

www.facebook.com/ninestarpress

www.facebook.com/groups/NineStarNiche

www.twitter.com/ninestarpress